Paddy O'Reilly

GW00467795

THE SONS OF LEVI

Darach MacDonald

The Sons of Levi
is published in Ireland 1998 by
Drumlin Press, P.O. Box 15, Monaghan

Copyright © 1998 Darach MacDonald

The author has asserted his moral rights

ISBN 0 9533438 0 4

Printing: R&S Printers, Monaghan
Cover illustration: Joan Mallon

The author gratefully acknowledges the help and encouragement of
Eugene McCabe and the kind assistance of Len Graham
who supplied the song verses of The Sons of Levi

For Ross and Sam

A note on characters and sources

The main characters in this book - Sinclair, Albert and Sadie Armstrong, Bob Sinclair, Roy and Robert James McConkey, Dorothy Hall, Alex Johnson - and most of the minor characters are entirely fictitious. Any resemblance to actual persons, living or dead, is purely coincidental.

However, this work of fiction is based on real events and some of the secondary characters were actual people of the time and place described. They include M.E. Knight, J.C.W. Madden, W.T. Cosgrave and Sir Basil Brooke. I am indebted to Johnny Madden of Hilton Park, Clones, for access to his grandfather's papers. Other contemporary sources were used, particularly those in the Public Records Office of Northern Ireland, Trinity College Dublin, the National Library of Ireland and newspapers including *The Northern Standard* and *The Impartial Reporter*. **The Sons of Levi** was inspired by research on the Irish Boundary Commission and the papers relating to it, including all the available contemporary records.

The names of Orange lodges and the Royal Black Preceptory are fictitious. However, details of the loyal orders are accurate insofar as possible, with information derived from the Laws and Ordinances of the Orange Institution of Ireland (1924) and other reliable sources.

In this work of fiction, I have attempted to convey the experiences and thoughts of the community it describes. For that reason, I am also indebted to artist Joan Mallon of Glaslough for the cover illustration of a scene at Drum, Co. Monaghan, and to her art class students at Monaghan Collegiate School for their contributions to its accuracy.

Darach MacDonald, June 1998

The Sons of Levi

Darach MacDonald

The Grand Design

Come all ye craftsmen that do wish
To propagate the grand design;
Come enter into our High Temple
And learn the art that is divine.

For we are the true-born Sons of Levi,
None on earth can with us compare:
We are the root and branch of David.
The bright and glorious Morning Star.

From both sides of Hadrian's Wall we came, a lost tribe in search of a Promised Land. From Cumbria, Dumfries, Fife and Northumbria - disciples of John Knox and reivers from the border marches. We were farmers by trade and soldiers by birth, sent to tame the rolling drumlin countryside that bounds the Black Pig's Dyke. There, along the southern reaches of the Erne Valley, we found our homes. God was our Guide and Protector. No mortal hand could put us from them. Armstrongs, Johnstons, Elliots, Grahams, Nixons, Crichtons and Sandersons, we came there from the "Debatable lands" of Hawick, Denholm, Jedburgh, Lustruther, Liddesdale, Southdean and Carter Bar. Planters, settlers and undertakers, we buried our dead and defended our living. Under the eyes of a just God, we carved out a Protestant Ulster on the skeleton of the once-defiant province. Through the ages, it became our loyalist bridgehead, holding out against native secession, colonial treachery and Papist rebellion. Bound together in solemn league and bearing with fortitude the Ark of the Covenant that was our birthright, we rode out the storms of uncertain times, praying for glorious deliverance under the union flag and the crown-topped Red Hand of Ulster. With Bible and sword, ploughshare and musket, we were descendants of Scottish and English settlers who matched their wits, and also their myths, to the Gaelic order we displaced.

****

The land basked in the unaccustomed warmth and Sinclair felt tempted to repair once again to the cooling shade of the hedge at his back. Yet the work had to be done and he lulled his brain back into a rhythm as he forked hay into the cock, the squat haystack in a line of similar formations down the length of the field. Another hot summer's day raised a haze before his eyes as he worked silently, pausing occasionally to look out over the surrounding hills, right down the Erne Valley, a lush, verdant land interpsersed here and there with buildings.

The hay meadows had been closed off to the livestock in mid-March and the mowing with scythes had been completed in June. Over the following weeks, Sinclair and his father had shaken and gathered the cut grass into coles, or wind-rows, before beginning the task of lapping - gathering the grass against the leg and folding it into small muff-like heaps. These were then smoothed down on both sides so that the rain would run off, yet left open so the air would pass through and dry them out. With the Twelfth now out of the way, the hay had to be saved.

In the background, Sinclair could hear the steady clanking of the crude raking machine drawn by a farm horse being led along by his Uncle Bob. The machine was pushing the coles of hay back into piles for stacking. Nearby, his father worked methodically at the same task as himself, and Sinclair knew that it would be now or never. Several days had passed since the Twelfth field. He had gone to Newtownbutler with Roy on the pretext of merely visiting Dorothy at her home. Nobody had noticed the change in his manner, but he could not conceal it long.

He worked his way over towards where his father was hoisting a final pitchfork-full of hay onto the top of the ruck. As he waited for the older man to pause, he swept his gaze again over the neat hedgerows that divided the green drumlins into small hill fields.

"Dad, I've been meaning to have a word with you," he began at last, cautiously as Albert patted the top of the ruck with his fork. "I was going to the other day, but you were off on your spree with Uncle Bob."

Albert did not look up as he grabbed a handful of hay and began twisting it into a crude rope to fasten down the ruck.

"About what, son?"

"I'm thinking of joining up."

Sinclair felt himself recoil from the words. They were so inadequate. His father looked up in mild puzzlement. Sinclair busied himself by using his fork to scrape loose hay from the side of the ruck. It fell in clumps which he hoisted back on top with his pitchfork.

"For what," said Albert, now looking directly at his son who paused and rested his weight against the upturned pitchfork. "Talk sense, son. They don't need you in the forces. We're not at war, unless you'd call this sorry mess here honourable combat."

"Not the army, dad, the Special Constabulary. I'm accepted for the A Class."

A shocked expression registered on Albert's face. "What? You mean you've done it already then?"

Sinclair blushed with guilt now, caught in the subterfuge of his last few days. "Aye, suppose so, in Newtown. Near as makes no difference in any case."

"Then I doubt nothing I say will hold you from it at the latter end."

"Don't worry about me. I'll be all right and, sure, Roy McConkey's going to be ..."

Too quickly, Albert showed his shock and sense of betrayal: "Sure, Roy's every bit as big an eejit as you are ...."

The two men worked in silence for a while. Albert resumed knotting his crude hay rope and Sinclair took up a nearby rake and began to tidy up the fallen hay around the ruck. As he did so, he searched his mind for something to say, something that might comfort his father and convince him that this would be merely a temporary absence. Yet he knew that his father was absorbed in the thought that he could lose his second son, now off to follow his brother into uniform to hold somebody else's battle line.

Albert broke the silence at last, "Tell me, what's to become of the land here. I'll not hold out much longer and Eric's gone in the War...."

"Och, dad. You're not bate yet and, sure, Uncle Bob's retiring from the railway in a few months. So he can lend a hand if you need it."

Albert mulled over the possible contingencies, aware that his son had been preparing for his mild objections, maybe even his strong ones if it came to that.

"What about Dorothy?" he asked his son. "Does she know?"

Sinclair knew he had won the tussle, even through his ineptness. With the conversation shifting to this vein, he realised in a surge of relief that his father had given his consent, or at least as much consent as he ever would.

"Aye indeed, with me earning on my own, maybe we can talk about that wedding you've been planning for us. They need more men in Fermanagh and I think they'll post me near enough home."

"So there's no stopping you. But there's too many going the same way you're taking across that damned border," said Albert, his voice now echoing the defeated resignation that flooded his very soul. For the past month, he had thought of little else. The final hope of reprieve had been dashed when King George had come to open the new parliament of Northern Ireland in Belfast. In that royal act of investiture, His Majesty had shattered the final lingering hopes of Albert and thousands of other Ulster loyalists.

"Och, don't worry. We'll be back when all this blows over," said Sinclair, his voice in turn registering relief and the forced optimism he knew his father needed to hear. "Aye, and with money to spare, too. This is still home."

With a visible sigh, Albert dropped the hay rope and turned his gaze again on the surrounding countryside. In his mind, he traced the imaginary line of the new frontier he knew cut right through the land he held within his gaze. It cut through his heart and soul, too, and now through his own little family.

"I doubt I find that harder to believe by the day. Matter a damn what Attorney Knight and Rev. Burns say, I think our days is gone about this country here. There's too many going the way you're now fixing to go. They're gone and others are looking for ways of getting out. Now it's only the old and the very young, widows and fools like myself being left behind...."

Sinclair turned to meet his father's full gaze now and he saw the pain in the older man's eyes and in his heartfelt words. "You know, we always say things like No Surrender or What We Hold We Steadfastly Will Maintain. Huh, the surrender began long ago and we should have known it when they shut us out of the Ulster Hall and opted for their six counties. Och, they can still march to fife and drum all right. But the surrender. The surrender was begun when they ditched us. After that, it's only words and puffed-up pride. That's all it is."

Sinclair followed his father's gaze across the land, over Drumkirk, Corragarry, Magherashaghry, Lurganboy, Creeran and Lisnageeragh, the names of places that summed up his entire life. As he listed the townland names silently in his mind, he fixed them in place for his leave-taking and thought again of the road that faced him and the route that had brought him there.

****

The Power that led his chosen, by pillar'd cloud and flame,
Through parted sea and desert waste, that Power is still the same;
He fails not - He, the loyal hearts that firm on Him rely,
So put your trust in Him, my boys, and keep your powder dry.

The power that nerved the stalwart arms of Gideon's chosen few,
The Power that led Great William, Boyne's reddening torrent through;
In His protecting aid confide, and every foe defy -
Then put your trust in Him, my boys, and keep your powder dry.

****

The Lambeg drums thundered in syncopated unison, their noise filling the small enclosed space where the crowds gathered and the ranks were forming. As one drum rose to a deafening crescendo, the other subsided into a temporary lull before gathering strength and taking over. The beat rumbled and echoed off the walls in a great tidal rush, quickening the heartbeats of those who stood listening in the near-stifling morning heat. For five solid minutes it continued to waft through Erne Square, the drummers competing for tempo and endurance.

Occasionally, a drum on the upbeat changed in mid-stream, embarking on a new trevally that caught the tempo of familiar tunes.

Lilli-bolero-bullen-a-la.

It thundered off the surrounding buildings and numbed the ears.

As the other took over the ascendant, it occasionally changed the tune, too. Some people in the crowd waited, listening intently for a song they would recognise. Earlier many of them had stood around in clusters as the drummers helped each other prepare. One man held the large oak frame in a firm grip while another tightened the linen ropes that criss-crossed between the rims, pulling the goatskins on each side to a new tautness. The drummers asked for help from some men standing by while they worked their way into the harness. Then backs bowed in a concave arch as they strained against the weight, heads almost concealed from view behind the big frames, they settled back and raised their cane sticks. The rolls began, soft and slow at first, then rising in intensity as each searched for the true heart of his instrument, the heartbeat of Ulster.

The drums themselves drew a crowd of onlookers. Painted on the side, they proclaimed their loyalty. One goatskin featured an image of the shutting of Derry's gates by the apprentice boys of 1688, the other drum a scene of William's landing at Carrickfergus. Both had biblical scenes, one the desert wandering of the tribes of Israel, the other the crashing walls of Jerico. The Lambeg drums, however, did not need to assert their loyalty. They had come to Ulster with William and were pounded as battlefield background to the fife bands which marched into the fray ahead of the infantrymen. Since then, no loyal gathering was complete without them. While the fifes bowed to the more sedate accordion bands now, the Lambeg drums still roared out their defiance and their loyalty to the Protestant cause.

Finally, the drum thunder relented, dropping off into sporadic brattles heard amid the shuffling of feet, the babble of voices and the occasional sounds of trains shunting and hissing in the nearby railway yard. Hearts settled back into their familiar beats, as spectators ranged along the sides of the square grasping union flags and favours and scanning the ranks of besuited participants for the familiar faces they knew would be there. Throughout the ranks, ornate silk banners hung limply from poles in the vanguard of each cluster of marchers, as lodges sidled into place. In the absence of a breeze, the banner-bearers stood listlessly and it was only with difficulty that the spectators could recognise their own. Yet they were all there, or arriving in the rearguard. There were the Clones Hearts of Steel Loyal Orange Lodge, the Clough Disciples of Freedom, Treehoo True Blues, Killeevan Ulster Heroes, Drumully Northern Stars, Killyfargy Ulster's Pride, the Rising Stars of Ture and the Drum Sons of Levi, the latter banner held by Sinclair Armstrong and Roy McConkey.

His tight, starched collar bit into Sinclair's neck as he stood rigidly waiting for the off signal. The sun blazed down causing a glimmer before his eyes as he stared hard at the broken surface of Erne Square. He glanced cautiously about him. His father Albert was up in front, positioned among the lodge elders. Sinclair knew them all - Wilson Latimer, Cecil Anderson, Robert James McConkey, Roy's dad, and the Rev. Robert Burns, the County Grand Chaplain who would go off shortly to join the other officers of the Monaghan County Grand Lodge at the head of the parade. Sinclair stole a glance sideways and saw Roy now signalling to somebody standing in front of Lendrum's Monumental Sculptors, but as the crowd on the side moved, he could not quite make out whoever it was. Behind him, he knew, there were others lined out in ranks, three deep along the road. He turned briefly and saw his Uncle Bob grinning broadly as he strapped on another large Lambeg drum with the aid of two helpers. Bob Sinclair winked at him and Sinclair turned back quickly. He counted them off, eight lines back and three across, that made, let's see, twenty-four. Still six missing, he thought. Maybe that's the hold up.

A single brattle of a kettle drum up ahead sounded above the happy banter and Sinclair could feel his body lean forward as if to commence marching. Realising that this was not the signal, he sought to regain his balance, but stumbled slightly and skipped forward a pace or two before scurrying back. He could feel his face growing even more red in the burning sun as several onlookers laughed, but glancing around again, he could see that others had made the same mistake

Bob Sinclair's voice came from behind, "Mind yourself there, ye big glipe ye." The elders looked around and Bob continued, shouting up to his brother-in-law, "Hey, Albert, that nephew of mine has got terrible clumsy of late. Must be in love or something."

Albert laughed, "Aye, indeed Bob, he has his mind on a wee lassie from out by Gortraw all the time now."

"Well, he's frisky enough, by the hokey. Aren't you Sinclair?"

"Sure, he's hardly fit to do a hand's turn these days. Should have seen him out trying to lap the hay only yesterday. Footering about and getting nothing done. Worse than useless. Big moon face on him staring off into the distance at a cow in Billy Crawford's back meadow."

"Then the sooner you get him hitched the better, eh?" Bob said, before turning to talk to some others in the ranks behind him.

Sinclair fidgeted with the brass trim of his sash. He looked over at Roy who was grinning broadly at his expense.

"Wipe that grin off your snout. Bad enough having to put up with thon pair of ould begrudgers."

"Couldn't help it," said Roy, trying to regain a serious composure as Sinclair inserted a finger between his own neck and collar, feeling the sweat. Rubbing the moisture between his index finger and thumb, Sinclair now said, "Well, that settles it for good."

Roy was interested, picking up immediately on the allusion to the sole subject of their conversation of late.

"You mean, you'll join up then?"

"Aye, we'll go over to Newtown the morra night and see about it."

"Good man your da," said Roy, "Aye, and I mean that and all."

No more needed to be said. It was about the notice, the one they had seen as they alighted from the train in Enniskillen and made their way out of the station. Its contents had played over and over again in Sinclair's mind, opening a world of possibilities and difficulties at the same time. He had tried to focus on it then, but decided instead that he would just ignore Roy's persistent questions. How could he make such a decision so quickly? He barely had time to enjoy his day with Dorothy since they had arrived in Enniskillen along with Roy and Eileen Anderson. From the station, the two young women marched on ahead and they had spent much of the day traipsing around the town. In a few of the drapery shops, Dorothy and Eileen tried on outfits between comments and giggles. All the while, Roy kept up his incessant chatter. The notice had fired his imagination too, but he was anxious that Sinclair share his enthusiasm for a new-found cause. The possibilities were real - a secure job with prospects and standing in the community, full board and lodgings after training and a chance to serve.

The notice had appeared as an open invitation: "Wanted," it had read, "Loyal and able-bodied young men for the Ulster Special Constabulary - A, B and C classes." In smaller print, there were details of how to apply and the training offered. Sinclair read them as avidly as Roy had while they stalled, allowing the young women to dander on ahead. Roy had shown immediate enthusiasm, but Sinclair was more reticent. As a sole remaining son, Sinclair knew that was needed at home. More so now that his father was getting on.

The tragic death in a faraway battlefield of his eldest boy, had robbed Albert of his will to maintain and improve the land. Mourning for his eldest, Albert had been overly strict with Sinclair, treating him as a child no matter how much responsibility he wanted him to assume on the farm. Yet, it would not be too long, Sinclair knew, until he would have to be prepared to take over the 100-acre holding of hilly farmland. He was resigned to the prospect, yet felt that he would welcome the chance to know another life before he did so. After all, he had lived all his life in Drumkirk. Apart from occasional trips into Clones or Cootehill, or further afield once before this to Enniskillen, his future would continue as his life before. Farming all week, church on Sunday and, even when he married Dorothy as he hoped, he would never have a chance to know more of life than he already knew. When Eric went off, after all, Sinclair had been only 15 years old, too young to join his brother and the other young men who marched off on that Spring day back in 1915 behind Col. John Clemens Waterhouse Madden of Hilton Park and the King's Own Fusiliers. Eric had not come home, and Sinclair recalled with a chill the telegram arriving on that cold winter day a year later. He and his father were busy in the house field, gapping a hedge that some live-stock had trampled. When they noticed the telegram delivery boy, he was already at the back door, his bicycle propped against his hip as he handed the envelope to Sinclair's mother, Sadie. Immediately they knew what it contained and, as they made off silently for the house, their steps quickening as they hurried along, they could see the confirmation of their fears in the horrified expression of the woman who had opened the envelope and glanced at its contents. There on the doorstep, Sadie's face registered the horror of their worst nightmare. Eric, son and brother, had been killed in the service of his King. In the gore-splattered mud of a place they called Thiepval Wood, he had fallen with scores, hundreds, thousands of his compatriots. Ulster blood drenched the Flanders field where Eric lay that day, his corpse surrounded by legions of others. Sinclair remembered the pleading of his mother and the stoical strength of his father as they embraced each other in their shocked bereavement on the cobbled street outside the back door of their home. "Don't go, son," his mother had entreated him, drawing him into their embrace, "don't go. You're all we have left."

Sinclair shuddered and gathered his thoughts, before settling back to his steady gaze around the crowd, searching for Dorothy among the smiling faces of parade onlookers. He knew she must be out there somewhere, probably craning her neck to get a view. Perhaps he should have told her first, Sinclair thought, before Roy even. No, it would be fine, she would understand surely. Indeed, it was only right a man would make a decision like this without having to ask a woman what she thought of it. Dorothy would admire that, his decisiveness and his independence from his family. Had she not been teasing him all the time about how he was under the thumb of his father, his mother, Rev. Burns and even Roy. He would show her that he was his own man now. He gazed, searching still for her face so that he could be reassured, even as his nervousness of the road he had set himself to embark on loomed ahead.

A single brattle again on a kettle drum, a fresh thunder of Lambeg skins and a band at the front of the parade struck up. It was the off signal, at last, and Sinclair marvelled at how the assembled brethren set off in perfect pace. Years of practice and marching together had honed their skills, joining together the members and their lodges into a formidable and impressive force of marching men.

Stepping off, Sinclair measured his pace against those in front as the lodges swung around into Fermanagh Street and began the gentle ascent to The Diamond, past the Butter Yard and into the narrow main street where the sounds of the bands bounced off the walls in a loud cacophony. All along the route, small clusters of onlookers gathered, some calling to their men in the ranks, others watching guardedly and with more than a trace of resentment at this annual spectacle of Protestant ascendancy. Sinclair's heart swelled with pride, even as he noticed the surreptitious glances from behind upstairs curtains over closed shops. A band ahead played *The Union We'll Maintain* while the Lambeg drummers, criss-crossing each other's paths to the rear, spared no Fenian ears in their thunderous show of loyalty. Glancing around, he could still see hundreds of besashed men following in close ranks, banners fluttering slightly in the breeze caused by their movement, men erect and proud. Sinclair remembered his own induction into the lodge, the pride of his father and his own acceptance that this was his passage into full manhood. For weeks he had been instructed in the beliefs, tenets and procedures of the lodge. He had learned by heart the prayers as he had learned no lesson with such zeal in school. The Orange lodge was the summation of all the education he wanted or needed, for it was the great bulwark of his Protestant heritage, the institution that encapsulated the fervent belief of his people in the freedom, liberty and salvation of their Protestant faith, as well as their fealty to the Protestant Crown of Britain and Ireland. In his mind, he recited the opening prayer of lodge meetings:

"Gracious and Almighty God! Who in all ages hast shown Thy Almighty power in protecting righteous Kings and States, we yield Thee hearty thanks for the merciful preservation of Thy true religion, hitherto, against the designs of its enemies. We praise Thee for raising up for our deliverance from tyranny and arbitrary power, Thy servant, King William III, Prince of Orange; and we beseech Thee, for Thy honour and Thy name's sake, for ever to frustrate all the designs of wicked men against Thy holy religion, and not to suffer its enemies to triumph; defeat their counsels, abate their pride, assuage their malice and confound their devices. Deliver, we pray Thee, the members of the Church of Rome from error and false doctrine, and lead them to the truth of that Holy Word which is able to make them wise unto salvation."

The lodges proceeded up the final stretch of Fermanagh Street and onto The Diamond. There, the wide expanse allowed the bands to give full vent to their playing. Looking back again briefly, Sinclair saw his Uncle Bob, flailing unmercifully with two cane rods at his big drum. Those sticks, he knew, would not see the end of this glorious day.

Dorothy Hall rested her bicycle against the stone bollards of the town water pump and hurried quickly over to the front of the line of spectators. The shutters had come down on the news kiosk and the proprietor Jemmy Reilly had taken up position alongside Hughie Maguire directly behind her as the first lodges approached. Preceded by the County Grand Lodge members, the foremost band was in full tune, ringing out the strains of *The Nine Counties of Ulster*. Yet above the music,

Dorothy could hear the conversation of her two unwanted neighbours as she scanned the ranks for sight of Sinclair.

"Here they come now, the True Blue Sons of Freedom, who would fight to the death to deny us ours," Reilly said aloud to several chuckles from onlookers.

"Thought you'd make a stand the year, Jemmy, and keep the shop open," said Maguire.

"I may be a true Irishman, but a I'm a lot cuter than to stand there selling the *Freeman's Journal* when those boys are abroad on the street."

Dorothy suppressed her annoyance, thinking to herself that she would not have to endure that kind of remark if she had gone with her family to the Fermanagh field in Lisbellaw. She had considered the option, but like many of her neighbours, had chosen to go to Clones as a show of solidarity. How much longer, she wondered, would such displays of loyalty be countenanced by those who mocked? She felt a wave of sympathy for Sinclair and the others who marched, and a sense of pride, too, in their fortitude even against the tide of history engulfing them on this hot summer's day.

"Be God, would you look at the peelers over these standing till attention," she heard Reilly say, even as her gaze followed his over to the small cluster of Royal Irish Constabulary members at the Ulster Bank corner. The broad-chested, ruddy faced men lined the route blocking off through traffic which had backed up behind them, the vehicles abandoned as the occupants ambled over to watch the procession.

"Next thing, they'll be saluting the ould bigots," said Reilly.

"Aye, them that's not already in the ranks with them," Maguire replied.

Feeling decidedly uncomfortable amid this exchange, Dorothy wondered whether she should go elsewhere to enjoy the parade. But she was aware that if she moved off, she would only draw attention to herself and she felt a curious embarrassment at the prospect of doing so on this of all days. For the first time, she was struck by a sense of utter alienation in this town she had known all her life.

The County Grand Lodge group was now approaching and Dorothy saw Reilly doff his cap grandly to the Grand Master who was smiling broadly in acknowledgement of the spectators. Reilly called out, "Good day to you, Mr Knight sir. It's a grand day for what you're at."

Knight nodded in recognition as he passed and Reilly immediately turned back to Maguire. "Don't think he'll be fit to get beyond the foot of Whitehall Street with the size of him."

"Won't have to," Maguire replied. "There's a car waiting at the canal bridge for the big nobs."

"That would be them all right. Let the foot soldiers slog it out in their ranks while they ride off to Corcummins in the best of style."

Dorothy resolved to ignore these snide remarks as she saw the Drum Sons of Levi banner approach and, with a beat of her heart, she saw Sinclair at last, holding the silk print aloft with Roy. She marvelled at its scene of a blessed people wandering in the desert in search of a Promised Land, bearing along before them the Ark of the Covenant. She tried to attract Sinclair's attention, but he was gazing fixedly ahead. When he did turn his head, it was to the other side. She called out, "Sinclair, here Sinclair." But he was already striding past and at the final moment she caught the gaze of Roy, her neck straining forward as she called. Roy tried to attract Sinclair's attention, but they had already gone by and a few paces ahead of her, she could see Sinclair wheel around, causing the banner to slump, before he regained his pace and drew it tight again. She would set off immediately, as soon as he could get through the crowd, but they were pressed tight around her and, as she waited for it to ease up so that she could regain her bicycle and go on out to the field, she was trapped within earshot of those two again.

"Hey, isn't that Bob Sinclair beyond with the Drum lodge?" Reilly asked.

"Tis in sowl," said Maguire, recognising his fellow railway worker.

"Would you look at him banging thon big drum. You'll not get much work out of him the morra. He'll be flailing that and whiskey all day."

"Damned but you're right there. He'll be nursing raw paws and a sore head for the next few days, I doubt."

Reilly coughed up a glob of phlegm and spat it dismissively to the ground, beside her foot. "Aye, and too soon for him at that."

Dorothy, feeling almost sick, broke through the crowd at last, relieved to get away. As she retrieved her bicycle and hurried off for Corcummins, she felt a deep and growing sense of anger mixed with trepidation for the future. What would it hold for the loyalist families of the district, families like Sinclair's who might be marooned and held captive in a place dominated by boorish, resentful and duplicitous men like those watching the parade.

****

They came by darkness to plunder what they coveted. Those of us who survived were herded like swine into the castle yard, whence I escaped at dawn while the rebels caroused. I saw Art Roe MacMahon slay William Elliot and I witnessed Teague O'Connolly drown Alexander Frizell in the castle well where he lay wounded. Honorah Beaumond, the innkeeper's wife, said and I verily believe that she saw 16 women and children drowned in a boghole. On my return, I found ruined property, desecrated graves and other results of wantonness and licentious cruelty. My home was in ruins, the cattle driven off or butchered. Stray animals roamed, feeding on carrion and half-starved at that. The church was desecrated, its doors pulled asunder, books scattered. The survivors were little better than the dead. Wracked by hunger and destitution, they could barely greet their liberators as we proceeded in mighty host from Enniskillen to free the land and save its titled owners from Satan's wrath. I thank the Almighty Lord for having delivered me. I, Andrew Edward Aldrich of Clones in the Barony of Dartrey, so swear on this 9th day of September in the year of Our Gracious Lord, 1642.

****

Just beyond Comber Bridge and hugged in under the brow of Corcummins hill by the River Finn, the gently sloping meadow was a blaze of banners, flags and bunting. At its entrance, a magnificent arch had been raised, its motto, "Our Protestant Rights and Freedoms We Firmly Will Maintain." Interspersed between the dark suits of the lodge members who passed under the arch and then fell out of rank, summer dresses, white shirts, tablecloths and picnic rugs added a blaze of colour. By spotting the lodge banners, neighbours and families drew together to sit on the grass or on the blankets many had brought. It was a geographical picture of the region. Along the river bank at the side of the large platform, groups from Scotshouse, Newbliss, Smithboro and further afield clustered. Beyond them on a slight knoll, the people of Tydavnet, Threemilehouse, Aghabog and Doohat held sway. Across the way, neighbouring Co. Cavan lodges from Cloverhill, Bailieborough, Cootehill, Redhills and Ashfield gathered. And so on, throughout the field where the members and supporters of 65 lodges formed a united crowd ranged around the platform.

Making his way through the gathering, his arms clutching the furled banner of the lodge, Sinclair marvelled at the turn-out.

He had loosened his collar and looked forward to the chance to take off his jacket as the sun baked down still. His body ached from the march, even though the two-mile route was nothing compared to a normal day's work. The heat, however, had made this a test of endurance for them all. But even as they had crested Teehill and relaxed the pace for the long walk to the field, his almost flagging spirits had been buoyed by the martial airs that rang out from the leading bands ahead. The lodge members had soldiered on, conscious that this demonstration of loyalty harkened back to a glorious past and forward to an uncertain and risk-filled future.

Intermittently, the stride had been broken when Bob Sinclair and Albert paused to pass between them a silver flask from which they drank surreptitiously and which progressively made their gait less certain. When this happened, the Orangemen faltered briefly as the ranks behind skipped along to regain their steps and their places. Rounding Comber Bridge, one band had struck up the air of *Croppies Lie Down*, safe now to echo off the hills without fear or favour to those who might not share the sentiment.

Children cavorted through the assembly, darting here and there in a carefree game of tag, as Sinclair picked his way along in Roy's wake. A dull pain of cramp seared though his legs and the lodge banner weighed even more heavily in his arms. Young mothers drew blankets around them as they nursed their babies, others busied themselves arranging tablecloths and picnic baskets. Men doffed hats and shrugged off jackets. An umbrella here and there provided welcome shade for some from the blazing sun. Sinclair noted that some had brought along wicker chairs for the occasion, while several wrestled with bright canvas backed deck-chairs, to the obvious discomfort and annoyance of those in the vicinity.

The air was a hubbub of chatter. Shrill voices called out in greeting occasionally. A final joust of the Lambeg drummers had commenced in a corner of the field near the entrance archway. Looking back in that direction, Sinclair could see enthusiasts lining up for a turn on the skins. He recalled his own experience only last year, or was it the year before, when he had congregated with other young lodge members intent on trying out their talent for the job.

Now his mind was on different concerns as he scanned the crowd. Suddenly, he saw her, straight ahead, settling down beside Sadie and some others, including Eileen and her mother. Dorothy's face was radiant in the sunshine and she had taken off her wide-brimmed bonnet as she settled herself on the blanket. Seated, she replaced it on her shining hair. Sinclair felt he had come home at last.

"Och, there you are," he announced as he drew to a halt and Roy helped him unfurl the banner and stick the poles into the surprisingly yielding earth.

"I was waving to you in at Clones there," said Dorothy in greeting, her voice registering a tone of mock scolding. "But you never passed any more remarks than if I wasn't there at all."

Sadie hovered solicitously as the two young men settled down in the grass. "Rest yourself, son," she told Sinclair as he and Roy slumped back on their elbows, plucking blades of grass with their free hands.

"I'm baked from that road," said Sinclair. "Anything to wet the whistle, is there?"

Dorothy reached for the basket, "Aye there's a sup of nice cold spring water here in the bottle. We've not set up for the lunch yet till the speeches is finished with." She retrieved the bottle from beneath a linen cloth and handed it over to Sinclair. As he took it, their hands brushed briefly and Sinclair searched for and found her eyes on his. They smiled as Roy whistled briefly in the background.

"Man a dear, Sinclair, she looks after you fierce well, doesn't she now? Thought you'd be off to the Lisbellaw field, Dorothy?"

"Och, no, there's a fair wee crowd in from out our way," Dorothy said as she settled back into her position on the blanket. "To keep up the numbers for you ones."

The remark threatened to crash like a stone in the company. Nobody wanted to be reminded of their isolation, not just yet anyway. Sinclair prepared to say something to distract attention when the surprisingly loud voice of his father rang out. Sinclair wheeled to see Albert and Bob Sinclair arriving into their little circle, their faces flushed and their broad grins revealing their high spirits.

"Don't you worry one wee bit, Dorothy," Albert called out, "there's still more than enough of us here to hold the numbers about this country. Aye, and when you and the lad here's wed, sure we'll have a few more on the way, won't we?"

Albert and Bob laughed, drawing the attention of Sadie who had been rearranging the baskets. "Would you listen to thon," she remarked sternly. "Don't you go minding him one wee bit, Dorothy. Aye and you," she continued, turning to face Albert, "Doubt you maybe had a sup or more out of our Bob's flask along the way to slake your own thirst, Albert Armstrong. You just hold your peace now and leave Dorothy alone."

With that rebuke, the group circle settled at last, just as a hush fell over the crowd. Sinclair could sense a murmur of anticipation rippling through the family groups and, looking up towards the platform, he could see the County Grand Lodge officers ranged on chairs at the rear as Rev. Robert Burns stepped up to the podium. A tremor of anticipation surged through the crowd, a few catcalls rang out, a Lambeg drummer gave a short burst on the goatskin. Sinclair could feel Roy nudge him, yet he kept his gaze fixed on the platform, even as he listened to his friend.

"Here it is now, Sinclair boy. There'll be a few Lundies roasted now."

"Aye, plenty of them about the year, too."

The crowd had lapsed back into silence as Burns arranged his notes on the podium table and began, his voice ringing out in a crisp clear Ulster accent that Sinclair knew so well from Sunday services.

"Yea, mine own familiar friend, in whom I trusted, which did eat of my bread, hath lifted up his heel against me. Psalms 41, Verse 9. Brethren in Christ and the Protestant...." Burns began. Sinclair felt another nudge from Roy, who whispered almost too loudly, "You mean it? What you said about Newtown?"

"I said it, didn't I?" said Sinclair urgently, annoyed at the interruption as he tried to concentrate on the words from the platform.

Burns was warming to the task: "You will have heard of the truce agreed in Dublin and now the cause of much speculation in these parts. When we saw it announced, I am sure it gave many of us the nastiest jar of our lives...."

"The morra night?" Roy interrupted again.

"Aye, now wheesht a minute."

"It means," Burns intoned, "that the government has granted the status of belligerents to men who hands are dripping with the blood of their fellow countrymen. It means that they are allowed to treat as honourable foes, while they are in reality skulking cowards whose diabolical cruelty cries aloud for the sternest punishment. It means that the Prime Minister has acknowledged as an equal, and invited other men to meet as an equal, the chief of the Murder Gang."

A roar of disapproval at the very idea rang out, as Burns paused for effect. Cries of "Traitor," "Hang him" and other slogans were shouted

aloud. Sinclair could fell himself strain forward, as he turned to Roy.
"Truer words were never spoke."
"Aye, a good dose of this is what we need for what's ahead of us."
Burns had resumed, causing the voices to plummet into silence again: "Are we to be handed over to the tender mercies of our deadly enemies who are thirsting for our blood; and who, if they dared, would murder us on the slightest pretext, or without any pretext at all? And simply because we are Protestants? For the crime of being a Protestant and standing in the way of realising a long-held ambition of Ireland for the ultra-Irish?"
Again the crowd surged forward, Sinclair felt himself and saw the others around him rise into a standing position. He joined the cries of "No, never" and "For shame," that rippled through the crowd.
All around him, others had risen to their feet and were pressing closer to the platform. He felt Dorothy's arm link his in a welcome embrace. Even in this moment of almost forlorn realisation of what his people must endure, the terror of uncertainty and betrayal, lost to the fold, wandering alone in the desert of treachery and insurrection, he felt a stronger bond than ever with the young woman who pressed her arm to his in a gesture of abiding faithfulness.
Right at that moment, he resolved to tell her of his plans. And, as he steeled himself to do so, his certainty was strengthened by the words from the platform which began to find a new crescendo for an enraptured audience.
"We of the Loyal Orange Institution stand for loyalty and our first resolution here today, and every such day, says so. But one would think that we could get far more consideration from the government if we plotted against the King and murdered His Majesty's forces from behind stone walls and hedges. The patience of every loyal subject has been tried by the government's unwillingness to root out like a pestilence the very name of the IRA."
"We've made up our mind to join the Special Constabulary," Sinclair whispered loudly into Dorothy's ear as he held her close to him.
"You and Roy? When?"
"The morra. I'll see you in Newtown, about seven or so...."
"Is it definite, so?"
"Well, not final like. But if we get in...."
"Suppose, whatever you think is best yourself, love..."
"Civil strife may be let loose in these Monaghan and Cavan hills,"

boomed the voice of Burns. Looking up, Sinclair saw the clergyman throw out his arm in a great gesture, the crowd following it, their gaze sweeping over the hills and fields and roads.

Sinclair thought of Drumkirk, just on the other side of the high hills beyond where they now stood. Those hills, roads, steams and rivers had marked the passage of his journey to manhood. This was the place he had always called home. Neighbouring places, Dorothy's own home place, would soon be separated by the new frontier. He felt a wave of isolation, a feeling that chilled his very bones on this still hot day in Corcummins field.

"Suppose it's none too safe about here now anyway," said Dorothy, echoing his thoughts.

"Doubt so. Thanks, love," Sinclair reassured her by drawing his arm out of the link and putting it around her shoulder as the speaker wound up to his final admonition.

"Just one more word in closing, Brethren," he said. "I would like to pass on that well-worn and tried order of Cromwell - Trust in God and keep your powder dry. God has never failed to defend the right, and although a just and righteous cause may for a time pass under a cloud, yet as sure as God is in His Heaven, it must ultimately triumph. God has always worked through human nature, and we must be ready...."

"Tell your father yet?"

"Not yet. But I will now."

"He'll not be pleased."

"You can say that again. But I feel I have to do it."

"Maybe it would be best if you allowed him to enjoy his day anyway?"

"Bid to be you're right."

Sinclair relaxed at the reprieve for now from announcing his intention and allowed himself to be swept up again in the closing words from Burns.

"The Spanish-American president of the so-called Irish Republic has been throwing out sinister threats of an intensive campaign against those he calls the enemies of Ireland. Brother Orangemen, that is you and I. But we will keep the old flag flying, here in these wee hills, as long as a man of us is alive...."

A mighty cheer burst from the gathering, accompanied by a thunder of drum rolls. As Burns stepped back from the podium, the crowd surged forward. Sinclair found himself punching the air with his fist, while hugging Dorothy with his other arm as she moved along beside him

Knights in Shining Armour

Come all ye Knights Templar of Malta,
Forth in glittering armour shine,
Assist your good and worthy master
To protect the Ark Divine.

For we are the True born Sons of Levi
None on earth can with us compare;
We are the root and branch of David
The bright and glorious Morning Star.

In a land of unspeakable wickedness, we walked with God towards His Day of Judgement. We guarded the ancient rites and knowledge - the rituals of Sword, Spear, Grail and Dish. We were a royal bloodline of the tribe of Levi, sons of David, children of the perfect seed by the intercession of Michael, Gabriel, Raphael, Zaphriel, Camael, Azarael, Uriel and Mazaldek. We entered the Inner Chamber, Nasorean priests of the Essene, to a sanctum draped in black where we stood between the mighty pillars of Boaz and Jachin, guardians of the kingly and priestly Messiahs. Before an altar of skulls, the Sovereign Grand Sacrificer wearing the head-dress of the High Priest of Yahweh, the golden mitre of Thebes, Amon-Re and James, greeted us with the words, "If you are fearful, go from hence; it is not permitted for men who cannot brave danger without abandoning virtue." We remained, steadfast in the everlasting Truth. We became guardians of the Holy of Holies, keepers of the secrets of the Temple of Jerusalem, protectors of the Ark of the Covenant, marksmen of the Royal Arch Purple, Kings of God, Knights of the Holy Temple of Jerusalem.

****

Even by the exacting standards of Ulster, Drum was a model village. Set in the rolling Monaghan hills about five miles south of Clones, it did not boast a single public house, tavern, hotel, betting shop or dance hall. Instead, the settlement of about 40 buildings comprised a thriving Church of Ireland congregation worshipping in the Anglican communion, a Presbyterian chapel of almost equal size and a Methodist meeting house. There was no Roman Catholic chapel in the vicinity, and no need of one. For, apart from those who attended the three most recognised Protestant religious institutions, others flocked to small meeting houses and prayer groups which were at least as averse to the doctrines of Rome. Drum, the hilltop village in the barony of Dartrey, was and remained as solidly Protestant as the Vatican City was Popish.

Albert Armstrong had entered the village by the small winding road which followed the crest of the hills from his farm in the nearby townland of Drumkirk. As he walked along purposefully, his feet crunched through a virgin blanket of crystallised snow which now bore the imprint of his long, sloping paces. The snow glimmered with frosted light and, before him, his steady breathing formed an enveloping cloud of steam through which he strode. In the absence of street lighting, the early winter darkness was pierced by a full moon and a blanket of stars which lit up the village.

Albert's subconscious registered the neat row of cottages on one side and a recessed group of buildings on the other, behind a tidy, but small, village green. These buildings included the village post office and shop over which the name of the proprietor, William Anderson, was inscribed. But as he crunched along through the frosty snow, Albert regarded them only with the lack of attention paid to everyday familiar objects and backdrops. His mind was deep in concentration reflecting on words of scripture he had read and re-read many times in preparation for tonight. They were from Psalm 133: "Behold, how good and how pleasant it is for brethren to dwell together in unity! It is like the precious ointment upon the head, that ran down upon the beard, even Aaron's beard; that went down to the skirts of his garments; As the dew of Hermon, and as the dew that descended upon the mountains of Zion; for there the Lord commanded the blessing, even life for ever more." Through the past year or more, Albert had sought and found reassurance from these words. Even in these darkest of hours, he could remain true to the institutions that bound his people together.

Albert clutched a neat parcel with one hand, tucked carefully under his elbow. Wrapped in heavy brown paper, it contained an ornate collar of a deep blue colour. It was not that he wanted to conceal this emblem of membership. On the contrary. But it was a cold December night and the respect he held for the badge of his lifelong apprenticeship to the cause of Ulster loyalism, dictated that it could not be worn under his heavy overcoat. Membership of the Royal Black Preceptory was a singular honour and Albert was utterly conscious of showing his collarette the respect that was its due.

Albert recalled vividly his inception into the Imperial Royal Black Chapter of the British Commonwealth. Almost ten years ago now it had been, during the golden era of Ulster loyalism when the Black was reincorporated into the loyal institutions to rank alongside the Orange. An Orangeman of good standing, holder of the Orange and the Plain degrees, he had long since taken his third degree, the purple. Raised from the dead into the truth of the living by the blast of a live gunshot from the ceremonial pistol, he had entered the Royal Arch Purple, the degree of the Marksman. A guardian then of the old system - the rites and traditions of the Orange Society brought to Ireland by the soldier followers of William III - he was called to the Black before a cross which bore the legend, *In Hoc Signe Vinces*. He remembered his own discomfort with the Latin inscription, the language of Romanism. His fears were dispelled by the obligatory averment of membership, "I was born of Protestant parents who were in no way nor at any time connected with the Roman Catholic faith and I was born in wedlock. I am married and my wife is a Protestant." So he had come into the ranks of the Sir Knights, the guardians of the faith, the holders of secrets, the lords of tradition, the foremost of the Orange.

As he covered the last few yards to the hall, glad to be getting indoors at last, he saw other men heading for the same destination. They were coming in the opposite direction, from the village forge. Back there, he could see, a group was still gathered around the scorching brazier while the blacksmith rang out metallic notes on a horseshoe held over a sturdy anvil. The forge was a favourite gathering spot for local young men. It offered the warmth, comfort and conviviality that other village communities sought in their local hostelries when abroad of a winter's night. Among the men approaching him, Albert spotted Robert James McConkey, another local farmer and Brother Knight. He hadn't encountered Robert James since both their sons had departed from Clones railway station for the special constabulary training camp in Newtownards, Co. Down, nearly six weeks ago.

"Och, Robert James, how are you?" Albert called out as the two men met up on reaching the steps that led up to the hall door. "Haven't seen you this good while."

Robert James, a big, thick-set man with sloping shoulders and a long, purposeful stride, gave a half-hearted smile of greeting. It was the best he could manage with his deeply creased face, a face which seemed to bear an eternal dour expression. Albert was well used to this. Although they farmed at opposite sides of Drum village, they had grown up in each other's company, attended the same school and the same place of worship. Now their sons, Sinclair and Roy, were best friends. They carried on a tradition among the males of both families that stretched back through many generations, possibly even to the border marches of England and Scotland where they had distant, now half-forgotten roots.

"No indeed, Albert."

"Suppose you're for the meeting?"

"Aye, just taking a wee warm up at the forge beforehand there."

"Many in yet?"

"Only a few. Plenty of stragglers the night."

"Time of year for it, I doubt."

They entered the door and, as it shut to in their wake, they both placed their small brown-paper parcels on a table in the box-like entrance, removed their hats and overcoats which they hung on hooks mounted on the gable wall beside the door. Then, they both went to the table and carefully opened their parcels. They donned the collarettes of the Rising Knights of Drum Royal Black Perceptory straightening out the brass trim, smoothing the wrinkles with big, coarse hands. Together, they then pushed through the interior door into the small hall where about seven other men were standing about at the far side chatting between several rows of chairs and benches.

"There you are now," said Robert James, "Many are called but few arrived."

"There's time yet."

"Aye, surely. So Albert, we see more of your young fellow nowadays."

"Aye, him and Roy's always been great."

"Companions is important when you're young."

"Any word from the pair of them up at the training camp in Newtownards? We haven't had a line since two weeks after they left," said Albert, not bothering to conceal his disappointment. Since his reluctant acquiescence in Sinclair's decision to join the Special Constabulary, he had hoped that it would not actually come to pass. For weeks, through the late summer and early autumn, he had hoped that the letter calling him up for training might not come. But it had and the young men had set off for their two-month training, far from home.

"Hadn't you heard, Albert? Roy's home this past week."

"That a fact? Never heard a word about it. Is he not well?"

"Och no. Just couldn't settle till it. I think it was some of those wide boys from Belfast was making it tough for him."

"Surely so. But Sinclair never sent word."

"Sudden enough. Time yet."

"Mind you, maybe that's why he hasn't been in touch."

"Bid to be."

"Wish to goodness Sinclair was clear of it, too. Sure, that's no place for him."

"Aye, right crowd of ruffians some of them Belfast boys, Roy says."

"Did he have any word on Sinclair so?"

"Aye, says he tried to get him home along with him. But Sinclair's to have said there was only a wee while more to go and he'd stick her out."

"Sure I thought myself a while back there, they were that long waiting to be called up, maybe they'd be forgot about entirely," said Albert, as they moved on into the hall and nodded greetings to the others already gathered there.

"Och well, Sinclair's well fit to look after himself. Wouldn't worry on that score."

"Never could take to the city myself, any few times I went up till her."

"Aye, same to myself. But Roy says there's plenty of decent young men there too. Sinclair and him was great with this boy called Morton, David Morton, I think. From down by Rockcorry way."

"Aye, think I know the family. Suppose it's not so bad he's great with a near-enough neighbour. And I'm sure there's others about."

"Deed there is, Albert. Roy says they're there from all over this country - Monaghan, Cavan, Fermanagh and all over."

"Sure, then, there's no need for him to truckle with those Belfast boys too much," Albert replied, just as his brother-in-law Bob Sinclair approached from across the hall, having just arrived from the forge gathering and now wearing his own collarette. Bob was obviously in high spirits, his face slightly flushed, whether from the heat or the cold or something taken internally, Albert could not be sure.

Since his very recent retirement from the Great Northern Railway company, Bob had moved out of his lodging in Clones and was now living permanently with his sister and her husband. But in the intervening period, he had been roaming the countryside around and dodging back into Clones to visit cronies. Albert suspected that Sadie would see little in the way of maintenance rent from her brother's pension. But he was not totally against Bob's decision to come and live with them. Goodness knows, with Sinclair gone, help would be needed about the farm and, whatever he might do in his spare time, of which he had more than enough at present, Bob could pull his weight when he was needed about the place.

"I see we're giving it to that Belfast crowd again," said Bob. "Too good for them. I doubt thon shower of blackguards would sell their young to get their way, forby what they done to us."

"Robert James was just telling me Roy's back home from Newtownards," Albert said, looking now at Bob. He realised immediately that, in his travels about the area, Bob would probably know this already. He would also have decided not to tell Sadie and him in case it might add to their deep concerns for their son. His suspicions were confirmed as he heard Robert James begin to say, "Sure, Bob...." But the sentence was not completed. Bob, with a flick of his eyes in the other man's direction, cut in, saying to Albert, "That a fact, now? When was that?"

Robert James got the signal: "We were just talking about the numbers from hereabouts that's up training to be special constables."

"Seems Roy couldn't take till it at all," explained Albert.

"Funny you should say that," said Bob. "In at the station there the day, I got talking to a wee man on the Belfast Express. The fireman like, wee fellow name of Rankin from up Portadown way. He told me they're getting up a whole go of special constables to operate along this frontier business now."

"Aye indeed?" said Albert. "Well, we can do with all the guns we can get about this country now. Judging from this Dublin news we've been getting about the so-called treaty and all."

"Speaking of the same," Robert James. "Hear tell it allows for transfers, across the frontier like. Some sort of a boundary commission will be sorting it all out."

"Transfers? Of counties, you mean?" Albert asked.

"Aye, that maybe, though I doubt Sir James won't be giving up any of his territory. But districts too, where the most of the people want moved or suchlike," said Bob. "Maybe about here like, where we have fair good numbers and are right close to the line."

"Well maybe there's hope for us yet," said Albert. "But the way things have been going, I'll not bank on it, so I won't. Though, must say, if they're moving this whole go of special constables into the area, maybe something could come of it."

In the background, a gavel sounded on the rough deal table as the meeting was called to order. A voice called out, "Sir Knights, Sir Knights, could we come to order now?" Albert noticed that there were about three dozen men present, a good turnout for the night that was in it. He also noticed the presence of the chaplain, Rev. Burns, and the guest speaker, Attorney M.E. Knight, out from Clones even on this inclement night. Maybe there would be good news, after all.

****

I have no news, but there is a hundred families gone through this town this week past for New England and all the Forsters as I gave you honour account. Mr Bellsore of Lisnaskea has set us fifty tates of land on the cross of Clones this day that is all waste, the tenants being all gone to New England. I believe we shall have none left but the Irish at last; but I hope your honour's estate will be safe enough for they complain most that the hardships of the tithes makes them all go; which is true, for the Clergy is unreasonable.

Letter to landlord Dacre Barret from his Clones agent, March 1718.

****

The low corrugated roof over the platform trapped the clouds of steam which billowed back down around the alighting passengers. Cases and trunks lowered from carriage doors were piled high and groups of people, awaiting porters or looking around in confusion as they sought out the way, clogged her passage. Whistles blew, shouts echoed and the persistent hiss of the steam engine caused a bedlam. Amid the chaos, she heard a harsh city accent announce the arrival of the early express from Enniskillen, Clones, Monaghan, Armagh and Portadown. Picking her way through the obstacle course, she fell in behind a group of elderly travellers making slow progress towards the ticket-collection booth. Hesitating intermittently, she paused and looked back to see if she had missed him. But her view was blocked by other passengers who had fallen into step behind her. Finally, she passed the engine and the exhaled steam was wafted back and dispersed. Handing her ticket to the collector, she emerged into a wide expanse of tiled floor crowded with people, some hurrying to catch a train on the other platform, others taking leave of them and yet others engaged in the frantic business of selling newspapers and other more mundane commercial affairs. It was all too confusing, Dorothy thought as she searched the crowds for sign of Sinclair. She felt agitated and a little frightened as her frantic gaze met a wall of unfamiliar faces. Then suddenly, from out of one large cluster of people, he emerged, his face beaming with a broad smile of greeting.

Dorothy's heart leaped in relief. She had longed for this day, again and again having to remind herself that, although he was in Newtownards now, she and Sinclair were seeing more of each other in these past few weeks than they had when he was at home in Drumkirk. Yet, always conscious of the distance between Newtownbutler and Belfast, she worried for him and anticipated anxiously these hours and moments they spent together, twice a week now, while he waited for his permanent posting. Please God, she prayed nightly, he will be sent down here with all the others who were coming in from throughout the North to form a growing frontier garrison.

Now, as he crossed the floor shouting needlessly, "Dorothy, here Dorothy love," she felt her entire being relax in his presence. Automatically, she fell into his wide embrace as they came together at last. Her head nestled against his broad chest and she squeezed him as tightly as she could, before breaking for a brief, but intimate kiss. Their lips caressed and parted, the sensation lingering as she noticed several onlookers staring at them in disapproval for even this cursory show of affection.

"Sinclair, love. Thought I'd miss you in the crowd."

"Och, not at all," he replied, smiling down on her, a smile that banished all her worries. "I was just checking with the information desk when the train was late. I'm here now."

They linked each other's arms and, like the two young lovers they were, began to make their exit onto Great Victoria Street at the heart of Belfast. Dorothy noticed with a sense of wonder, how nonchalantly Sinclair moved, wheeling her into the bustle of the city as if it didn't exist, sure of his direction and of his place in the affairs of this burgeoning industrial metropolis of the north. Dorothy was simultaneously aware of her own reaction to the confusion of it all. A country girl in the big city, nervous and overwhelmed. She thought again, and was conscious of the persistence of the thought as it arrived, that all the people she could see, and thousands more of them, tens of thousands in this city alone, were totally oblivious to any knowledge of her way of life. City people, she thought, think they know so much, but they are thoroughly taken up by their own wee patch. None of the people she could see now, she found herself thinking, probably knew of the existence of Newtownbutler, or any of the people who lived there, never mind her own wee community in the townland of Gortraw. How could that be, she wondered, when back at home we are so familiar with thoughts of Belfast and what the people there were doing and thinking? City life was a mystery, sure enough. Look at these people coming towards us, city girls out shopping and traipsing about. They are probably even incapable of thinking that Sinclair and I don't belong here, that we know somewhere else.

The anonymity of the city engulfed her, even frightened her more as she thought to herself, how would you know your own people here? That is, how would you recognise other Protestants in a big city? She had heard all that stuff about the distance between the eyes, but it made no sense now as she examined each passer-by trying to determine, is he or she ours or theirs. Back in Newtown, and all about it, she could tell. Dress, mannerism and the odd spoken word were as good a signal of who was what as name, school or any of the other labels we all wear on our sleeves. Even if they kept that frontier business in place, we will still know our own, she thought, relishing the security of thoughts of the familiar. Here in Belfast, so smug and secure in itself now, they move in a sea of uncertainty. They are different from Sinclair and me.

Dorothy tightened her grip on Sinclair's arm as he spoke, barely making out his words, a running commentary of all he had planned for their few hours together before she would get the late afternoon train back home. She didn't want to anticipate the day in its plans, just savour each moment as it came. She trusted Sinclair, even more so now in his newfound confidence here in the big city. As his assurance grew, she realised that her own confidence had faltered, probably because he was here and she was there at home, missing him, missing him all the time.

She thought of her arrival at Clones railway station today, cycling into town from Gortraw in the early morning dusk because the express train to Belfast did not stop in Newtownbutler. She was wheeling her bicycle into the small shed off the ramp, when she noticed a large black car pull up at the main entrance. A chauffeur had got out and opened the back door, from which emerged a very tall man sporting a drooping dark moustache, expensive hat and coat and a military bearing. Without by or leave, he had marched past Dorothy as she waited at the ticket booth and proceeded down the platform towards the first-class carriages of the Belfast train which was idling there. Then, as Dorothy counted out her change for the ticket, he was back, standing behind her and berating the official behind the glass partition. "You," he barked, "get me a porter. First-class carriage is a damned disgrace." Dorothy had withdrawn from the scene and was walking towards her own carriage, while hearing the ticket-seller saying, "Yes, Colonel. Immediately, sir." That little episode had delayed their departure for more than a quarter of an hour, she remembered now with a sense of resentment at the man. She remembered with some pleasure, however, seeing that railway porter, Maguire, hurrying along the platform towards the colonel's carriage with a bucket and brush. There would be no mocking remarks from him now, she thought, as there had been when he and that news vendor were making those jibes about the Orange parade in Clones.

Seems so long ago now, she thought. Then when she arrived in Belfast at last, standing there, looking and searching for Sinclair, anxious with the thought that he wouldn't see her. And now here, sitting in a teashop just off Royal Avenue and around the corner from Belfast City Hall. Funny, she remembered that scene at Clones station vividly still, yet she could barely remember coming in here now. Must be love, moving in a dream, sort of, with a man she trusted. A man who was now sitting there, across from her, chatting as if the words would cause him to explode if he didn't get them out fast enough. She, sitting here opposite a large plate glass window looking out onto bustling Royal Avenue, the crowds milling back and forth, some pausing to cross the street and waiting for clanging trams to pass by, thinking and not paying attention, just smiling and indulging herself in the pleasure of his company. Must pay attention now, she thought, else he'll think I've lost my reason sitting here with a stupid grin on my face . . .

"The marching and drilling is bad enough," Sinclair was saying, "But they have us our running and leaping as well. You know, the kind of thing that you'd have Joshua, you mind thon wee gelding I sold at Clones fair, up to ...."

"You must be exhausted with it all, Sinclair love."

"Then there's what they call recreation. But, sure, that's near as bad with the football and what have you. I take to my bed the odd time I'd get the chance."

"Are you getting out much from the camp?"

"Aye, well still the two times a week of a Saturday or today maybe. You know yourself. Last Saturday, Davy, mind I told you about him, and me, we went to the pictures in here in Belfast. Holy terra what they can do now."

"But you miss Roy, do you?"

"That much happening all the time, things you have to think about as well, the shooting and drill practice and all. But, aye, betimes you'd miss him about, annoying you head with his whinging and gurning, as they say here. Tell us, though, any word from him much?"

"Sure, you know he brought over your letter when he come home. He's in grand form, but I think he regrets leaving you behind here."

"Longest we've ever been apart, and it's only a wee bit over a week now, from the time we were childer."

"Did he have any trouble getting out of it? He didn't really say."

"Not a bother to him. Couple of day of whinging in the right quarters and he had the bag packed and away."

"Suppose there's that many going through, he'd not be missed anyway."

"Aye, and they're still coming in. Can't get us trained fast enough."

Dorothy sipped from her cup of tea, deciding not to indulge for now in the plate of sticky baps that somebody, a waitress she supposed, had placed on the table. She took the plate now and proffered its contents to Sinclair. He took one, sliced it open and began to slather on a thick coat of bright yellow butter from another small plate piled high with rolled pats of corrugated portions.

"Thanks, God, but I'm starved with the hunger," he said, munching a large bite.

"Must be all the running and leaping."

"Aye, but the mess, as they call it, you know the food like, it's not up to a whole terra."

"Aye, well, suppose when they're cooking for that many, it wouldn't be great fare."

Sinclair laughed, "Be God though, you'd want to see the way some of them boys from the city tuck into it. They'd ate just about anything that wouldn't ate them. You'd swear you could tie a nosebag on any of them and they'd just ate away all day."

"Roy says you still don't get on with them, the Belfast boys."

"Och, not as bad as at the beginning. But they stick to themselves a lot now. Them and the ones from Londonderry, you know, city boys. The rest of us find our own company and we get on the best. They don't bother us the way they did at the start when we knew near nobody."

"Och, sure you're near enough done now, I suppose."

"Aye, and I'll not be too sorry to see the back of it either."

"Any word on your posting?"

"Well, it's near definite it's Fermanagh anyway."

Dorothy was thrilled at the news, yet she wondered why he had not said so since her arrival. Goodness knows, they had talked of it often enough, worrying that he might be sent somewhere else, even further away or somewhere that was simply more inaccessible. Then there was the danger and all the other worries they did not mention. Good enough that she had this hope, she decided.

"That's great, Sinclair love. We'll be beside other again soon."

A scurrying movement outside, people gathering in a cluster that spilled out from the footpath and onto the road, traffic paused as everyone craned for a view of something across the street. Inside the scraping of chairs on the tiled floor as customers and staff became aware of the distraction. Outside a cheer and handclapping. Dorothy rose to her feet and the slight platform on which their table rested allowed her to see out over the crowd. She saw a car on the opposite side of the street where a few policemen stood guard as two men emerged and began to ascend the few steps to an imposing door adored with a shining brass plate. The tall man with the imposing moustache was ascending the steps with another man she recognised immediately as Sir James Craig. Dorothy grabbed Sinclair's hand across the table where he too had arisen and, nodding in the man's direction, she urged him to look.

"That's him now," she said. "The man held up the train at Clones station. With Sir James Craig."

Sinclair laughed, "Held it up? Robbed it you mean?"

"No, not at all. Delayed it for his carriage to be cleaned."

"That I can believe. That's Colonel Madden of Hilton Park. You know, out our way from Clones."

"Och, deed and I heard tell of him, sure enough. On the Ulster Unionist Council and big in the Ulster Volunteers, wasn't he?"

"Aye, he's a director of the Great Northern Railway company, too. Always up and down to Belfast here."

"Well, he fairly had them hopping the day with buckets and what have you."

"Aye, they'd be more feared of him nor the IRA," said Sinclair, laughing and causing Dorothy to giggle and snort as she tried to suppress a loud guffaw. As their laughter subsided, she glanced over at the customers at an adjoining table, one of whom was intermittently looking over at the laughing young couple nearby. His quizzical look, no doubt an indication that he was wondering about their political allegiance after the premier of Northern Ireland had arrived outside. It brought a fresh paroxysm of laughter from Dorothy, which only set Sinclair off again.

That is what she would remember of the day, she thought later and often, the laughter, the closeness, the sharing of secrets and experiences as they explored their growing intimacy. And later, after the teashop, the stroll through busy streets, even a brief visit to a picture house with its dazzling projections on a big white screen, and then a final stop for afternoon tea. They clung to each other as they entered Great Victoria

Street station. Her earlier sense of being overwhelmed by the city had disappeared, simply dissipated in his company. She reflected on the other Sinclair of only a few months before. The unsure, indecisive young man held in awe and deference by his father. The young man she had teasingly mocked for his lack of confidence in himself, now transformed into a strong and sure escort even in the big city. Although they were about to part, she knew she would always be in his heart, as he was in her's. Yet, all around, there were reminders of the wider world. Inside the station, posters proclaimed the news, Dublin Accepts Treaty, an announcement taken up by small boys carrying bundles of newspapers and shouting out to passers-by in almost incomprehensible accents.

"Hold on," Sinclair said, extracting his arm from hers. "I'll just get one of these."

He soon returned with a copy of the *Belfast Evening Telegraph* which he scanned quickly.

"Is it all over then?" she asked, trying to read the headlines.

"Only one thing for sure. You can't trust thon crowd down there," he replied as a train whistle cut through the noise in a shrill signal. Dorothy tugged his arm, "C'mon love. I'll miss my train."

Sinclair took a grasp of her elbow and, as they ran down the platform, he virtually lifted her along, causing her to call out at one stage, "Easy there. I'm not training for the constabulary, you know."

Laughing again, he helped her on board a carriage and waited as she rushed through to a seat and opened the window to where he stood. "Thanks, Sinclair love. I had a really great day."

"Pity you can't stay on a wee while more."

"Och, never mind, I'll be back up in a few days. Next week, anyway."

"Aye, Wednesday'd be good. I'll be here to meet you. And I mean that about giving you the price of the tickets. Damned the much else to do with the money."

The whistle blew again and the guard walked along the platform calling out for immediate boarding of the express train for Portadown, Armagh, Monaghan, Clones and Enniskillen

"Regards to all at home," Sinclair said, anxiously filling the silence of their last moments together.

"Aye, come here, love," she said. Sinclair grabbed the window ledge and hauled himself up for a final kiss.

"Knew that training would come in handy," he said, not quite breaking the tenderness of the moment. The train began to move slowly, chunting out of the station as they kissed warmly and he dropped back down. And, as the carriages receded from view, he stood watching and missing her already.

She took her seat as he disappeared from view, there alone on the platform, and she missed him too.

****

It is allowed by all Moralists, that the love of our native country is not only one of the noblest, but that it is also one of the most universal passions that influences the human mind. It would be a mere waste of words and time to enlarge on so known a Truth, and especially when it is to be followed at the heels with this melancholy reflection, that there is hardly a spot on Earth on the Globe where it seems to have less influence than here in Ireland. Whether this proceeds from the ill usage or misfortunes too many among us meet with in it, or from its being so often in a very unsettled precarious way, and what is worse, so frequently a scene of War and Rebellion, Poverty and Famine, which has weaned man's affections from it, or that there is less of profit or pleasure to be found in it than in other parts of the World, which makes us fond of rambling abroad, certain it is that most of us seem to regard it, rather as a nurse or fosterer, than as real parent and use it accordingly.

Dr. Samuel 'Premium' Madden, Hilton Park, Clones
Resolutions & Recommendations for the Gentlemen of Ireland, 1733.

****

"Many things have happened in recent times which would be calculated to take the heart out of an Irish Protestant, and especially an Ulster Protestant from one of these excluded counties," boomed the voice of the Rev. Robert Burns. From his vantage, right in the front row, Albert Armstrong could see that the minister was in the throes of a full frontal assault. All around him, he could feel the congregation straining at the bit on the preacher's every word.

"But, while we can testify that our Glorious Heritage is still a living and vital force among us, the latest dastardly betrayal is almost enough to drive us to despair. We must, therefore, learn to protect ourselves. We must band together and ruthlessly cast out any person who would dare to sow dissension among Protestants. We must take all possible measures for the time when we shall be as sheep left in the midst of wolves. Because, humanly speaking, we are left defenceless."

Burns paused and Albert coughed. He wondered immediately why he did that. Indeed, why did others scattered around the pews do the very same thing? Nervousness maybe, he thought as he raised his eyes and found the minister staring directly at him. In a moment of fresh anxiety, Albert averted his eyes, looking up at the stained glass window to the rear of where Burns stood. The window depicted a flaming bush with, underneath, the single word, "Redeemed." Hardly seems appropriate for what's been happening to us, Albert thought, as he renewed his concentration on the sermon.

Burns was now reading from the heavy tome on the lectern, "For I have heard a voice as of a woman in travail, and the anguish as of her that bringeth forth her first child, the voice of the daughter of Zion, that bewaileth herself, that spreadeth her hands, saying, woe is me now, for my soul is wearied because of murderers. Jeremiah, 4, 31."

The clergyman paused, closing the book and now continued in a more even, explanatory tone. "The British government has shown that its chief end is to placate the foe, rather than protect the friend. The Northern Ireland government has shown that it stands for itself alone. Having bolted the door on the three counties, it has no further concern for their fate."

Another brief pause, more coughs. Albert restrained his urge, despite the tickle at the back of his throat. Burns began again, this time punching out his words with thrusts of his fist, adding conviction and force to his pronouncements. Albert could almost feel himself flinching at the message.

"Thank God we have a stronger protection than either of these two parliaments can offer. We have the protection of Almighty God Himself. I therefore counsel you not to put your trust in princes, nor in politicians, nor in any child of man, but in the Great Eternal God. I counsel you to put aside everything which is not in accordance with God's will in order that your cause may be more truly His. I counsel you to stick together, determined to resist by every means, every encroachment on your hard-won liberties. For there are times when resistance is not only lawful, but a solemn duty."

Albert wondered briefly if the congregation would rise to its feet and cheer. His inclination to do so was now every bit as urgent as had been his urge to cough earlier. But this was church, he reminded himself. Time for cheering, or crying maybe, later.

"So brethren let us remember," Burns admonished his congregation. Then, turning to the side to indicate with a sweeping gesture of his arm the window, he bellowed his final sermon observation, "Though Horeb's bush is burning, it shall never be consumed."

Loud coughing again, but glancing around him as he reached for his pocket handkerchief, Albert could tell that others were equally impressed as he was. Goodness knows, they all needed a few words like that to stiffen their resolve. Things had been going badly, not least in the absence of Sinclair from home in these trying and troubled times. The pity was he had nobody to talk to about it. In the past, before Sinclair left, he'd maybe go down by the forge sometimes, talk with the other men, his neighbours. But he'd only find Bob about there now and he'd maybe have a wee bottle on the go and, sure, Albert knew that he had no head for strong drink. Maybe about the Twelfth, or around Christmas time. But the rest of the year, he'd leave it alone, thanks all the same. Wouldn't be worth it anyway for the tongue-lashing he'd get from Sadie if he came home with a smell of strong drink on his breath. The same Sadie as wouldn't say a cross or untoward word to her own brother that took a drop, and maybe a lot more, every day of the week now. Funny, he thought, how women will tolerate more from blood kin than they will from others. Aye, maybe even especially from their husbands. No sign of him here at service, either. He wasn't gospel greedy, the same Bob. But you couldn't say that fornenst his sister.

Well, if Sinclair was here they could talk, he knew. Those last weeks, before he went off, they talked all the time, discussing not only how Albert would manage the farm, but also about these Troubles. Sinclair knew a fair bit from his wee jaunts over about Newtown and his chats down at the forge. Man a dear, he devoured a few newspapers too in those weeks, cycling down to Anderson's every day to pick one up and poring over it for hours for the news from Belfast and Dublin and all about.

If Sinclair was here now, he'd be fit to tell him all that's happening, stuff Albert knew wouldn't be making it into the papers that they'd have up in Belfast or Newtownards. Stuff like the growing concern about the flight of young Protestant men, just like Sinclair himself, and even older men across this new frontier. Bob had told him of whole families taking the trains to Belfast and Enniskillen. Goodness knows, even the wee gatherings down at the forge these days included fewer young men, apart from Roy McConkey who had come home, of course. He'd tell Sinclair, if he could, about the recent meeting he and some of the other lodge elders had with Attorney Knight and Councillor Carson. Albert was surprised himself at the venom which greeted Knight's assurance that the Protestants of Monaghan would get full backing from Sir James Craig's government if they were threatened by the rebels down in Dublin. They were right, of course, to doubt the so-called Ulster loyalists with whom they had signed a solemn and binding league and covenant back in those bygone days of yore. Robert James had summed it up for them: "They sold us out already," he had declared. "Why give them the chance to do the same over again?"

Knight had talked of binding together in common cause. Made sense and, for a while, Albert had recalled the days of the volunteers, the memory of standing shoulder to shoulder with loyalists from all over the province of Ulster, drilling, camping out at Knockballymore House that time, getting the guns that were dispatched from the docks at Larne and stored in the big house at Hilton Park and even down in the local Orange hall here in Drum. Glorious times, surely, even if there was that impending sense of doom to it all in the end. He thought of the Ulster Hall rally only, what was it, eighteen months ago, when the fate of loyal Protestants in Monaghan, Cavan and Donegal was sealed, not by rebels and traitors, nor by the trickster politicians over in London, but by their very own. The bitterness of the betrayal swelled in his throat again and he knew that there would be no great mobilisation of armed loyalists about here now. No, the young men were being sucked out to defend the very people who had sold them out. Their own people were left defenceless and alone on this side, trapped between two armed camps. Lambs to the slaughter, it might transpire at the heel of the hunt.

The thought reminded him of how life had changed in only a few short years. How the Protestant community now clung to home, eschewing many of the pastimes that used to bond it together. Pastimes like hunting maybe. He remembered the thrill and exhilaration of the hunt, the gathering of the beagle hounds, the pursuits over the hills and down through valleys, the dogs always ahead, fanning this way and that in search of the scent of a hare, the sound of the horn at the sighting, the dogs taking off in a pack and the huntsmen following on foot, moving along at a canter, scrambling over obstacles to maintain their view of the pack, anticipating the chase. Then there was always the build-up of the excitement in the chase itself, men running as hard as they could for a vantage to see the action, urging on their dogs and the hare too betimes if it was putting up a good contest.

He used to keep a couple of hounds himself, a pair of cross-bred beagles from the same litter out of a pack they called the Corragarry Blazers. He called the dogs Fife and Drum which always raised a few eyebrows in mixed gatherings. But the hunt was common ground and it was the dogs and their prey that were the centres of attraction. The dogs died within two weeks of each other and, despite several offers of pups from neighbours, he had not felt inclined to replace them. Then he just got out of the habit of it. He regretted it now, of course, not least because the hunting used to make for great fun of a winter Saturday when there wouldn't be too much happening about the place. The other side hunted on Sundays mostly, so it was not usual that the packs would be mixed. Yes, indeed, even the hounds carried the religion of their owners and Albert had often remarked that Protestant dogs worked harder in the chase and weren't as easily distracted as those from the other side. It said something of their breeding maybe. But it was the adventure of it mostly, going to a new but maybe wee bit familiar area and joining in with local men and dogs from about there for what they called a drag hunt. There were few entertainments to beat it surely.

That time beyond in Ashfield when they had tramped through several townlands after the pack, leaping across sheoughs, climbing over fences and pushing through broken hedges. Finally on a wide hill meadow, they ran the wee puss to ground, dogs dodging this way and that after the animal. At several points, it seemed like the wee hare would actually give them all the slip, but she was caught eventually and there was a collective groan from the men who watched, each by then hoping the prey would escape their own dogs. It was Fife that ran her to ground in the end and he recalled the brief anger he felt towards his own dog at that time. But wasn't he only following his own nature, the God-given urge to hunt for survival.

He had seen some of the gentry hunting, too, the Maddens of Hilton Park, the Dawsons of Castle Dartrey and others, but always on horseback. It somehow didn't seem the same fun to him - all got up in fancy hunting clothes and jackets, horses tramping the hedges round about. The wee hare or fox or whatever they were chasing didn't have the same chance in that game. In his youth he had also beaten the heather and ferns for a pheasant shoot, but that too seemed less fair than the simple pursuit on foot of a pack of hounds. Lord Erne beyond in Crom Castle raised flocks of pheasants for the shoot, penned up in an enclosure on the wee island between the big house and the walled gardens. But wouldn't that be like shooting your own livestock in the heel of the hunt. Whatever others might say, the drag hunt with dogs and men on foot was a fair contest as far as he was concerned.

There was no fair contest here now. And it was the Protestants who were being hunted into the bargain. The threats had been real enough, too, and too damned close to home for any comfort or doubt. In the *Northern Standard* only last week, there was a letter from Eoin O'Duffy, the Sinn Feiner who had led the rebels hereabouts. Used to work with Bob down at the railway station, too, didn't he? Albert had been alarmed by the tone and the words. They left little enough to the imagination as O'Duffy poured his scorn and bile on those who would deviate from his line and he pointed the finger at the so-called "Robber Gang from Drum." The wee fenian scut, Albert now thought, excusing himself such a sentiment in church, for it was well deserved and more besides.

O'Duffy, of course, was still smarting from that day, three years ago, when he led his Murder Gang out this way to intimidate the good God-fearing loyalists of Drum from opposing him in the election. They came armed with their hurley sticks, but the boys in the village would have none of it. They went to the forge and they got the caulkers from a barrel and the hurley sticks had to go.

Then the rebels sent for reinforcements, but they never got up Pump Brae for all their big talk and rebel ways. O'Duffy's motor was smashed, Albert recalled with pleasure, and he had to run for his life. Now, he had the cheek to tell us that the eyes of the British army and the eyes of the IRA are on us. We'll let him know that Drum always welcomes His Majesty's Army, and the army knows that too and they always welcomed the people of Drum. But if O'Duffy or any of his rebel scum put their noses into Drum, they'd hear about it, and no mistake.

Albert could feel a slight tug on his sleeve and remembered with a start that he was in church now. The congregation was rising to its feet as Rev. Burns urged them to do with his wide-armed gesture. Albert scrambled to his feet as Burns intoned, "Now, let us rise and sing ...."

Sadie helped him to find the right page in his hymnal as the strains rang out:

O God our help in ages past,
Our hope for years to come,

Our Shelter from the stormy blast,
And our eternal home.

As he joined in with gusto, his voice rising in volume but not quite finding the right key, Albert reflected that he could not have chosen a better anthem for the times.

Rev. Burns was greeting the members of his congregation as they filtered out the door after the service. Giving a word of advice here and a word of warning there, Sadie had no doubt as she prepared to join the general exodus. Sure, it was ever like this since he came about the place. But he was a good man, she knew, only he thought that he was dealing here with simple people, him not being from the country like. She knew he meant well, but maybe he spent too much time laying down the law for people who were strong and resolute in their God-fearing ways in any case. If he listened a bit more and talked a bit less, maybe he would find that out.

"Come on, Albert," she urged. "They'll have us locked in here if we don't get a wee bit of a move on."

Poor Albert, she thought, he's aged a lot this past wee while. Seems distracted all the time, like during the service there. He usedn't to be like that though, not till poor Eric was killed. Even then, his distraction wasn't nearly as bad until Sinclair went off. Not dead, of course, but gone from home. Who knows if he would ever come back, or even be able to come home if he had a will to do it? You heard so many stories now about other families, the raids and intimidation. Mrs Anderson was telling her only the other day about the Fergusons over by Magherashaghry way, how they came in, the rebels, and started asking about their son, Jackie, who went off to join the constabulary way back a good while ago. Put a real fright on the Fergusons, and more besides about here, Sadie knew. An awful thing it is that honest, God-fearing families can't go about their own business without the thought they might be killed in their own beds. Hunted by the army of Herod seeking their first-born sons. Now only herself, Albert and Bob about the place and Bob's seldom enough there. And sure, look at Albert now, shuffling along like that.

"Albert, Mrs Armstrong, how are you?" Rev. Burns greeted them as they finally emerged, the last of the stragglers.

"Inspiring words, Mr Burns," Sadie remarked.

"Indeed, grand sermon altogether," Albert agreed.

"Well, hope springs eternal from the words of the Lord," Burns said. "The Lord of hosts is with us; the God of Jacob is our refuge. Psalm 46, 11. Tell me, any word from young Sinclair? He's managing up in Newtownards, is he?

"Och, grand entirely, by what we hear tell from Dorothy," Sadie said, noticing that the mention of Dorothy's name was dismissed cursorily by the minister, although she thought she did detect a slightly raised eyebrow.

"His place really should be at home with his family in these trying times," said Burns. "I have been a stranger in a strange land, Exodus 2, 14."

"Och, sure you know the ways of the young," Albert said. Sadie herself added, "Aye, and Dorothy says he's near finished up there now."

Again he failed to take the bait, Sadie thought, as Burns proceeded to ask, "Anybody helping you out at home, Albert?"

"Well, Bob's there now," Sadie replied. "My brother, you know, retired from the railway."

"Not too much needs doing about these times," said Albert. "Dorothy was ...."

"That is the young girl from Newtownbutler?" asked Burns, to Sadie's relief. She thought he had gone soft or something, the way he had ignored earlier references and Sadie wanted this out in the open.

"A word of advice, scriptural, you know," said Burns. "As a jewel of gold in a swine's snout, so is a fair woman which is without discretion. Proverbs 11, 22."

Sadie braced herself and struck home, "Aye, Mr Burns, but remember, 'Who can find a virtuous woman? For her price is far above rubies," Proverbs 31, 10, I think you'll find."

Burns reeled back slightly and Sadie could see that Albert had turned to look at her in wide-eyed amazement. Let that straighten his hump, she thought.

"You're a righteous woman, Sadie Armstrong, and you read your Scripture," said Burns, clearly taken aback. "Let's hope you're right, though. Good day now."

"Aye, good day, Mr Burns," said Sadie, linking Albert's arm as Burns repaired into the church, and together they walked towards the gate.

"That was a powerful bit of quoting you did there, Sadie," said Albert.

Sadie stopped and smiled up at him, "Aye, wasn't bad, was it?"

"How did you come up with it at all?"

"Sure, I've been saving it up his good while now. I knew from the way he ignored Dorothy and disapproved, that he would say something at the latter end. So I read up and learned that wee bit to throw back at him."

They laughed and left for home.

The news got worse, not better, of course. Raids, shootings, armed men marching about in broad daylight, the British forces confined to barracks, pending a total withdrawal. They would be gone any day now, the word went. The rebels in control of everything and the Royal Irish Constabulary, themselves under sentence of dissolution, unable to do anything to curtail the advances of the growing rebel forces or their excesses. Men were hauled before make-shift rebel courts to answer to so-called judges.

Harsh and bitter words were traded openly, mocking and warning Protestants all through the area of who called the tune now. And the tune would not be sweet.

A frontier which had not existed this time last year, slowly became an impenetrable line, demarking two distinct orders. Over there, not but a few miles or even yards away, Sir James Craig was battening down the hatches. With Capt. Basil Brooke to the fore, armed constables, including thousands of new special constables, were being set up in garrisons along the line. Nearby Fermanagh was almost entirely an armed camp. Young men who answered the call from Monaghan, Cavan and Donegal could not even come home to spend Christmas with their families. Too dangerous, everyone agreed. The rebels knew who had gone too. Looks, off-hand comments and open threats warned their families. It was a bitter greeting for the festive season.

The words of the prophet echoed ironically through the lacklustre Christmas celebrations: "Art Thou not our God, who didst drive out the inhabitants of this land before Thy people Israel, and gavest it to the seed of Abraham Thy friend for ever. And they dwelt therein, and have built Thee a sanctuary therein for Thy name saying, If when evil cometh upon us, as the sword, judgement, or pestilence, or famine, we stand before this hour, and in Thy presence, (for Thy name is in this house,) and cry unto Thee in our affliction, then Thou wilt hear and help. And now, behold the children of Ammon and Moab and Mount Seir, whom Thou wouldst not let Israel invade, when they came out of the land of Egypt, but they turned from them, and destroyed them not. Behold, I say, how they reward us, to come to cast us out of Thy possession, which

Thou hast given us to inherit."

As the new year dawned, it was more of the same. The awful bitter legacy of 1921 was compounded by the headlong rush of 1922 to destroy all we had built.

People waited for the worst. Too often, they got what they expected.

Dorothy was shaken to wakefulness and confusion, her body sore from the hard wooden bench on which she had been sleeping across from the near-exhausted embers of an open coal fire. Slowly she became aware of her surroundings, a waiting room at Clones railway station. She remembered now, coming in here earlier this morning. The face in the back window of that motor car as it sped past her where she had dismounted on hearing its approach. Even as she stood there in the hedge, holding her bicycle, the car's wheels had sent up a spray from a puddle, splashing her good coat. There were armed men in the car, she knew, holding that poor man who stared out from the back, a look of fear and pleading in his eyes. She remembered one other face as the car receded from view, turning also and staring back at her. The eyes were cold as steel. It had frightened her, but not enough to stop her going on to catch the train. She had to see Sinclair who was still waiting for his permanent posting, all these weeks, hoping he would come soon.

She had reached the station at last and there was that other face at the ticket booth, Maguire again, Hughie Maguire. She now knew his name, but never let on as she asked for her same-day return ticket to Belfast. Maguire simply said, "Don't know if she'll be running, Miss." Dorothy remembered asking why and being told there was "some bother out the road." Nothing more, just that intending passengers were to be warned of the delay and possible cancellation of trains. She had said she would wait and came in here, to the glowing fire, the welcome heat. As minutes stretched to hours, she waited still for the sound of a train, resting now and then, and then this. The voice now waking her.

"Dorothy? Hey, Dorothy? You awake?"

It was Sinclair's uncle, Bob. She was relieved to see a face she knew and trusted.

"Sorry to frighten you, daughter."

"Och, it's you, Mr Sinclair. Lost track of where I was."

"What has you here anyway?"

"Waiting for the Belfast train."

"Sure, it's been cancelled until the noon express and they're not certain of that yet."

"I was to go up to see Sinclair. He'll be worried, for he was to meet me at the station."

"Time enough yet. They'll have told him at the other side anyway."

"He'll be fretting by now."

"Listen, he'll know and you can send him on a telegram maybe."

"I'd better. What's happened Mr Sinclair? They said there was trouble out the road."

Bob sat down beside her, his voice a near-whisper, "Have you not heard? There was raids all round this country early the day. Men lifted from their homes right, left and centre, I hear tell."

"What men?"

"From out your own way and nearer. Up to forty of them, I hear tell, and all our side too. The Shinners are holding them up at their barracks in the old workhouse."

"What for?"

"Seems they're to be traded for the men from about here was lifted up at Dromore last Sunday," he said, and Dorothy remembered now. The IRA gang on the way to a gaelic football match somewhere in Derry, lifted at a checkpoint around Dromore in Co. Tyrone and guns found on them. She had been cheered by the news then, but not now.

"Sure the roads is all closed now, and armed men on them on both sides."

"Has there been any shooting? I didn't hear any."

"Not yet, but it's touch and go, as they say. Tell you, though, it's no day to be abroad."

"But I've got to get home, Mr Sinclair. Mum'll be worried there too."

"Best you stay put here in the town, for now anyway. It's not safe to try and get home," said Bob, whose comforting arm now brought Dorothy to her feet. "Come on, I'll take you round to Mrs Hutchinson, my old landlady. She'll make you a wee bit to eat anyway."

"I want to send that telegram first."

"Aye, right, I'll take you to the post office too, soon as I get on my coat. Hung it back of the ticket office when I came in to see the boys."

As Dorothy waited on the platform for Bob who went through a door marked "Staff only," she could hear a conversation from the ticket booth. Out of sight, she recognised the voices of that man, Maguire and his crony from the news kiosk, Reilly. She quickly realised they were talking about her trips to Belfast - twice a week, Maguire reported.

"Was thinking she must have got a big job for she's up and down as often as ould Madden himself," he told Reilly.

"Not at all, it's courting she's at, young Sinclair Armstrong from out Drum way. He's up there learning to be a Special constable."

"Must be a good lock from about here in the Specials now."

"Aye, and maybe more in the IRA, specially since the Truce," said Reilly. "There'll be bad trouble yet. She has all the signs of it."

Bob Sinclair emerged and, as the door slammed shut behind him, the voices went silent.

By the time the regular army departed, it was a spent force. For months, the officers and men of His Majesty's Forces had been confined to the barracks on The Diamond. Now a small token garrison, no longer even able to show the flag, they had waited. From the barracks windows, they had to endure the constant sight of those who had shot at them from behind walls and hedges assuming the role they once had played. The makeshift rebel force marched across the large market square. As the south of Ireland slipped from Britain's grasp and the Irish Free State was born, those who had waged a reign of terror assumed the reins of control. Young IRA men, the fugitives from justice of a few months ago, now strutted around in full view - like peacocks in their green military tunics, brandishing guns and stopping decent, loyal and God-fearing citizens from going about their business. The ignominy of the changeover was felt keenly within the loyalist population of Clones and the surrounding area. Try as they might, they could not countenance the abject reality of it all. Tea parties and other occasional social gatherings had only accentuated the imminence of the time when the garrison would be withdrawn. Attorney Knight's wife, Clemina had organised a small committee of loyal local ladies who hosted the little gatherings, as much to maintain heart in the local Protestant community as to assure His Majesty's officers and men that they were still more than welcome among them. But all the time, they knew it would not last. Then, loyalists would be truly at the mercy of the gunmen.

No use looking north either, as Robert James McConkey had warned so poignantly a few months ago. Just as the Irish Free State became an armed camp of rebels, so too the North was preparing for the siege with no concern for those who had not made it inside the walls of the new frontier. For days now, the main roads had been closed, armed groups facing each other after the kidnappings. As the hostage-taking became the subject of delicate negotiations, with London acting as the arbitrator between Dublin and Belfast, we waited for war. In the ominous silence, a great unheard cry went up from the people as they prayed, "Cast forth lightning, and scatter them: shoot out thine arrows, and destroy them. Send thine hand from above; rid me, and deliver me out of great waters, from the hand of strange children; Whose mouth speaketh vanity, and their right hand is a right hand of falsehood. Psalm 144, 6-8."

And today, February 3, 1922, was the day of the final leave-taking, a sombre, almost ridiculous affair. Loyalists gathered around the platform erected beside the Queen Victoria Jubilee monument on The Diamond. The decorative fountain in the monument itself had been shut off, because some vandal had emptied soapy water into it and bubbles had wafted across the platform to the amusement of the rebel supporters gathered beyond at the Ulster Bank corner and outside the Market House, small clusters of disaffected clowns. A small band of stalwarts stood in front of the platform now. Most were missing, afraid to identify themselves openly for fear of what might come next. We tried to put a brave face on it. If we had nothing left but decorum, then that was what we would show.

In the background, a few Free State soldiers mingled with clusters of their local supporters. Their jibes and catcalls were hurtful, piercing us to the quick. But none of them dared say it to our faces.

Dorothy, staying over at Mrs Hutchinson's until the roadblocks were lifted, met Roy McConkey. He seemed on edge, loitering on the periphery of the loyalist gathering. But he was glad to see her nonetheless, she knew. They spoke in low voices, looking all the time, not at each other, but at the platform itself on which the local unionist leaders and their wives were ranged in a semi-circle of chairs.

"Said they knew I was in Newtownards and wanted to know who else from about here was up there," Roy said.

"What did you say?"

"Told them nothing, But then they started on about Sinclair. Sure, they knew all anyway."

"What was the point then, Roy?"

"A warning, I suppose. For him as much as me."

"Cassidy was the name of the leader, you say?"

"Aye, from down below Scotshouse way. He'd know Sinclair, by sight if nothing else."

"Aye, seems it's well known hereabouts. I was telling you about what happened down at the station? The talk about Sinclair?"

"Aye, I heard from Bob Sinclair. Listen, best if you can get on home. Aye, and maybe stay away from the town while all this is going on."

"And yourself, Roy? What about you?"

"Sure where else could I go but home. It's safe enough out our way."

"You sure?"

"Aye, they don't come about Drum too much."

"Seems they like to have it on their own terms, right enough."

Taking leave of Roy, Dorothy moved on through the crowd as a regimental brass band played in the background. Martial airs, she thought, doesn't seem right for a retreat. A small group of soldiers approached the platform from the direction of the barracks opposite. An officer ascended the steps and was greeted by a number of the local loyalist dignitaries, among them Mr Knight and Col. Madden. The ladies committee stood to the side, Mrs Knight holding a beautiful shining trumpet that the local loyalist community would present to the regimental band as a token of abiding loyalty and appreciation. Off to the side, some whoops came from among the band of rebels, or Free State soldiers as they now called themselves. Dorothy saw Sinclair's mother in the crowd and sidled in beside her.

"Och, Dorothy pet, how are you?" Sadie asked, as Dorothy noticed her eyes welling with tears. "That's it now. They were all that was between us and this IRA crowd. Now they're away too."

"Och, don't worry Mrs Armstrong. Sure isn't the police still here."

"Police, you say? Sure most of them is as bad now."

"How do you mean?"

Sadie sounded angry, her voice on edge, "Sure they did nothing when all them poor men and boys was taken off. Just let them at it and they still have them out the road beyond. God knows what will happen now."

"Aye, I saw some of them on the day it happened. Put the heart across me, it did. And you say, do you, that they did nothing in them kidnappings, the police I mean?"

"Sure it's not the police any more, is it?" said Sadie. "They call them Civic Guards here now. All the loyal police in the RIC is retired on pension or else gone off across the frontier to join the constabulary there."

Dorothy had heard that, of course, but she had thought that with some of the same RIC officers in the new police force of the Free State, they would behave as they always had.

Sadie grasped her arm and drew Dorothy close, "Hope to goodness

Sinclair's safe. He's well clear of this anyway."

****

Bide your time, for we are ready,
Treason shall no longer thrive,
Ye are hot, we cool and steady,
Mad ye are with us to strive,
Mock philanthropists now hear us,
Rotten patriots attend;
If you don't, we'll make you fear us,
We are not the men to bend.

****

Sinclair Armstrong relaxed as the Belfast train rounded the track under Gough's Bridge and eased into the final stage of its journey to Clones station. Up front, the engine released a long shrill blast of the whistle as it chugged at a quickening pace along the mile-long stretch into the station, anxious to make its timetable schedule. To his left, Sinclair saw the lazy hill of Clonkirk townland recede behind the enclosed carriage in which he sat. It dropped away bluntly giving way to Largy, another squat drumlin which nosed its way into the town. Along the lower reaches ran the lane which once served as a major coach road between Enniskillen and Monaghan town here in the lowlands of the Erne Valley. On the opposite side was the new road, cutting across the bogland. The train began to slow down as it entered the final stretch. Sinclair peered out beyond the glass-panelled door and the windows on the far side at the familiar landscape beyond the short stretch of flat bog, where once a lake formed a defensive bulwark for the fortress of Clones. The lake had long since receded and the marshy bottom now drew the eyes to what lay beyond. Drumlin hills cascaded off into the horizon. The highest, out there beyond Ture, enveloped his home in Drumkirk.

How long had it been now? Almost four months. He had never been away so long. Come to think of it, he had never been away more than a night or two. Yet, even now he knew he could not return easily. Six weeks of training, followed by two months in the Belfast barracks at Mount Pottinger, his life had changed remarkably. Then, when his transfer had finally come through for a fixed posting, he hardly expected it to be as good. Enniskillen - it would be just like coming home.

Sinclair loosened the top buttons of his ill-fitting tunic, dyed dark green with mismatched brass buttons. In the rush to turn out reserve police officers, the constabulary had improvised with what uniforms came to hand. They would just have to do until more could be manufactured. They would suffice for now, as long as there were enough guns to go around and despite the fact that the outfits appeared unkempt on a lot of the young men being turned out of the training camp. Sinclair twisted his neck against the mandarin collar, which gave way to the pressure, and felt some relief. The rifle he had held so anxiously between his knees since crossing the frontier at Tyholland between Armagh and Monaghan, about 20 miles back along the track, he now allowed to lie casually against his crotch. Back in the familiar countryside of his birth, he felt his apprehension disappear and give way to a surge of confidence that surprised him. It had been so long since he had felt such a sensation.

"This is Clones coming up now, Sergeant," he needlessly informed the man sitting opposite him. Sgt. Alex Dougherty, a man of maybe only a few years more than Sinclair himself and the others, was only distinguished from the his charges in the carriage by the three white stripes on his right sleeve. "She'll not be long more till we're back inside the Six Counties."

"Aye, not before time either," Dougherty replied curtly.

"Don't we have a wee bit of a wait?" asked Davy Morton, the young man who sat alongside Sinclair, his close companion of the past few months. They had bonded together as outsiders from the day they had reported to the training camp in Newtownards. Morton, from the Rockcorry area of Co. Monaghan, had also endured the snide remarks of the other young recruits from Belfast long after Roy McConkey had gone home. Had it not been for Davy, Sinclair knew, he might have cut out of it himself.

"Aye, about half an hour for the other connections to come in from Dundalk and Cavan way," said Sinclair. "You won't notice it, Davy boy."

The train now slowed considerably as it pulled into the Ulster Yard, losing speed by the seconds marked out now in the sound of the tracks underneath. From the steady rhythm of beating they fell to clanking and jarring as the train moved from one parallel line of tracks to another.

Cattle pens to the right, crowded by morose beasts, slowly disappeared from view. At a long low warehouse on a flat platform, bundles of retted flax in Raygo bags were stacked up for their journey to scutching and spinning mills in Portadown and Lisburn, whence the linen fibres would be sent on to Belfast weaving mills. A coalyard opened up to view, where a couple of blackened faces simultaneously moved back reluctant dray horses for the final load of the day. To the left, the open countryside had given way to a long line of coniferous trees, an inadequate screen to the backs of houses on the hill opposite, The Diamond.

Another shrill whistle and the Belfast train chugged lazily past the signal box at the level crossing on Lower Fermanagh Street at the foot of Church Hill. Several children had clambered onto the gates and, as they waited for the gates to swing home, they waved at the train passengers. The train chunted along, into the West Yard, brakes grinding intermittently as the metal wheels screeched slowly on the rails and the leading carriages pulled along the platforms. With a long, grinding final lunge, the train came to a halt and a thick, hissing blanket of steam enveloped the carriage window. Sinclair felt his back lift fractionally from the seat and then slump back. Already, he could hear carriage doors sliding and banging shut as passengers alighted. Rising to his feet, Sinclair slung his rifle across his right shoulder and grabbed a small brown cardboard suitcase from the rack above.

Others in the carriage were making their way into the narrow causeway and Sinclair joined them now, a silent group sidling their way onto the flagstone platform. He saw Dougherty signal ahead to others in similar uniforms who had alighted from the door further along towards the main station buildings. As other passengers moved past them, some with sidelong glances, a group of about 18 special constables huddled in a scrum around Dougherty, their platoon commander. Last to arrive, Sinclair inserted himself into the group beside Davy Morton, just as Dougherty began to speak.

"Right, men, you all know the drill. Nobody leaves the station here until we're underway again," said Dougherty, now looking over at Sinclair and Davy. "You especially, Armstrong and Morton. I know you're back in your home country here, but remember we are in enemy territory. So stay alert and stay armed. Nobody is to be alone. If you want to do something, go in pairs or groups. We have a little over 25 minutes for the next train. Stay alert."

With that the group broke up and moved off. About a dozen headed towards the station waiting room; Davy and Sinclair moved over to a wooden bench. As they slumped into it lazily, the train doors were slamming shut, thrown to by the guard as he moved to the end carriage where he boarded. Then, with a signal from his whistle, the train began to move noisily from the platform to make way for the next arrival.

Evening was closing in fast and, as the last carriage passed from view, Sinclair looked over at the hill opposite where the Roman Catholic church stood, twin sentinel over the small town with its Church of Ireland counterpart on the hill behind the high stone wall which blocked the view behind them. Sinclair had no need to see it. He was in familiar country. As Davy sat alongside him, neither of them talking, Sinclair knew that they shared similar thoughts of home. Since the previous summer, the IRA had assumed a new and shocking role in the area. It was that which had strengthened the resolve of both these young men to join up, even against the opposition of family and neighbours. They were all uneasy that the loyalist areas were losing their young men, just as they faced the growing tide of Sinn Feinism that threatened their liberties and faith in the embryonic Free State. Cut off from the truncated state of loyal Ulster, members of the new frontier unionist community were clinging to an almost forlorn hope that they would somehow be restored to their brethren in the Six Counties.

Yet even the very institutions of the new state had been rapidly eroded or replaced. Only six months ago, for instance, the Royal Irish Constabulary had policed this area, just as it did the new state of Northern Ireland. But, in the meantime, the RIC had been disbanded, leaving only the Royal Ulster Constabulary to carry on its traditions in the North. Ironically, those traditions of policing were rooted firmly in the land of Ireland. Unlike the British Bobbies, the unarmed civilian police officers who traced their lineage back to the Bow Street Runners and the parish constables, the Royal Irish Constabulary was born out of the Peace Preservation Force set up by Sir Robert Peel during his sojourn in Dublin Castle. Efforts to introduce a police model on the same basis that applied in England had failed miserably. As Irish unrest persisted, sometimes breaking out into violent confrontations, local magistrates continued to proclaim the Insurrection Act and call in the troops. The new paramilitary police force would take care of that unnecessary expenditure and burden on the army. Organised on military lines and armed, the RIC centrally controlled and paid for by the Crown Exchequer. Like the RUC which inherited its traditions, the RIC was a standing army that performed police duties. Now in the Free State, the police had gone, replaced by toady Civic Guards in the control of the Dublin government and drawn in many instances from the ranks of the Murder Gang itself. Loyal subjects of the King were at their mercy.

Even in distant Newtownards and Belfast, Sinclair had been fully aware of the precarious foothold his community held. Though confident that it would not be swept aside by the Sinn Fein hordes now emerging from the hedgerows and dark alleys to assume power as the British withdrew, he was shocked by the recent events. Only three days ago, he had learned from senior officers of the kidnapping of loyalists from their homes by thugs who carried out the raids in the dark of night. Here in the Clones area, marauding gangs of armed men had swept across the new frontier into Fermanagh and south Tyrone, dragging men from their families and carrying them off to a nightmare of captivity.

Yet even in the horrific details of the raids, there was cause for a surge of pride and optimism. He had heard how old Anketell Moutray of Favour Royal near Aughnacloy defied his captors, even as he stared into the gaping mouth of death. The 70-year-old Deputy Lieutenant of Tyrone had mustered every strain of his defiance and sang out *God Save the King* and a chorus of hymns as his captors bundled him roughly across the border – a fate far worse than Babylonian captivity. Sinclair knew that negotiations were now underway for the release of Moutray and the other captives, about 40 in all, including young Capt. Coote, the son of Fermanagh MP William Coote.

Then he had heard of the ambush at Wattle Bridge, only out the road a wee bit from Clones, where a cowardly gang of assassins had laid in wait for a patrol of special constabulary. Against overwhelming odds, Sinclair was told, his comrades had stoutly resisted before capture by the IRA murder gang. At Newtownbutler, too, shots were exchanged between a police patrol and a raiding party before reinforcements arrived and drove off the rebels. The possible consequences of that incident now struck home for Sinclair as he waited in silence on the railway platform only four miles away. In his throat he felt his anger rise like a bile and his body rivet to attention as he remembered that a machine-gun had been used in the cowardly ambush by the fenians. Its bullets had raked the roadway. Two constables had been gunned down and a woman, Sinclair had been told, had also been caught in the hail of bullets and reported dead.

His heart heaving like a choking lump in his throat, he had imagined the worst, seeing his beloved Dorothy lying in a pool of her own blood, her skin ripped apart, gaping wounds lanced open as she jerkily stumbled to her death. For two full hours he had carried that vision in his head before her telegram arrived. "Safe and well, stop" it had said. And, even as his fear subsided, he felt his entire being turning to thoughts of revenge against the murderous perpetrators of this atrocity and others. In a seething and, at times, despairing silence, he had nourished the prospect of coming face to face with those cowardly rebels.

I'll soon have my chance, he thought, glancing around at the station clock. Five minutes more and the train would be in. Then ten minutes more and they would be off.

A pall of terror descended with the darkness. Angry clouds scooted across the sky as a gust of wind whipped up litter on Fermanagh Street. Shopkeepers went to their doors and looked out. Stragglers ran for cover, sure of an imminent downpour. In the background, a roar could be heard. Thunder, perhaps, or the loud report of a motor engine. The shopkeepers waited.

The Crossley tender sped across The Diamond, its driver swerving to avoid a young boy leading a malingering donkey by a rope towards the water pump. With a loud report of its Klaxon horn, the tender careered down Fermanagh Street, its rear occupants holding on to the sides with one hand, while grasping their rifles in the other. Three men sitting on the flatbed nursed a large machine-gun. All of them were dressed in the green worsted tunics of the Free State army. The grim-faced young officer in the front wore a Sam Brown belt and holster. His duty lay ahead. For now, he waited.

Hughie Maguire swung open the large wooden gate as the Crossley tender pulled up, allowing it to proceed up onto the side of the tracks. The men on both sides jumped out and set off in two lines, one towards the waiting room, the other onto the platform and along the side of the train. The three men grabbed the large gun and carried it up the wrought-iron steps of the pedestrian bridge, pausing on the stair return to ensure that the muzzle remained pointed at the train below. At the top, they rested it down on its tripod stand, fed a belt of ammunition into the top. They aimed again and waited.

In the distance, there were shouts and the sound of running feet as boys and young men rushed across the rutted surface of Erne Square to see the action. Others huddled indoors or made for home and a file of would-be passengers stole quickly down the ramp and off into the night. They were hastened along by Maguire who had now taken up sentry duty at the gate, barring entry to the first of the mob who had reached it, just as he was shutting it to. Peering though the grills of the gate, the mob waited.

The town waited. The station waited. The train waited.

Sinclair settled into the compartment, taking a seat beside Davy Morton who had grabbed the window spot for the final leg of their journey. A civilian passenger, a middle-aged man, paused at the door, eyeing the vacant spot on the seat beside Sinclair. He hesitated, then moved on. Sinclair recognised him, Patrick Crumley, former Nationalist MP for South Fermanagh. Well, they're the very boys got us into this mess, Sinclair thought, as he arranged his rifle between his feet the barrel pointing upwards. He had seen Crumley once before, just last year it was, addressing a small rally in Newtownbutler about the evils of partition. At the time, Sinclair had been surprised to find him echo some of his own fears about being a minority caught on the wrong side. Today, he could not find it in his heart to do so. The train was already five minutes late and he was as anxious as the others to be out of here and back across the frontier.

As other passengers settled in their compartments and doors were slid shut, Sinclair became aware of some activity outside. He could hear shouting and, as the shouting grew louder, the noise of the passengers trailed off into silence. In his carriage, the others were rising to their feet now, moving towards the door. Sinclair slunk along the seat and peered through the glass panel towards the platform. Somebody slid the door open, to hear better. It only moved part way and then became stuck. The shouting continued, moving closer. He could heard the words now.

"We have the entire train covered," the voice shouted, a local accent, a man. "Surrender now and come out with your hands up."

Sinclair almost obeyed, feeling his grip on the gun relax. It was an automatic instinct now to obey barked orders. The voice was addressing him and the others, he knew. If the rebels were kidnapping civilians from across the frontier, then they would likely arrest uniformed constables too

"Christ, they've caught us," he groaned, too aware of his profanity even as the words left his mouth. In the weeks since leaving home, he had felt this instinctive urge to blaspheme, something that would not have been tolerated in him at home. He thought of Drumkirk, only a few miles away, close enough to walk in a couple of hours or even less. Now he would be held prisoner here, he thought quickly. Would they visit him? Would they be allowed? He prepared to rise. The others were crowding the space between the seats, blocking the way. He slumped back into the seat again.

"Damned driver," he could hear Dougherty saying. "He must have known ...."

Davy's voice now, frightened, "What'll we do, Sergeant? Give up?" Sinclair looked up, but could not see Davy in the jumble of bodies pressed to the door, looking out, hunched in a group before him.

"No, sit tight a minute. I'll go out," the sergeant said, grabbing the door handle, just as the man who had been shouting appeared in the frame of the window outside, still moving towards the front of the train. He was young, no more than a few years older than Sinclair himself, dressed in a Free State army officer's uniform. He wore a Sam Brown belt across his chest and around his waist, the holster flap open, the revolver in his hand, outstretched, pointing at the train, at the carriage ahead.

Suddenly, a single shot, its report a sharp crack. It came from somewhere nearby, next compartment maybe. The scene froze to a tableau in Sinclair's mind. In the numb pace of action as the shot echoed around them, Sinclair saw a clean wound opening up in the forehead of the young man outside, a spurt of blood gushing from it. Then the man crumpled and collapsed sideways out of view. A smell of gunpowder invaded his nostrils, pungent, stale, and Sinclair felt himself falling forward, collapsing to the floor between the legs of the others, who were now scrambling to get out of the half-opened door. They had no chance to do so, as the glass shattered in a hail of bullets which began to splick and splock into the wooden panels of the carriage itself. That first hail of bullets became a torrent as the heavy machine-gun began to open deadly pock marks in the roof of the train, the ceiling panels splintering inwards, a hail of wood specks raining down, a cloud of dust.

Screams and groans, as several heavy bodies slumped and collapsed on top of Sinclair where he hugged the floor, trying to scramble underneath the seat itself. A strangled scream and, suddenly, Davy's face beside him, contorted in pain. Sinclair could see a fresh, gaping wound in Davy's neck. Surprised at how clean it looked, like the first gash in the pig's throat when his father had slashed it open as the animal hung upside down in the barn over a bucket to catch the blood. The pig's squeals died then. The screams now continued around him. Sinclair placed a hand on the opening in Davy's neck to stem the blood he knew would come. But when it came, almost immediately, it spurted though his fingers. He could feel the warm splash strike the side of his face, oozing down his cheek. He pressed harder in a bid to staunch the flow and could feel the very life of his friend force its way through his fingers again. Davy's mouth moved in silent words. He pleaded silently for life as death gripped him and pulled him down. Sinclair grabbed Davy's tunic, coated now in slick blood, and tried to drag him under the seat. He became a dead weight. Sinclair groaned aloud with his friend's last silent breath, a frantic gasp of nothing that ended in a sigh of submission. Davy's face relaxed, his expression composed now amid the chaos and hysteria. The shattered railway carriage had become the place of dragons, covered with the shadow of death.

Rallying now, Sinclair knew he had to get out of there. He edged through the door opening, crawling sideways because of its narrowness, scrambling with his feet as he felt them trapped by falling bodies. Behind him, only the muffled groans remained, interrupted by fresh shots that tore holes in the fabric of the seat covers. Crouching low in the passageway, Sinclair scurried along the floor towards the front and away from the sound of the gunfire and shouting. Away from the ratt-a-tatt of gunfire, interrupted by the screams and shouts from behind. He pressed forward in a mad scramble for his life. In the gloomy darkness, he felt ahead frantically with his hands. The carriage ended in a small recess with a window that had been shredded by the gunfire. Taking off his jacket, Sinclair draped it over the shards of glass on the bottom, pushed other fragments from the side and vaulted through into the opening and onto the tracks, his jacket dragged behind him, pulling it now as it tore from its jagged moorings.

He scrambled to his feet again, his mind blank but for a single thought of getting away. Keeping close to the side of the train, he ran for his life in the shale-covered trough between the tracks, seeking the darkness beyond the engine. He could feel his cheek now gripped in a sticky congealed film. Davy's blood, he thought as he ran on, stumbling and falling and scrambling to his feet again, his breath a cloud of gasps, steam in the cool air. The engine idled, pointed to safety, rooted in danger. He could feel the heat of the engine as he clambered past it now, the noises receding behind him.

At last enveloped in the shroud of darkness beyond, he became aware that the gunfire had ceased. He stumbled on, tripping over a rail and falling to the ground. As he scrambled back to his feet, he could see the faint outline of a clump of bushes to the side and he ran for it in a final lunge, throwing himself into its thorny embrace. Panting heavily now, he struggled into the jacket he still held in his hands. It was sticky with blood. My rifle, he thought then, knowing he had left it behind on the train and worrying briefly if it would land him in trouble. He paused to find his bearings. The border, he thought, not too far. Clontivrin, he knew, was only a short distance away, a few hundred yards and over a small river. There was a bridge, he knew, maybe a shallow ford underneath. Or maybe Carn Lane, nearer and quiet. There was a bridge there, a footbridge over the wee river. Into Knockballymore. He would be safe there. He traced his route of escape in his mind, seeking out the cover, seeking out the protection of darkness. He scrambled out the far side of the bushes into a trench which ran parallel with the side of the tracks and hurried along to safety.

****

In Nineveh or Gomorrah, I do not recollect which, five righteous persons could not be found to save it from destruction; at Clones, the inhabitants set judgements by fire and water, pillars of salt and lakes of sulphur at defiance, for they are all righteous or Methodist, which are the same. They are mild, unassuming men with short hair combed sleek behind their ears, sanctified looks and an assumed English accent.

Gabriel Beranger, 1779.

****

The sound of the gunfire had been carried along on the easterly winds and Dorothy had known immediately that it came from Clones. She also felt a tightness in her stomach as the image of Sinclair's face popped into her mind. She had received his telegram only yesterday, telling her of his transfer to Fermanagh and the time of the train. She had gone down to the station in Newtownbutler in the hope of seeing him, even if only for the few minutes of the stopover there. Now she knew to the very core of her being that he was somehow implicated in the gunfire. With others waiting on the platform, she had hurried along to the station-master's office where, after what seemed like an interminable wait, word came through that there had been a "spot of trouble" at Clones station and the evening train departure for Enniskillen would be delayed for now.

No word on casualties or anything else? Dorothy had asked, others joining in. Best to go up to the police station, they were told. Dorothy had gone alone, running as fast as she could down the main street and turning right up the hill. But there, too, news was sparse. They had a report, yes, but no confirmation. Were any special constables involved? So we heard, but we're still awaiting confirmation on that.

"What about names?" Dorothy pleaded. "A Special Constable Sinclair Armstrong?"

The desk sergeant, a kindly man in his fifties with a soft Mournes accent, was understanding but unable to help. She had been here now for the past hour, waiting and asking. Always the same name. He wished he could help, but what could he do?

"Look, daughter," he said, a puzzled expression on his face, "We weren't even told they were coming this way on the train. We don't know."

"Somebody must know."

"Listen, come back in the morning and we'll be able to tell you more. You'd best get away on home now."

"The morning?" Dorothy was nearing despair.

"Well, you could try later on, couple of hours maybe. We may get word from Enniskillen by then."

Dorothy had left the police station in a quandary, eventually deciding she should come back later. Who knows, she might hear more from neighbours who had been in the town maybe. So she walked through the village again, retracing her steps towards the station and beyond. Clusters of men stood outside the few public houses, looking off intermittently towards the station and towards Clones beyond. She hurried by them in silence and quickened her steps as she made for home.

Now beyond the village, Dorothy moved through the darkness, her coat flapping around her in the heavy winds, her mind a jumble of confusion. Ahead a dog barked persistently and she could see a shadowy figure loping along towards her home. She ran towards the shadow, oblivious to peril and she could see now that it was a man. Dear God, let it be him. Let it be Sinclair. And, as the features became clear, it was.

Dorothy's entire body trembled with a surge of relief and tears welled in her eyes as she ran forward to gather him in her embrace.

"Sinclair, Sinclair love.Thank God you're alive."

He was mumbling through his panted breaths, words, single words of horror and dread, "Clones, ambush, dead."

"You're safe love, you're safe."

Sinclair slumped in her arms and she had to spread her feet wide to bear his weight, but she clung to him.

"They're all dead, Dorothy. All dead but me."

"Wheest, wheest, love. Take it easy now," she comforted him, drawing her head back from his shoulder to stare up into his face. It was caught there in a grimace of terror.

"The blood, Dorothy," he groaned. "Tried to stop it, but I couldn't. Blood everywhere. Davy's dead. They're all dead now ...."

Dorothy inserted herself under his arm and moved him towards the house, along the last few yards to safety. He continued to mutter and groan. She could not tell if he was wounded or if it was just shock and exhaustion. The final steps and the door. Dorothy pounded with the fist of her free arm, the other clutching him around the waist. She kicked the door and pounded.

"Open up, mum," she called. "It's me. I've got Sinclair here."

Sounds of bolts being unlocked quickly and the door swung open.

"I think he's hurt, mum. Help me, please."

Together they dragged Sinclair to the sofa beside the open hearth fire, her mother saying all the while, "Och, the poor cratur."

Sinclair slumped and they examined him, his bloody hands and dishevelled torn uniform. No wounds, just cuts and tears. Dorothy touched his face tenderly and said, "It's over now, love. It's over. You're safe here."

Loud Shrill Knocks

With trembling steps I slowly advanced;
Sometime I knocked both loud and shrill,
Till lo! a knight in armour bright
Demanded of me what was my will.

For we are the true born Sons of Levi,
None on earth can with us compare;
We are the root and branch of David,
The bright and glorious Morning Star.

After some questions being asked,
To which I answered with some fear,
He told me neither Turk nor heathen
By any means could enter here.

For we are the true born Sons of Levi,
None on earth can with us compare;
We are the root and branch of David,
The bright and glorious Morning Star.

We were the children of Zadok, the Righteous Seed, the Sons of Dawn awaiting our resurrection in the light of the Morning Star. Fleeing the destruction of the great Temple, we guarded the secrets of Enoch's pillar, the Font of Knowledge, the Truth of Ages. We obeyed the Duty inexorable as Fate itself. Scattered to the winds, we refused to bend our knee to Pretenders who would come between us and our Salvation. We pursued our great destiny, our sacred covenant. We cast our seed and grew and prospered. Some went west, over the great sea to the perfect land of Avalon, guided there by the star of Merica. Those who remained, guarded and protected the Holy Grail, the beacon of hope to those who would build God's Dominion. Woe unto those false teachers of Gog and Magog whose damnable doctrines will reap them horrible punishment. They have gone in the way of Cain; they ran greedily after the error of Balaam. They will perish in the gainsaying of Korah when the earth will swallow them up. Raging waves, foaming out of their own shame, they are wandering stars to whom is reserved the blackness of darkness forever.

****

A flurry of flames danced over the coal bricks, shooting here and there through the pall of smoke being sucked up the chimney with a whooshing sound. Alex Johnson grabbed the poker from the hook on the side of the fireplace and jabbed its point into the heart of the bank, spilling coals to either side. A steady blaze erupted, sending a waft of warm air into the small dayroom. Several of the men now loosened tunic collars and basked in the comfort of heat, before settling back into their daydreams or their newspapers. Two of the group, in shirtsleeves, pulled back their chairs and resumed a silent game of cards on an upturned tea-chest. Sinclair flexed his shoulders and tried to make himself comfortable on the hard, straight-backed wooden chair. He thought of the funeral only a few days previously at Magheraveely, the horse-drawn hearse, the coffin draped in the Union Jack, the small lonely cluster of mourners around the open grave.

Sinclair had been among the pallbearers, shouldering the coffin to the graveside where it had rested on two ropes of heavy linen. The clergyman, visiting from Rockcorry, proclaimed the graveside eulogy, drawing inspiration from the 34th Psalm: "The eyes of the Lord are upon the righteous, and his ears are open unto their cry. The face of the Lord is against them that do evil, to cut off the remembrance of them from the earth. The righteous cry, and the Lord heareth, and delivereth them out of all their troubles."

Yet nobody but Sinclair had heard the silent cries of his friend as he lay in that railway carriage. The clergyman said, "David Cecil Morton gave his life for King and country." Standing in a wet biting wind that whipped around the yew trees, trees of graveyards and death, Sinclair knew otherwise. Davy did not give his life. It was wrenched brutally from him and from the others who had been killed that day at Clones station. As the sole eyewitness among the group clustered around the grave, Sinclair harboured the pain of wondering if he could have done something to alter the outcome. It would be me in that coffin, he thought, if only I had got to the window seat sooner. He remembered the sharp crack of that initial gunshot and the reflex that sent him diving to the floor. Was it cowardice then? Could he have done something to save the others?

The memory had sent a chill down his spine as he gathered the folds of his tunic tighter around him. And now Davy's mortal remains could not even be taken home for burial at Rockcorry for fear of reprisals against his family and neighbours. Sinclair had looked over at that family - father, mother, younger brother, sister and her husband. They stood there, the women crying bitterly, the men with expressions of hurt and anger so visible to those who stood around and prayed for the repose of a young man who had been killed in cold blood so near his home place. Sinclair had choked back his own tears as the coffin was lowered and, with each dry thud of the soil on its lid, he resolved to avenge his friend's murder. A gravedigger perched on the mound of earth, struggled to control his shovel as chilling gusts of wind threatened to disrupt the interment. And as the mourners prepared to leave, it whipped a shower of sleet into their faces.

Sinclair shivered again at the memory before relaxing into the warmth of the dayroom. A sergeant entered from a side door, a man with a kind face in a regular police uniform. Several of the men looked up as he closed the door softly behind him, but the card players continued their game. Some shuffled their feet on the bare wooden floor and looked around in anticipation.

"The inspector will see you now, Armstrong."

"Right, sergeant," he replied, rising to his feet and checking to make sure that his tunic was fully buttoned.

"Well, get a move on you then," the sergeant said, stepping to the side to allow Sinclair enter the room from which he himself had just emerged. Before he opened the door, however, Sinclair paused briefly, straightened his tunic again and knocked gently before turning the door handle. He then stepped inside, pulling the door after him, and moved forward in a brisk march.

The station inspector did not look up immediately as Sinclair came to attention about two paces from his heavy, overloaded desk. On the wall behind, a large ordnance survey map of the area was dissected by a heavy red line delineating the new border. Here and there throughout the area centred on Newtownbutler, small red and white thumb-tacks had been inserted to mark the permanent outposts of the detachment. His head bent in concentration, the senior officer read down lists of names which Sinclair assumed were duty rosters and patrol schedules. With a blunt-nosed pencil, the inspector trailed a barely visible line to the bottom of the page and, without raising his head as he turned to the next page in the clipboard, he used the pencil to point to a chair placed slightly to the side. Sinclair stepped up to the chair as the inspector continued to read down the quarter page of names, not daring to sit down until he had an explicit invitation.

The inspector raised his head at last, "Take a seat, constable. You came back on duty today?"

"Yes sir," Sinclair replied as he sat down, remembering to hitch his uniform trousers over his knees and keeping his back erect, not touching the back of the chair. "I had a week's leave, sir."

"Yes, indeed. And how do you feel now? It was a bad episode you went through over there."

"Yes, sir. I feel better, thank you."

"Four dead, eleven wounded and two others still held. We hope to secure their release though official channels, of course. We still have a few trump cards up our sleeve, or in Londonderry Gaol to be more exact."

"Yes sir."

"Understand you requested this posting rather than Enniskillen. You're from the area, I hear."

"Yes sir. A few miles away across the frontier. Drum village area, if you ever heard tell of it."

"Somebody told me of a young lady as well."

Sinclair blushed. "Yes sir. House I went to when I got away from

Clones station."

"Good, good," the inspector mused. "Well, I think we can use your local knowledge to advantage. We have a lot of men here, three full platoons, or about 100 men in all drafted in from outside."

The inspector pointed to the clipboard he had been studying on Sinclair's entry. "We can't really rely on the local B and C force members, however. Although, heaven knows, they try hard. They just don't have the training that you and the other A constables have received. We have to take the front line, as it were."

"My local knowledge, sir? In what way?"

The inspector, turned to the map and gestured in a sweeping movement of his hand. "Well, for the moment, I'm sending you to one of our more difficult outposts."

"That's all right by me, sir."

"Lackey Bridge, know it?"

"Think so, sir," said Sinclair, his mind's eye now conjuring up an image of the small country road, quite near Magheraveely where they had buried Davy. "Just a mile or so from Clones town, sir. Road to Fivemiletown, isn't it?"

"Exactly," said the inspector, rising now and pointing to a spot on the map. "We're coming under heavy sniper fire in that area, as you have probably heard. It seems to be one of the more difficult parts hereabouts, though God knows why."

Sinclair had heard of shots exchanged in the aftermath of the station ambush. Clones area was all he had been told. He imagined various outposts, his colleagues pinned down by gunfire, returning shots when they could. There had been similar reports from other locations all along the new frontier. Wasn't that the very reason he and all the others were being sent here. He stored away this information now with a memory of the area.

He had gone there as a boy with his father and Eric, a cold day like this, it was. They set out before dawn on the pony and trap, and were through the town and going down the brae to Lackey Bridge itself just as the day broke. He recalled a heavy metallic clunking noise, like slow shots from a gun, as they rounded the turn at a small cross-roads just before the bridge itself and pulled up at a small mill which straddled the river. Inside, a furnace blazed and several men stood around a heavy hammer from which the thuds emerged as they beat spade heads into shape. Along the walls, rested row upon row of finished digging instruments in all shapes and sizes - spades, shovels, loys for harvesting turf, graips and other digging forks.

His father and Eric had spoken to the mill foreman and then walked along the rows, examining this one and that, discussing their relative merits for what they had in mind. The foreman, shouting above the noise of the hammer and the rush of the furnace, had pointed out proudly that they made almost 150 different types of spade in the factory for customers throughout the length and breadth of the country, each one forged and milled to local specifications. The foreman pointed to the long gripless handles favoured in the west and south of the country, the shorter crutch-ended Ulster spades in all their various forms – the expanding edge which extended a half inch or more beyond the shank shoulders, the acute "cranked lift" below the socket of the Cavan spade and the more gentle, yet pronounced, angle lift of the Fermanagh and North Monaghan spade; the Armagh spade which tapered from a wide mouth to broader shoulders in a curved, rather than cranked, lift. He laughed as he said, "You've heard tell of the saying 'a face as long as a Lurgan spade?' Well there she is now."

Sinclair just stood there, his body immobilised and tense as he awaited the next crack of the hammer, staring into the belly of the furnace and savouring the astringent smell of molten metal. He recalled now that they had left with a few spades, their faces shining in pristine newness and their heavy wooden handles still smelling of the sap of felled trees. Sinclair had nestled in beside them under a blanket on the journey home, touching them every so often and remembering with each chilling sensation from their icy faces, the inferno of their creation at Lackey Bridge.

The inspector rose from his chair and traced an invisible circle around a spot on the map with the unleaded side of his pencil.

"You may know of other crossing points in that general area," he said. "Accessible to a man on foot.

"Yes, I do, sir. Least I know of them."

"Excellent, when you get the lie of the land, you may be using one of them. For the mission we have in mind, we need someone with the local accent and knowledge. We have to establish contact with our people on the other side," said the inspector, resuming his seat and looking closely at Sinclair now. "We've had reports that an invasion force is building up in Clones. But after the railway station ambush, the lines of communication with our people have been cut off. So we don't really know what is happening there."

"Are we expecting a major attack then, sir?"

"Seems so. But we need to know more about the strength and level of equipment. Precise details, if we can get them, will equip us to repel any incursion on our territory here. Because of the high level of activity on the other side, we feel that Lackey Bridge is a likely target for any push, or it may be just a diversionary movement. The latter seems more likely to me, in any case. Think you can find out what we need to know, Armstrong?"

This was it then, thought Sinclair, the real thing. Invasion, defence, the very stuff of war. His concerns for the people who would be caught in any major battle, disappeared in the knowledge that he would be a key contributor to the defence strategy for Northern Ireland. While he worried that maybe he was not up to the job, he resolved to demonstrate that he could do it. His escape from Clones station, he realised, had raised his value in the constabulary. The innate local knowledge he possessed would ensure that he got across the border quickly, while others might set off in the wrong direction even and be captured easily by the enemy.

"Well, I can ask, inspector," he said, careful not to over-emphasise his confidence or ability. "I know a few people around that country - at Aghafin and Clough on the other side there. They'd be contagious enough to Lackey, and I know people in Clones of course."

"Good, good. When you have had a chance to see what you are up against, you can see about making contact. We don't know when the attacks might be launched, but our information is that an attempted invasion is imminent enough. There's talk of guns being moved up from the south and what have you. Maybe even the Howitzers that were left behind in Dublin. We just don't know. Your local knowledge should prove invaluable in filling in the missing pieces. We need to know what the enemy is doing over there."

"Thank you, sir," Sinclair said, his mind racking up several people who could help him find out. His uncle Bob, he knew would be a prime source. Maybe he could even get home to Drum on one of his forays.

The inspector lifted up his clipboard again and nodded, "Right then, you can go now, Constable Armstrong. There will be a relief patrol leaving for Lackey Bridge shortly and you will join it. The sergeant know."

Sinclair rose and saluted. As he moved to the door, the inspector added, "You could ask Sergeant Murphy to step in here for a minute."

"Yes sir," said Sinclair, turning the handle and stepping outside into the dayroom again. Several heads among the group still clustered around the fire turned around. He wondered if he should tell them of his mission. Better not, he decided. Less said, the better for now.

Outpost was a rather grand title for the pair of labourers' cottages that had been commandeered beside Lackey Bridge. More like an outhouse, Alex Johnson had remarked frequently since their arrival from Newtownbutler by a circuitous route through Magheraveely that avoided close contact with the frontier. The ten men who had disembarked from the tender, now made do with the basic facilities, using one two-room cottage as their dayroom and eating area, and the other as sleeping quarters with four beds, used in rotation. The wall surrounding the tiny front gardens of the cottages had been reinforced with sandbags, allowing peepholes through which the constables could fire on the enemy, or simply at random as occasional bursts of sniper fire came from the steep hill on the far side of the bridge, just inside the Free State. And across the narrow country road, two walls of sandbags had been erected from each side, not quite closing the road, but impeding traffic within a staggered stage where inspections and searches could be carried out. In the two days since their arrival, however, there had been no traffic. The only contact with the outside world had been the regular visits of children from neighbouring farms who brought fresh milk and eggs, and their fathers who occasionally called to chat with the men, assuring them they were comrades in arms as members of the ancillary reserve detachments of the Special Constabulary. These conversations were dominated by Alex Johnson, older by about five years or more than his colleagues. As he quizzed the local children and their fathers about the lie of the land, his main concern was to build up an inventory of the local young women. Indeed, his sole interest, it seemed to Sinclair, was women.

On the journey there from Newtownbutler, Johnson had singled out Sinclair for attention as they made their way to what he called this God-forsaken hole. Not bothering to check with the platoon commander, a young corporal from Portadown, Johnson had announced that Sinclair would be bunking down beside him. The younger man had been flattered by the attention.

"I hear tell you're a ladies man hereabouts," Alex had said. "I'll want you to mark my card on the local women."

Unsure of how to deal with the tone of sarcasm that oozed from

Johnson's every word, Sinclair had been embarrassed by the implication in his remarks and had mumbled something about there not being much likelihood of courting about Lackey Bridge. He cringed in embarrassment afterwards, when he recalled how the older man had guffawed and slapped his back as the others laughed along.

Now Johnson lounged on a dishevelled sofa as Sinclair donned a heavy overcoat over his uniform. It came down well below his knees, hiding the uniform trousers which were stuffed into a pair of rubber Wellington boots. As Sinclair did up the buttons of the coat, he could hear a spluttering sound of gunfire from off in the distance. Johnson appeared not to take any notice as he rose from the sofa, just as Sinclair put on a tweed cap, its brim well down from his hairline and almost obscuring his eyes.

"They're at it again, Alex," he said, nodding in the direction of the gunfire and taking a revolver from the kitchen table nearby. He checked the gun for ammunition and slid it into the right pocket of his overcoat.

"Aye, make you wonder what the hell they're firing at."

"Us, I doubt."

"Och, no need to worry, Sinclair lad," said Johnson now, inspecting the younger man by walking around him slowly. "Sure, not even your own mother will know you in thon get-up."

"Well, I hope to God she's not abroad in this country," said Sinclair, "what with all the sniping going on. It's enough to drive a body mad."

Johnson laughed, "Aye, well, you just leave that to us, Sinclair. Off you go on your wee mission now and take care of yourself out there. I wouldn't want to have to comfort your wee lassie beyond in Newtown if you got shot or anything."

Unsure yet again of how to take Johnson's remarks, Sinclair mumbled a cursory thanks and exited the cottage. He took a left turn away from the border and then slipped down a small lane that doubled back, further down from the bridge. He soon found himself at the Finn River, above the millrace, a spot he had checked out over the past few days and again that very day before night fell. With his wellington boots on, he easily traversed the shallow water that trickled over a stony bottom here and, clambering up onto a hedge-lined road, he turned to the right and made off in the direction of Knockballymore, near Magheraveely. His footsteps were silent in the rubber boots as he hurried along, aware that on the hill to his left, the snipers lurked with their guns trained on the bridge and the cottages beyond. But in the eerie silence of darkness that surrounded him, he wondered if he could suppress even the barely audible sound of his steady breathing. His stomach tightened as he rounded each corner in the twisted road, preparing to bolt for safety if he should meet anybody. But about a mile or more from the bridge and just after he had passed a small, silent farmhouse, he had already gone too far to retreat when he became aware of the bulky shadows ahead of him. Breathing heavily, the shapes moved slowly towards him and it was only as they loomed into view a few feet away that he realised it was a herd of dairy cattle. There were about 10 animals in all, ambling back towards the farmyard he had just passed. A slap on flesh, and Sinclair saw a man at the rear of the small herd, driving the lumbering animals ahead of him. Sinclair stepped into the side, his left arm resting against a small ash tree in the hedge as his right hand closed around the revolver in his pocket.

The cattle drover seemed nonchalant as he approached, barely bothering to look up from the rear ends of the cattle when more shots rang out in the distance. Occasionally, he swung his stick, beating the road surface or the rump of a beast which scurried forward briefly and then settled back into the slow gait of the herd. Sinclair could feel his body tense as the man drew alongside him. Then, without warning, the man stopped in the middle of the road. He put the stick under his arm, holding it there as he reached into his pocket. Sinclair flexed his grip on the revolver as the drover pulled out a pipe and a box of matches. Clamping the pipe between his teeth, he cupped his hands around the matchbox and stuck, turning and ensuring that the small pool of light extended into the shadows where Sinclair was now exposed. The man then lowered his head and drew the flame into the bowl of his pipe as he spoke out of the side of his mouth from clenched teeth.

"Thon's a brave evening now," he said, punctuating each word with a waft of smoke.

Sinclair stepped forward, his right hand still cradling the gun. He could now almost make out the man's features - coarse, unshaven, a wry smile curling the sides of his mouth as he withdrew the pipe.

"Aye, it is. Not too bad."

"Draws in very early still. But I'd say we've seen the last of winter."

"Hope so," said Sinclair, anxious to be off.

"From about this country, are you?" the man asked, examining Sinclair's features, or as much of them as he could make out as Sinclair pulled the brim of his cap further down over his eyes.

"Och, not a big way off. Just making my ceilidh up the road here a wee bit more."

"Hendersons or Fosters, is it?" the man asked. Sinclair mumbled a non-committal reply.

"You'd want to move on then, I suppose." He nodded in the direction of the gunshots, drawing deeply on his pipe: "Those shots are real. You'd no problem getting by back there?"

Sinclair pretended he hadn't heard, aware that the man was still trying to get a closer look at his face. He kept his profile to the side as he began with faltering steps to move off. "Aye, right then," he said, walking off quickly. As he did so, he was aware that the man had remained standing there behind him. After about ten paces, Sinclair turned to see if he had moved, willing him to have done so. He hadn't and, seeing Sinclair turn, the barely recognisable shadow raised his stick in a farewell gesture. Sinclair turned and quickened his pace towards the next bend. Damn, he thought, that was too bloody close for comfort.

****

Notices have been fixed on the doors of some Papists in the town and neighbourhood of Drum desiring the inhabitants to leave their houses or that they and everything belonging to them would be destroyed. The Orange boys who are comprised mainly of Presbyterians sent a deputation to neighbouring areas inviting them to join their association, and following this, notices similar to those in Drum and signed 'Oliver Cromwell' were attached to the doors of Catholics elsewhere. I am very much afraid the Orange boys are becoming too numerous and too riotous around Drum. I went to the funeral of one of them yesterday, who was supposed to have been murdered, in hopes of keeping them quiet, which was the case, and I am certain there was not less than 1,500 of them.

Henry Clements, Ashfield, to Dublin Castle, 1796.

****

The raids came almost as a relief, said those who had already experienced the invasion of their homes by armed men dressed in the makeshift uniforms of the new Free State army. It was the waiting that was difficult, worrying constantly that we were being watched and observed, even as we went through the semblance of living normally. Constantly aware of neighbours and acquaintances, especially those from the other side, we knew they were just waiting for an excuse.

The few guns kept in farmhouses to control pests and vermin, were locked away securely now, or hidden in haylofts or cow sheds, far from the prying eyes. We only hoped that we would have a chance to get to them if the worst ever did happen. Some said it would be better to keep one old shotgun in the house, a lure to keep them away from more useful weapons if we had any about the place. Others said they could just use any old piece to charge us with worse, whether or not they found them.

For now, we waited, carefully avoiding attention if we could, trading information when it was possible, clinging together for support and comfort when we had the chance. We began to think of ourselves yet again as a besieged people. We were cut off from our natural friends and allies and from our lines of communication with the world. A new frontier right before us had become an armed camp on both sides. As our forefathers had done at Enniskillen and Derry, we watched, held out and waited for relief.

Through the darkness, the Lord was our light and our salvation; whom shall we fear? The Lord was the strength of our life; of whom shall we be afraid? When the wicked, even our enemies and our foes, came upon us, they stumbled and fell. Though an host should encamp against us, our hearts shall not fear: though war should rise against us, in this were we confident.

While our leaders spoke frequently of banding together and showing that we were still a formidable force in local affairs, we tried not to think of our precarious position as a tiny minority on the periphery of a new and hostile state, a state that eschewed everything we had stood for, a state to which we could not give allegiance so long as we had even the remotest chance of being reunited with our Ulster brethren. Daily, we clung to that hope, even as we waited for the raiders to come and ransack our homes. Yet, all the while, we knew that our own people were hunkering down across the line, so near and yet so far.

"So next thing he finds himself up in front of one of these courts they're running now," said Sadie. "Down about Newbliss it was and there was these two men sitting there like magistrates or judges ...."

Albert used a knife to slice the top of his boiled egg, and laying it down, picked up the teaspoon which rested on his plate beside a thick wedge of toasted soda bread which he had coated thickly with butter. "Any idea of who they were?" he now asked, dipping the spoon into the soft yolk and drawing out a lump of egg which he popped into his mouth and swallowed as he talked.

"Man the name of McKenna was one, according to Mrs Anderson. The other man wasn't from about this country here at all," said Sadie.

Bob, sitting at the far end of the table, chewed a morsel and swallowed, "Did he get any word on why they took him there? I mean, how did they say they found out he was in the B Constabulary."

"Well, the way Mrs Anderson had it, they said it was his wife gave the information. They had a big row, you see, and he's to have gone off from the house, across the border like. They got him when he came back to see the childer. Aye, Mrs West herself, she was to have been at the back of it all."

"But he come to no harm, did he?" said Albert now, cupping his index finger into the handle of the tea mug.

"Not unless you would class a hefty fine of £20 as any harm," said Sadie, her voice registered the indignation they all felt. "But they let him go because, at the latter end, the wife said she wasn't giving evidence. For the childer's sake, she's to have said."

"Change of heart, so?" asked Bob, who was sitting at the table but not eating the food before him. He sipped at his tea instead, the mug shaking slightly in his hand.

"Something like that. But that's what comes of marrying into the other side. You can't trust them from one minute to the next, if you ask me."

"Aye, specially in the times that's in it," Albert agreed.

"Good job Sinclair's thinking of getting hitched up to wee Dorothy so," Bob observed. "She's a grand wee lassie and one of our own too."

Albert poked at his egg again as he mused, "Not a word from the same boy from he went back on duty."

"Well, I pray to God that he's all right," said Sadie. "I can't rest easy in my mind for worrying after him, so I can't."

A furious yelping and barking outside froze the teatime scene. Sounds of a heavy motor engine approaching at speed. Albert shuffled to his feet, "Who can that be?" he wondered aloud, although each of them sensed they knew the answer. "You weren't expecting any callers, were you Bob?"

The motor screeched to a halt, as Bob also rose, "No, divil a one."

Sadie clutched her apron hem, tugging it between her two hands. "Oh, my God," she began to wail. "Something's happened to Sinclair. I know it."

Sounds of shouting outside as the back door thundered with loud knocking, even before Albert could get to it or to the window to peer outside. A voice, loud demanding, "Open up in the name of the Provisional Government. Open up, or we'll break it down."

Albert whispered to the others to be calm as he got to the door and drew back the heavy bolt. As he prepared to pull it open, the door was pushed through and three armed men with rifles at the ready tumbled into the kitchen, followed by a man in the uniform of an officer in the national army, the former IRA. The trio inside all recognised him immediately, young Francie Cassidy from nearby Scotshouse. His father was a farmer too, on the board of the local village creamery and a leading member of the Ancient Order of Hibernians in the region. Cassidy, no more than 25 years old, strutted about the kitchen with a brash confidence.

Wee pup, Albert thought, knew he was one of those skulking about the ditches only a while back shooting people in the back. Albert stood defiantly as the soldiers trained their rifles on him. He gestured to Sadie and Bob, "Sit back where you were and say nothing. I'll handle this."

Cassidy looked him in the eye as he removed his peaked military cap to reveal a shock of red hair underneath. "We're soldiers of the national army," he announced grandly. "You'll come to no harm if you answer straight. Where is he?"

"Where's who?" asked Albert, who felt his confidence growing ever since he had recognised his adversary - sending a boy to do a man's job. But it was true what they had been saying, about the relief of actually being raided. He would never have thought it possible before. But it was far better to look your foe in the eye, something these skulking rats had not known over the months and years they had terrorised the countryside round about. "Who are you looking for?"

"Your son, the one that's in the Special Constabulary," said Cassidy. Albert could see that the young man now regretted removing his cap. It was maybe the one thing that gave him at least the semblance of being of military age. He now looked like the young farmer's son from down the road got up for a drama group. But Albert knew the guns were real, the guns pointing at him.

"Sinclair's his name, isn't it? Sinclair Armstrong?"

"He's not here," Albert replied gruffly. "There's nobody here only us."

Cassidy signalled to the three men, drawing his revolver from the holster he wore on a belt that criss-crossed with a Sam Brown belt strapped across his chest. Albert felt more irritated by that gesture, than afraid of what the young man might do with the gun. He bit his tongue as the other men moved through the kitchen door into the rest of the house. They clambered heavily up the stairs, running almost as they began to search the bedrooms. Cassidy continued to hold his revolver at waist high, pointing in Albert's direction while they waited in silence. Loud thuds and the scrape of furniture being roughly moved about upstairs could be heard in the silent kitchen. From outside, the dogs continued to bark and yelp, and Albert knew that there were others out there searching through the hay barn, the cowshed and the tool shed.

Cassidy turned to Bob: "Who are you?"

"Bob Sinclair, as you know rightly young Cassidy. I live here."

"He's family," said Albert, heartened that Bob was equally prepared to defy this upstart.

"My brother," said Sadie.

Cassidy, brandishing his revolver, looked back at Albert: "You, Mr Armstrong. Albert Armstrong, isn't it?"

"You know that. Else you wouldn't be here."

"Where's your son?"

"Don't know. He's not about here is all."

Cassidy moved over near the range now, turning his back in a show of confidence. "Well, we hear he has been back in our territory. On this side of the frontier."

"Who told you that?

Cassidy wheeled around and rested his back against the rail of the range: "He was seen and recognised two days ago. He wasn't in his uniform and he was acting suspiciously near one of our positions."

"Know nothing about it. Haven't seen hide nor hair of him for a while."

"Was he back home since the invasion of Clones station? He was seen there as well."

Albert's voice rose with indignation: "Invasion? Invasion is it now? More like cold-blooded murder." He shouted at Cassidy, not caring about the gun or the armed men elsewhere in the house. "It was near a massacre there with your lot firing into a train of women and childer."

Cassidy struggled for the upper hand again: "Hold your tongue. It was a military engagement and those armed thugs invaded the station. The first shot was fired at Commandant Matt Fitzpatrick, a senior officer in the national army. He was shot dead from behind."

"You had set up for an ambush. They never had a chance."

"The Provisional Government is in control now. Remember that."

"Provisional Government? Couldn't govern themselves if you ask me. More like ruffians going about terrorising women and childer and scourging law-abiding and loyal citizens."

"Your loyalty is to the Provision Government now, or it should be."

"It's nothing of the sort. My loyalty is to the King and to my Protestant religion, same as it has always been. I'll bow before no rebel parliament, much less your Traitor's Republic."

Cassidy bristled. What could he do? He faced a trio of old people.

"Shut up, y'ould Orange bigot. Or you'll only make it worse for yourself. Bad enough your son is a traitor to his country. But we'll get him yet. Don't worry about that."

Cassidy's gun shook in his hand as he spoke. Sadie watched it, fearful that the young man might lose control altogether.

"Easy, Albert," she cautioned. "He's got a gun."

"Aye, Albert," Bob chimed in. "You're wasting your breath on the likes of him."

Silence reigned in the kitchen once again. Cassidy leaned back against the stove rail and waited. Soon, the sound of heavy footsteps came from the stairs as the men descended. The door was thrown open roughly and the three soldiers reappeared in the silent and tense kitchen. One of the soldiers addressed Cassidy: "Nothing there, sir."

"Checked the roof space, did you?"

"Aye, all over. Found nothing only a British uniform in a wardrobe."

Albert jumped back into the fray. "Keep your damned treacherous hands off that."

"Whose uniform is it?" asked Cassidy.

"Our son's. Eric's."

"Where is he?"

"Dead," Albert's voice faltered. "The Somme, Thiepval Wood."

Cassidy assumed he was back in control. The old man was shaken at last. He sneered: "Went to war, did he?"

Albert mustered what defiance he had left. "He served his King and country to the last. While lesser men, if you could call them men even, were scheming and plotting rebellion."

Cassidy dismissed the remark, signalling to his men with the revolver. "Well, you just listen here, Mr Armstrong. You just beware of your other scheming son, Sinclair. We'll have him yet and his spying."

The soldiers moved to the door on the signal. Cassidy holstered his gun as he followed, looking around the elderly trio. "And don't try any tricks to warn him off, or it's worse for you it'll be." He spoke directly to Sadie and Bob, "All of you."

Cassidy paused at the door and stared at them in silence for a couple of seconds, turned on his heel and went out calling his men: "Right lads, we're off. But I doubt we'll be back here before too long."

The sound of the heavy engine firing up filled the kitchen through the open door. The tender moved off, its noise abating as it headed down the lane. Albert went to the window and carefully peered out. He then went to the door and exited into the yard, returning a couple of moments later. He shut the door and threw the heavy bolt to fasten it securely. Bob and Sadie slumped back into their chairs as Albert turned to them.

"They've gone. Best see what damage they've done, Sadie. Aye and check Eric's uniform, will you? If they've harmed it, they'll answer for it somehow."

Sadie reached out to touch her husband's arm, "Calm down, Albert. We came to little or no harm, thank goodness."

Sadie went off and they could hear her lighter footsteps on the stairs. Albert sat down at the table, utterly exhausted after the encounter. Bob was agitated, he could see, his face creased with worry.

"What will we do, Albert? They'll be waiting for him next time, sure as anything."

Albert tried to focus. "We've got to get word to him somehow, Bob," he whispered. "I could maybe go over to Newtown and tell Dorothy to pass on word that they're out to get him."

"You can't go, Albert. They know you now and, after tonight, you'll be a marked man, if you ask me. Best I go instead."

"Bid to be you're right, Bob. Aye, and people were used to seeing you out late when you were with the railway." He didn't mention Bob's recent night-time jaunts around the district and beyond.

"Aye, I can slip over by the Annies. If I'm stopped, sure I'll just say I'm making my ceilidh with some of the boys from the station."

"Should you maybe wait till light?"

"I doubt she'll not hold that long. Sinclair may have been thinking of coming over the night. Maybe that's why they were here. Like, if they got information passed on or something."

"Aye, you're right, Bob. Thanks."

Bob rose to his feet, the chair sliding back across the floor as he eased it away with the back of his legs. "I'll go right now so and, sure, I'll be back here in a few hours or less."

He went to the rack near the back door and put on his coat and cap. Albert rose too, peered out the widow and then went over and slid the bolt. As Bob prepared to leave, Albert asked him, "What did he mean when he said Sinclair was seen on this side of the frontier?"

"Och, probably no truth to the half of it." Bob avoided Albert's eyes as he went into the darkness, "Nor any of it, for that matter."

"Aye, Bob. If they have guards posted, come you on back, mind."

He could hear Bob wheeling out his heavy bicycle and mounting it. Then the whirring clickety sound as it freewheeled down the lane. He closed the door, bolted it and waited for Sadie to come downstairs.

Few ventured abroad in the night. A curfew had been declared on both sides of the frontier as hostilities mounted. A knock at the door, which remained bolted now as never before, signalled danger and risk. Raids, attacks and intimidation on both sides unleashed a suspicion and wariness that sat uneasily on people whose very nature was welcoming and inviting. For women living alone, as Dorothy and her mother did, the risk was amplified. So when a heavy knocking had come on the door, Dorothy was terrified at first. When she opened it at last and heard the familiar voice of Bob Sinclair, her welcome was coupled with a vast sense of relief.

They stood inside the door, Bob still wearing his heavy overcoat, declining the offer of a chair beside the fire. It was not like him, Dorothy knew, to turn down the offer of hospitality. A warm and friendly man, he was welcome in any house in the entire region. Her apprehension mounted as Bob recounted the events of the night.

"You must have been terrified out of your wits."

"Aye, well we didn't let it show, mind you Dorothy."

"I'll tell Sinclair first thing. He said he'd be over as soon as he comes off duty at Lackey Bridge."

"Right, so I'll be going. Take care, Dorothy, and if the roads is open, we'll see you both over here on Sunday afternoon."

"Surely to God Mr Sinclair, you'll not venture out again the night? Stop over, can't you?"

Bob hesitated, clearly concerned about the risks of travel. Dorothy hoped he would stay. She could make up the day-bed for him beside the stove and he could set off at first light. It was not as if he had a job to go to, being retired from the railway now. But Bob's hesitation was only momentary. Apart from the impropriety of a man staying in a house with two lone women, they would be expecting him back at home.

"Och no, Dorothy. They'll be fretting beyond at Drumkirk."

"But the patrols?"

"Och, I come over a wee back road by the Annies. There's nobody that direction."

"I'd rather you'd stay the night. It'd be safer with the curfew and everything."

"Och, what reason have I for that? I know the way and, sure, nobody's going to bother an ould man like me."

Bob put his cap back on: "Just you take care of yourself and your mother, and take care of the young lad for us."

Dorothy unlocked the door and stood in the pool of light from the kitchen lamp while Bob remounted his bicycle and set off.

"You take care of yourself too, Mr Sinclair," she called out softly. "And thanks for coming over with the warning ...."

The Finn River trickled down from the Slieve Beagh mountain and began its circuitous route around the town of Clones. Keeping about two or three miles distance to the north, east and south, it flowed under Lackey Bridge, Roslea Bridge, Stone Bridge, Analore Bridge, Comber Bridge, Annies Bridge and Ballyhoe Bridge, finally entering the great waters of the River Erne at Wattle Bridge. It hemmed the town into its western flank, away from the rest of Co. Monaghan and almost into Fermanagh. For much of its course, it delineated the parish of Clones, an administrative unit pre-dating the county boundaries by hundreds of years. From the Finn's southernmost reaches, the parish swept north, back into the very mountain which harboured the river's head waters.

Bob Sinclair traced the route of the river as he cycled hard towards the Annies. The road was narrow and rutted. Ahead, he knew, an attempt had been made to block it off. But it was the only route on which there was, as yet, no permanent checkpoint. Having crossed the Annies Bridge earlier, he was confident he could get home safely. He had to concentrate on the road's twists and turns and avoid the potholes from memory, not having a bicycle light. He had deliberately left his paraffin lamp at Drumkirk, deciding that it would only attract unwelcome attention with the times that were in it. So, when he rounded a bend just before the bridge and saw a light on ahead, he assumed it was another cyclist out beyond curfew and less cautious than himself.

Bob pedalled on, his mind clocking the distance travelled from Gortraw and anticipating the few miles ahead. He knew he would have a difficult climb on the final leg as he reached the high country and ascended to Drumkirk. But, what matter. He would be as good as home then, safe and sound and, God willing, young Sinclair would be safe on the other side too.

The light ahead had not moved and Bob could see a few dark figures standing around it as he approached. Damn it, are they ours or theirs?

A voice calling, "Who goes there in the name of the Provisional Government?"

I'll show them the kind of government they are, thought Bob. He called back, "Sinclair's the name. Bo...."

A shout from the side, "That's him, the spy."

Bob tried to call out again. A shot exploded. He felt no pain, just a growing numbness, spreading from his chest. He fell from his bicycle, hit the road with a dull thump. Didn't hurt though. He felt winded. Just get my breath back. He began to feel cold now, and raised his hand to tighten his coat about him. It was wet and sticky. Must have fallen in a puddle of something. The numbness continued to spread. He tried to raise himself, but felt his body slump back as running feet approached. That damned light coming closer at last. Dark figures, uniformed, above him. Voices, receding even as they approached, growing faint.

"Did we get him?"

"Aye, done for, I'd say."

"Is it him?"

The light in his eyes. Moving back. Calling him home. The chill and numbness spreading still. Must sleep before the climb to Drumkirk ....

"Christ, no. It's an old man ...."

****

In relation to my own locality and particularly the village of Drum, I am very sorry to tell you that the sentiments of the people of this country are within these last 10 days totally changed from what they were. It was at that time a loyal and spirited people, determined to support their King and constitution and were bound to each other by the oath of Orangemen. But on finding they were in the exact same state with what they called the enemies of their country, the United Irishmen, both they and the free masons, who are very numerous in this country, joined the United Irishmen and I think I do not exaggerate when I say four fifths of the people of all persuasions are joined with them ....

Henry Clements, Ashfield, to Dublin Castle, April 1796.

****

Some situations are beyond comfort. When sorrow, blame and anger collide in the heart, they are beyond reason. Better to let it boil over and have its turn. Yet Dorothy was prompted as much by self blame as she was by her urge to comfort Sinclair. Seated here on the couch with him now, she had been awoken by his heavy pounding on the door shortly after daylight. Roused from her sleep, she was greeted by his news of the shooting.

"I'm sorry, Sinclair love. I told him to stay over. Said it wasn't safe. He wouldn't listen."

"Never would. Not your fault, love. More mine. Sure, he wouldn't have been on the road but for he was bringing me word."

"No use blaming yourself either, love."

"No, suppose not. It could have happened anywhere, any time."

"So pointless though .... an old retired railway worker."

Sinclair's anger returned as he twisted out of their embrace. Her hand moved to his arm. He looked away.

"Murdering bastards. Someone will pay before I'm through."

"Easy, Sinclair love. Don't dwell on revenge. It can come to no good."

"But there's no sense. What makes anybody a victim these times?"

"It'll get better. Don't fret, love."

He buried his face in his hands. She could only put her own hands on his shoulders, warming him, caressing him.

"It's just I feel totally cut off. Can't even go home for the funeral ...."

"I'll go over and see them for you. It'll be all right."

"What about my mother? Her only brother."

"She'll be concerned for you."

Sinclair's chest heaved and he choked back another sob. Dorothy drew him back into her embrace and waited till his breathing subsided. His face nuzzled her hair, his breath warm on her ear. She heard him sigh, preparing to speak. She would let him talk it out.

"Dorothy love? Hardly the time, but well .... could we get married sooner? Maybe in a lock of weeks? I need a family, a new family here. I need to belong again."

Her heart swelled with love. She patted his back as she would a child's, maybe their own child. She drew back her head, his face was full of longing, questioning, anxiety. She smiled, "Of course, my love. I'll take care of you now."

She kissed him then, a deep kiss, full of love, commitment and belonging to each other.

Albert shuffled uneasily as the gravediggers shovelled and neighbours came over to offer condolences. What could he say in such circumstances? His concern for Sadie paramount as she sobbed at his side. He was glad to see that there now remained only Robert James McConkey and his son, Roy. They would go through the usual exchange of such occasions, but at least he knew that Sadie would be released from the long procession of sympathisers and having to hold herself together. She could be herself in front of Robert James and Roy.

"Sorry for your troubles, Sadie," Robert James offered. "You, too, Albert. Shocking doing."

Roy mumbled in agreement and Albert noticed that Sadie now grasped the younger man's hand tightly, unwilling to let go.

"Och, thank you both," she said. "Good of you to come along."

"Least a body could do," said Robert James, lapsing into the embarrassing silence of futility in the face of grief.

Albert broke the silence, uncomfortable with this show of mourning. "Cold blood it was, Robert James. Bob wasn't armed or anything, of course. Just coming along on his bike ...."

Sadie sobbed openly: "My own brother. Shot and killed in the dead of night, without even a friend to hand."

"Never gave him a chance," said Albert.

"Didn't even know he'd gone," said Sadie. "Not till afterwards."

Albert grabbed his wife's shoulders, comforting her as best he knew how, his voice now losing the pitch of raw anger. It was replaced with a soothing tone, born of his wife's distress.

"Och, Sadie, don't take it so bad."

"Aye," said Robert James in support. "He was a good man and a God-fearing Christian. He can't be denied that."

"He'll not be forgot," Roy promised.

Albert wanted to talk with Robert James, but Sadie was too emotional. He patted her shoulders. "Why don't you go on over now to Mrs Anderson's. She said for you to come by for a wee drop of tea and a bite. She'll be expecting you."

Albert nodded over her bowed head, a signal. Roy got the prompt. "Aye, come along," he said. "I'll take you across, Mrs Armstrong. Eileen's over there helping out."

Sadie had recovered a little bit. "Aye, well maybe a wee cup," she said, moving off with Roy. Albert and Robert James watched them go. Clusters of mourners would impede their progress, but most had now left the graveyard.

"Any word on how it happened, Albert? If they had to have a reason at that, I suppose."

"Well, Col. Madden says the word is they thought it was our Sinclair. Bob's to have called out his name and they got it mixed up. They were lying in wait."

"Dirty cowards. Sadie know?"

"No. Thought it best she doesn't. She'd only worry more over the lad."

"Times like this, I think the Man Above took our Roy home."

"Aye, wish to God He'd taken Sinclair along with him."

The last of the mourners had now gone from the graveyard and Albert noticed Rev. Burns approaching. He signalled to Robert James as Burns called out, "Good turn-out, Albert. He was a liked man hereabouts. You can see that."

"Aye," said Robert James, "All his old comrades from the Volunteers."

"Indeed, and Mr Knight was here, Dr Henderson and Dr Elliott and Col. Madden himself for the railway company," Burns added, totting up the importance of the funeral as he drew alongside the two men.

"Aye," said Albert, "All god-fearing people."

"At least they leave us to bury our dead in peace," Burns observed, in what Albert took as an obvious reference to the fact that very few, if any, Roman Catholics had been present. Not even his former work mates from the station. It was a clear signal of the times. Even at such a tragic funeral, the sides were clearly drawn. Albert knew, however, that it was more due to the desire not to give rise to offence or provocation that many had refrained from coming. Yet, in his heart, he could not muster forgiveness. They caused this whole trouble, he believed fervently.

"Aye, it's bad the times we live in," Robert James was saying.

"Dark and troublous days," Burns agreed, adding "Satan shall be loosed out of his prison, and shall go out to deceive the nations which are in the four quarters of the Earth, God and Magog, to gather them together to battle. Revelations, 20, seven and eight."

"Hear tell both Braddox and Drumully Orange halls are gone from the same night," said Albert.

"Yes, like thieves in the night. Thou has given us like sheep appointed for meat; and hast scattered us among the heathen. Psalm 44, 11."

"They'll have all wrecked before them," Robert James sighed.

Burns had thought of something and was excited now as he spoke, "Col. Madden has just been telling the latest. Miss Adams of Drumelton, the High Sheriff's daughter ...."

Albert was alarmed, "Was she attacked?"

"No, thank goodness. She's been arrested for shooting a local member of the Murder Gang. Charged with attempted murder of a member of their National Army."

Robert James was cheered by the news, Albert could see.

"Well, good luck to her if she did. Certain sure it wasn't without call."

"Yes, indeed," Burns intoned, "Vengeance is mine, I will repay, sayeth the Lord. Romans, 19, 19. But as we know, the Almighty often moves through the intercession of mere mortals."

They stood there a while more, savouring the thought of fighting back. Albert thought it was just the sort of news that would cheer Sadie too. God knows, they needed their spirits lifted.

****

And now, God bless the yeoman
In Ulster's happy homes.
God shield them from their foemen,
Uphold when danger comes;
May the Orange still united
With their fathers' sturdy blue,
By factions breath unblighted,
Wave o'er their legions true.

****

Sinclair Armstrong was far from convinced by the newspaper headlines declaring peace. Nor was he reassured by the announcement that the head of the new government in the Free State and Sir James Craig would sign a pact to ensure that the border would not be threatened until the promised Boundary Commission had a chance to examine the issue. Wasn't the head of that government down in Dublin the same Michael Collins who led the Murder Gang of the IRA? Wasn't he the man who had cold-bloodedly killed men and women, or worse, had others do it for him? Wasn't he the same Michael Collins who had sent out his thugs to shoot at His Majesty's forces from behind walls and hedges? Wasn't he the same who led the so-called Belfast Boycott, forcing people not to buy goods from the Black North, as they called it, until the unionists climbed down from their opposition to Home Rule, Rome Rule? Aye, and when that didn't work, wasn't he the same Michael Collins that went over to London and bamboozled Lloyd George into pulling the British out and leaving the loyalist people of Ulster, the loyalists of Monaghan, at the mercy of his gangs? Swanning about London, he might convince the English that he was a man of honour. Battling for supremacy against his blood brothers in the south, he might convince Sir James Craig. But he would not convince Sinclair Armstrong.

The catalogue was still growing. Hadn't the same Collins presided over the very gunmen who had shot Davy Morton and all the others at Clones, killed his uncle Bob, terrorised Protestants at every turn? He could have stopped it, if he had a mind. He could have prevented them burning Orange halls, attacking special constables going about their duty, building up the forces in Clones that Sinclair knew were straining at the bit to come in here, harrying and worrying law-abiding citizens and their rightful protectors at every turn. Only last week, Sinclair had been caught in one of their ambushes. Two dead and four wounded from the platoon. Nor was that a first either. For months since he arrived here, there had been running battles along the frontier. Shots aimed to kill and maim. It was all the work of Collins, for wasn't he supposed to be in control? If he could guarantee peace with Craig now, could he not have stopped these endless attempts to harry and brutalise ordinary God-fearing people into submitting to his wishes?

But the continuing atrocities across the frontier were the true mark of the perfidious nature of the Dublin government and Collins. He might soft-talk the big shots, but people in Drum and other loyalist areas caught in the new Free State knew no freedom. Homes raided, people driven out, Orange halls burned at will, lodges prevented from walking, Protestants dragged before those so-called courts and fined or worse, and people reminded at every turn that they were captives, exiled in the Babylon of this latter-day Nebuchadnezzar. Now they even talked about forcing loyal subjects to learn their barbaric tongue if they wanted jobs in the public service or teaching. Next they would be insisting they bend their knee to Rome into the bargain.

No, Sinclair would not be convinced by Collins or by any of his henchmen. Nor would he be convinced by Craig either. Sure, hadn't he thrown his own people to the wolves too? What did he care, sitting up in Belfast in all his new glory, for the people in this country here along his precious border? Ulster needed defending, he said. By God, but Sinclair Armstrong would do the job, even if some were fooled into thinking it was no longer needed.

Even Dorothy, his own Dorothy, was convinced by the lies, insisting Sinclair was being unreasonable in not trusting the news. Did she not see that this was another trick, another ploy to get people off guard so that Collins could harass loyalist people on his own side even more? And maybe worse. Sinclair had seen the build-up in Clones with his own eyes. He had heard of the arrival of trucks from the south, of guns swapped with the so-called Irregulars under Liam Lynch in the deep south so they wouldn't be traced back to the munitions the British had supplied. What was all that for, if not to further his dastardly work? Sinclair would stand on guard, even if others were letting their guard down, even over Dorothy's protests.

"But surely it's all over now," she insisted yet again as they sat in the kitchen at Gortraw. "They've agreed, haven't they - Craig and Collins?"

"Aye, peace is declared today and next minute they shoot us in the back. We're still sitting ducks for them if we let ourselves relax."

"But you're all right, Sinclair love. That's all that matters. You've come through it safe."

"It's not what matters. We're all in this together. We're still at war, Dorothy, and it may be my turn next."

"Don't say that, Sinclair love. Don't even think it. For God's sake, Sinclair, think of our wedding," Dorothy pleaded, worried that the man she loved with all her being was changing before her very eyes. The unsure, faltering, even shy, Sinclair was gone. He had been metamorphosed into this hard, brutal, untrusting person who sat beside her and refused her caresses. She resolved to let him believe what he wanted to for now. She would be proved right in the end. She had to be. Then Sinclair would begin to trust again. Maybe after the wedding, maybe then it would all be fine.

Sadie noticed the change in Sinclair too, when they found him sitting at the table in Robert James McConkey's house a few nights later. His usual lack of confidence was replaced with a wee bit of swagger, an urge to let them know that he knew all that was happening now. He was less a farmer, more a policeman, she thought. But maybe that wasn't such a bad thing. For she fretted so about him over there, worrying that he might be taken advantage of just because he was softer than some of the others he'd be dealing with. Not soft in his physical strength, mind you, for her son was strong and fit after all the years on the farm with Albert. But in his emotions, that was where he would be vulnerable. God knows, after what happened to poor Bob, he had a right to be nervous and afraid. But now here he was and not a hint of his usual trepidation fornenst his own father.

Sadie and Albert had been rising from the tea table when the knock came on the door. She knew from the knock it was Roy, of course, for he often called out these days since the funeral and they liked to have him about the place. He had even said to Albert he could give him a hand when needed at any of the farm work. But, sure, they couldn't impose. And Albert had already spoken to Wee Willie Houston from down beyond the Pump Brae about maybe coming by to help out. With a house full of childer, Willie could use the few bob. Though, God knows, the pay wouldn't be up to much.

But Roy was doing more than just making his ceilidh tonight. He said they should come with him and they would see. They trusted Roy, of course. Who wouldn't trust him? So Albert had hitched up the trap and they followed him down through the village and round by the church and now here they were. She knew it had to be something to do with Sinclair, even though Roy had said nothing. She would have worried but that Roy had this big grin on his face as he turned around on his bicycle to check they were still there. Or maybe he was just checking the road. Goodness knows, Albert kept sharp too, no less than she had her own eyes peeled.

So here they had come through the door and there he was, Sinclair, larger than life, as they say, and his father not believing me when I said it as we set out. Well, suppose that's men for you, especially with the times that's in it. They'll always expect the worst. Takes a woman's intuition, though, in the heel of the hunt. But, sure, then we had to consider Roy. Him going to all that trouble to get us over here. Had to show a wee bit of concern to please him too.

"What's the matter, son?" Sadie had greeted Sinclair. "What has you over the line."

It was easier for Albert, him expecting the worst anyway: "Aye, you're taking a shocking risk, Sinclair lad. They'll have you if they get half a chance."

"Don't worry, they didn't see me coming over."

There it was, Sadie thought, the confidence. Not like the old Sinclair. Took the fretting and worrying after herself, she knew. Maybe her own mind would rest easier now. For, surely to God, he knew what he was about. Maybe that training and all had been good for the lad. Made a real man of him.

"But they're out scouring the whole countryside these days for what they call spies and traitors," said Albert.

"It's Belleek has me over," said Sinclair, causing Sadie to start with the fright.

"Belleek? Are they moving you to the far end of Fermanagh son?"

"No, they've gone in there, the Fenians. Set up camp in Belleek Castle and around Bo Island, over by Pettigo way."

"You mean an invasion?" asked his father.

Robert James was incensed. There he was, a widower man, him and Roy, trying to get a sup of tea wet and bread cut. And us only up from our own tea table. Robert James stood, bread knife poised in mid-air, like a ceremonial sword, as he declared, "By God, but they'll pay for that. Surely to God the British government can't stand back on that."

"Word is they're mustering again, the IRA like, all along the frontier," said Sinclair. "They may be going in from here. This was maybe my last chance to come across this way."

"Och wheest son," Sadie said. "Don't say things like that, for they put the heart across me, so they do."

"We've been expecting it. I came on foot by Clonagun, over by the Elliotts' place. That's a wee lane and a ford over the river they don't seem to know about. Anyway, I hear tell they're moving all about the roads down that way and all over the area hereabouts."

"Aye, they've been at it for days now," Roy chimed in. "I could have told you that."

"Och, all ould show, if you ask me," said Robert James, buttering bread now, big doorsteps cut from a loaf of shop bread. It's a terror to think of them without a woman in the house to do a wee bit of baking for them. But, sure, poor Pearl McConkey wasn't fit for much those last couple of years as she wasted away. How many years ago, five or six anyway. Aye, closer to six for it was during the war, right after poor Eric.

Robert James was saying, "Sure, they can't control theirselves and their own area, never mind Fermanagh as well."

"True enough," said Albert. "Mr Burns was saying he was down in Dublin and they've got two armies down there now - patrolling the one street on different sides. They'll be at others' throats before long, so he was saying anyway. Mr Burns like."

"Doubt it's not over about here yet either," Sinclair cut in. "They're still shooting across at us out by Lackey Bridge. Five of our men have been killed this week past. Nearly got it myself out by Wattle Bridge in thon ambush last week."

Sadie was alarmed, her motherly concerns awakened again. Her son was still in mortal danger. "Och, my poor wee lamb. What have they got you into at all, at all?"

"Aye, Sinclair," said Robert James, as he placed the bread on the table, beside great big mugs with chips out of them all. "Sure, it isn't our fight no more. We've enough of a job holding our own ground here."

"Wheesht, dad, there's no going back on that," said Roy.

Albert agreed, "Aye, it's a different situation now. We all know that. Sure, haven't they called to our house beyond several times since Bob was murdered. Looking for Sinclair here."

"Aye, brazen as you like," said Sadie, her voice sharpening again with indignation. "Walk all over your grave thon crowd would, and not as much as flinch while they did it either."

"That's why I came here," Sinclair explained. "Thought it might be safer."

Robert James was pouring tea now, a dense black liquid that gave off the pungent odour of stewed tealeaves. "You were right. Sure, we'd not see you stuck and you know that."

"Aye, but what's to happen with Belleek now took by them?" Roy asked Sinclair as he sat down with a big jug of milk and began to pour from it into the black tea. The creamy milk formed a cloud, then spread out into a deep tan colour. Sadie didn't relish the tea. You could stand a spoon up in it without a bother if you had a mind to, she thought.

"Don't rightly know. But they're transferring men from all over. When the word comes down, we may be going in."

"Going in?" Albert asked, excited. "You mean a counter attack?"

"That's the word anyway. There's some are very put out at losing ground in the first place."

"Aye, a mite sorrier than when they lost us and all along with us, I doubt," Albert remarked bitterly.

"Hope to goodness they're not sending you in, son," Sadie said. "Sure, you're needed about Newtownbutler there, where they know you and the whole seed and breed of you."

"Well, no word yet .... But that brings me to my other news. You're all invited to a wedding ...."

The day lit up for Sadie. "What? You don't mean to say ...."

The others cut in, offering congratulations, commenting on what a great wee lassie he was getting. Roy raised his mug in a toast; the others joined in. It was just like the old times, when there was a wee bit of fun to life.

"Aye, we're tying the knot," said Sinclair when he got the chance. "We were going to anyway, but it's sooner rather than later ...."

Sadie's heart skipped a beat. Surely not? "There's not a wee bit of bother, is there? Dorothy, like, she's no ...."

Sinclair laughed and the others joined in. So did Sadie. "Och, away on out of that," her son said. "No, we just don't want to wait, in case I'm transferred or something. It would be more difficult then maybe."

Albert was pleased. You could tell. And proud, too. "I suppose every dark cloud has a silver lining," he began.

But Sadie's mind was taken up already by wedding preparations. She would have to get over and see Dorothy and her mother now, no matter about this frontier business. "You'll have to ask Mr Burns of course," she said. "Your own clergyman should be there. And then there's ...."

But they were still caught up in telling Sinclair what a great fellow he was. Men, leave it to them and it would all turn out a right shambles. Aye, and if it did, wouldn't they just turn around and blame the women. Say it was their job to make it right.

****

We have hitherto succeeded in keeping the United Irishmen out of the town of Clones, though it has been threatened, and within these few nights they have committed depredations immediately in its neighbourhood. So lately as last night many guns were taken, and yet the yeomanry of both corps were out through the country patrolling in different directions. The two Clones corps are exceedingly harassed by constant nightly duty of patrols and are almost becoming dispirited through excessive fatigue and the uncertainty of their receiving any compensation for their extraordinary services.

Rev. John Wright, Rector of Clones, 1796.

****

It had been less than a year since they had danced in this very same hall, Sinclair recalled, after their day trip to Enniskillen. On a stage platform at the front, a small fit-up band of accordions, a fiddle and drums had played waltzes for about 20 dancing couples, the accordions threatening to shift from the two-two tempo into a martial air. At tables arranged around walls bearing a few emblems and pictures of investitures, other couples sat with their parents. Women sipped tea, saucers held chest-high, small fingers extended daintily. Their men folk sat, heads together discussing farming affairs and the state of the country. It was just a few of weeks before the Twelfth, a matter of days after the King opened the Northern Ireland parliament. In this wee Orange hall, it was a celebration. Sinclair remembered that Dorothy compensated with deft side-steps for his own awkwardness. Yet, as they moved, he found his clumsiness disappearing, Dorothy bearing him along in a loose embrace. If dancing allowed him only that physical contact, he could endure the embarrassment. He even remembered his chest swelling with pride as he glanced around, sure that everybody there was watching, some envying his luck to have Dorothy in his arms. It was then he felt a pair of piercing eyes. Rev. Burns, towering above the crowd was moving in their direction. They met near the centre of the floor as other couples took their seats during an interlude, Burns already in full flow as if delivering a sermon. He remembered the clergyman ignoring Dorothy, pointedly it seemed, saying something about being here to ensure "all things be done decently and in order," whatever he meant by that. They escaped him in the end, duking out a side door to see the small village below, its two streets bedecked for the marching season. Beside them, flags wafted proudly from the turrets of the Church of Ireland steeple, a perfect backdrop for the band inside which had begun to play *The Ould Orange Flute* in waltz-time. Sinclair remembered their embrace, Dorothy giggling occasionally and saying that Burns gave her the "heebie-jeebies." Sinclair embraced her closer still and kissed her. "We'll have to take care of that then, won't we?"

A year less four days, Sinclair thought, as he surveyed the scene now. It was changed, just like everything else. He was changed from then too. Sinclair wondered again if he could ever return home. In a year, his outlook, his prospects, his very chances of survival had changed utterly. What hope did they have back home now? No Twelfth, no comfort and no help from this side either.

He counted them quickly again. Seventy-two guests. No matter what Dorothy said about the suddenness of it all, it was a grand wedding breakfast and now his wife sat alongside him. His platoon over there at the side, raising a wee bit of ructions and whooping it up. Doubt that's not orange squash they're drinking either. But sure wasn't that only what happens at weddings, matter a damn what Rev. Burns might say and him sitting down there with Mr Knight, quoting scripture in his ear no doubt. He scanned the tables again, some full of laughing faces, others glum. Why did his own side seem so uncomfortable? The ones who had come across did, at any rate. They would put a real damper on his and Dorothy's day if they got the chance. Probably pining because they couldn't have their own parade this year.

After the wedding service, with his platoon lined up in a guard of honour, they had kept to themselves. Even Roy, his best man, was making a poor fist of it. Good job Alex was in the wedding party, sitting now on the other side of Dorothy, what would have been Roy's place as the best man if Alex hadn't grabbed it for a joke. But Roy didn't see the joke, and neither did Dorothy when Alex made that crack a wee while ago when she asked her new husband if he wanted some more meat. "Building up his strength for the night ahead?" asked Alex with a big wink. Sure, he was just having a wee bit of fun. Barracks humour, maybe. But isn't that where we are now? Those of us in uniform. Och, what matter now?

Soon the dancing would start and they'd all get into the fun of it. None too soon at that. At least he would get to hold Dorothy close. With only a couple of days off for the wedding, he would soon be embracing a Lee Enfield rifle again.

Why does Sinclair avoid my eye when I remark on him and Dorothy coming home to Drumkirk when all this blows over? It happened again there when I said something to Dorothy and she said, "You'd better ask my husband here about that." I looked at him, getting the wee joke, mind you and all, but he just turned away and said something about not seeing the end of the troubles. Sure, that wasn't what I was asking him and he knew that rightly.

Sure, haven't I my own information on that anyway, from Col. Madden and Attorney Knight, men that would know a wee bit more nor our Sinclair thinks he knows. They said the crowd down in Dublin are really sizing up for a fight and, sure, the whole country knows that too. Col. Madden said that when they get at it, the British army will be back and, this time, they'll go at it in earnest. Would Col. Madden not know now? Him a senior officer in the Ulster Volunteer Force and all? Aye, and a former member of the Ulster Unionist Council and a railway company director who has the ears of both camps.

Said as much to Sinclair a while back. What does he say back to me? His own father? Says he, if they do take other on down in the south, then they'll be just let at it to give the North a chance of making a go of it up here. Still, maybe he's right at the heel of the hunt. It'd just be like them to look after their own wee patch and to hell with the rest of us. But the thought doesn't make for much celebration, nor the thought of what will happen to Drumkirk. I tried to make Sinclair address that when I pointed out about our Eric's being gone and the cause robbed from under us as well. He said, "Dad, not here." Sure where else but here?

Only for Dorothy, maybe I'd be away home already. She was saying a wee while back she'll not be calling me Mr Armstrong from here out. I'll be dad or father or something like that. God, she's a great wee lassie. She'd be a great help to Sadie and me over in Drumkirk, to see us out the last of our days.

You'd think we'd get a wee break from it all, Sadie was telling Jean Hall, Dorothy's mother. Politics at a wedding, I mean. But there they go at it, Albert in the corner with Attorney Knight and Rev. Burns and the others, settling the fate of small nations. No fear of them joining in the dance anyway, I remarked laughing. Sure aren't me and Jean family now, all the one, thank goodness and doesn't Dorothy look radiant. Mind my own wedding day like it was yesterday. It never leaves you, I said to Jean and then caught myself on, her being widowed and all. I just didn't think. But, not a bother till her either. Just kept going on about how great our Sinclair is and how grand he looks in his uniform there. "You know," says she, "There's something about a man in uniform that will always turn a woman's head." We laughed at that, of course, there being so many of them young bucks about here got up in uniforms. Special constables, how are you. Nothing much special about some of them if the truth be known. Wish to God poor Eric was here though. He went off in uniform too. But needn't think about that now. Special occasion. Time of great happiness and celebration.

The talk of uniforms put us both in mind of the volunteers, of course, the Ulster Volunteer Force and them all gathered down beyond at Knockballymore House drilling and training and what have you. The open day, it was, with the newspapers there and all. A great show of force by the men of Ulster. I don't mind seeing Jean there, but wasn't there that many about. Thousands, they say, from all over Monaghan and Fermanagh, before this border business got going at all. No talk of any of it back then. Ulster will fight and Ulster will be right, they said. Didn't mean Ulster will split, did it? Her man Willie was lined out then too. Sure she misses him. Wouldn't I miss my own Albert if he was gone. But, sure, don't we all have our crosses to bear as they say. I've had my own losses too.

"What's it like over there now?" Jean asked. "Must be terrible for you altogether not knowing from ...."

"It's bad all right. They've taken over completely, the other side. Hard to imagine we're only five miles away or less even some of us. Getting so the county line is a real divide now."

"We haven't been across since this good while," said Jean. "Don't trust the journey and then, you hear so many stories."

"Don't hear the half of it," Sadie said, and wouldn't she know, her own brother Bob going like that only two months ago now.

"Why don't you move over here?" asked Jean, just like that.

"Maybe I would, but Albert's very strong on holding onto the land. His people have farmed Drumkirk for 300 years now. It holds you that. Aye, and if it came to the bit, maybe I'd not go either. It's home. It's where we belong, no matter what they say."

"Aye," she said. "That's understandable. But I wouldn't think Sinclair will go back now he's made the break. What with him and Dorothy settling down here in Newtownbutler now."

She may be right. But, please God, for Albert's sake I hope he does come home. It would break poor Albert's heart if his only living son forsook him and all he holds dear too.

If that Alex Johnson puts a hand near me again, I'll smack his face, thought Dorothy, even as she forced herself to give Sinclair a reassuring smile across the floor where he was dancing with Eileen. The cheek of him, pawing me like that on my own wedding day and making out it was just a joke.

"Just a wee kiss from the bride," he says, lips puckered up and smacking off other. He has a cheek, but I give him no quarter. Then he says, barefaced as you like, "Know what they say about forbidden fruit ...."

He has drink taken, I know it from the leer on his face. Mind you, that leer is always there when he looks at me, or any other woman for that matter. You can see the lechery in his mind.

Even Sinclair knew that wasn't just orange squash he and the others were drinking.

God, when Sinclair told me he would be in the wedding party, I tried to talk him out of it. What about, Roy? I asked. But he was having Roy and Alex, too, his best friends. A man like Alex Johnson is no fit companion for Sinclair, never mind a best friend. Just because they are in the same platoon. Aren't there many others there that would make better company than that sly fox, sly wolf is more like it though.

All through the dinner, he kept it up. One joke after another. Jokes! I was mortified in front of my own mother. And Sinclair, with the big open stupid grin on his face. Don't think he understood the half of it. Men are like that. Go along with what they think is manly.

At least we have our own cottage. Sinclair will be home with me when he's off duty now, not hanging about in that barracks with the likes of Alex Johnson. I'll make sure of that.

Even the other day, when we were moving in and the platoon was helping us, I let him know that he would not be welcome there. Said as much when he came in carrying a chair and the chamber pot. "Where'll I put this?" he asked me. I started to tell him where the chair went and he holds up the pot and says, "No, this." I didn't smile or anything, just grabbed it from him. He can see where his so-called humour is not appreciated. I'll make sure that Sinclair lets him know too. Just as soon as we're settled in.

But here comes Sinclair now. He looks so happy to see me. You would think we'd been apart for years, the look of longing in him. I'll not think any more of that Alex Johnson. There is only one man here that interests me and here he comes, sweeping me off my feet all over again.

****

Hearing reports that a numerous body had assembled at Leysborough, I led my troop of Yeomanry and a party of the North Lowland Fencibles to the place. When I got within sight of them I walked the troop to give them time to disperse; however, finding they were determined to stand their ground, I made part of my troop get into the same field and form in front of them, while I proceeded with the remainder to flank them; they let me ride quite close to them and when I desired them to disperse took no notice. I then fired a pistol over their heads and ordered the troop to charge them; some fled, while others made resistance with their spades (for it appeared they had not any firearms, which from their keeping their ground so confidently I was induced to think they had). From every information that I can get six of the deluded wretches were killed, several severely wounded and fourteen made prisoners. There were about 300 of them in the field exclusive of great numbers upon all the adjacent hills...

Alexander Ker, Newbliss, to Dublin Castle, 20 May 1797.

****

"Go on Sinclair, take a wee drop," Alex Johnson said, proffering the bottle of Bushmills whiskey. "It'll not do you a bit of harm."

They were lying in the grass with other members of Newtownbutler B platoon of the Special Constabulary at the edge of the field in the demesne of Brookeborough Castle. Around them, families were busy having picnic lunches, while some children cavorted and a cricket match between two lodges had commenced to their rear. The crack of ball on bat interrupted the steady thunder roll of Lambeg drums from the other side of the field. Somewhere nearby, a male voice had started to sing. Sinclair listened closely, trying to make out the words, but the bottle was still held before his eyes.

"Just a wee drop for the day that's in it," said Alex.

Sinclair shifted uneasily on his elbow. He should really go and look for Dorothy who was with some of her friends from Newtownbutler. But he had been unable to find them in a cursory search when the platoon had arrived late. That was during the middle of the speeches, after he had spent three night's duty at the Wattle Bridge outpost. When he had met up again with his constabulary colleagues, he abandoned his search. Alex persuaded him to sit a while and maybe Dorothy would come by, knowing he should be there by now. Since then, Alex hadn't stopped insisting that he have a drink.

"Stop pestering me, Alex. I don't need it."

Alex called out to the others, "Would you listen to him. Not a month married and the wee lassie has him well under her thumb already. Afraid to take a wee sup on the Twelfth, no less."

"Och, wheesht your ould blather," Sinclair said. "I'm my own man."

"Well, take a wee sup then and prove it. Come on, prove it so."

Sinclair, exasperated at the taunting, and anxious to prove to the others that he wasn't declining on Dorothy's instructions, reached for the bottle. "Och, if only to give my head peace."

He raised the bottle to his mouth and took a small sip, the fiery liquid burning a path down his throat and sending a warming waft through to the pit of his stomach. He could feel Alex grabbing the base of the bottle and holding it to his mouth. Sinclair's throat opened wider and he was forced to gulp it down, hearing the bubbles released into the whiskey as he did so. Alex laughed, "That's it. Take a good drop now, for that's good Ulster Protestant whiskey. None of your ould Free State drink here."

Sinclair managed to break free at last, twisting his head to the side, away from the rim, choking. A small splash of whiskey plopped onto his tunic as Alex righted the bottle again, laughing with the others. Sinclair coughed and spluttered, a burning trickle of whiskey escaping from his nose, his eyes watering and his body shaking. He took a deep breath and exploded in anger at Alex:

"Holyful God, are you trying to choke me with that stuff?"

"Sure, you only got a wee taste. Not bad, is it?"

Sinclair could feel the whiskey warming and relaxing his body, easing the tension that seemed to have been there for months. He could feel a faint lightness in his brain and the after-taste of the whiskey was pleasant on his tongue, now that he had stopped choking.

"Go on again," Alex urged. "I'll not bother you this time. Aye, and there's plenty more to go the rounds."

Sinclair looked around at the field, the lodge banners fluttering in the mild breeze. The Fermanagh field, he thought, guarded and protected now by men such as himself. Back in Monaghan, he knew, the Twelfth celebrations had been cancelled because of the worsening intimidation. Not safe to march, the County Grand Lodge had decided, urging district and private lodge members to travel if they could to the parades in the Six Counties. Few, Sinclair knew, had ventured across the frontier, afraid of being identified and marked. The Orange parades in the Six Counties were guarded and protected by the mighty army of the Royal Ulster Constabulary. The Orange lodges in Monaghan had no such protection. His resentment built, nurtured by the whiskey which pervaded his mind with a clarity he had not known for so long.

He looked back at the bottle, held before him again by a smiling Alex. The amber liquid glistened with an orange sheen in the sunlight. He shrugged and grasped the bottle by the neck. Keeping an eye on Alex, he raised it to his mouth again and drank gingerly at first, then steadily. This time, the spirit flowed easily down his throat.

Dorothy found him at last in the dayroom of Newtownbutler police barracks, slumped over a small wooden table and singing drowsily. She was shocked and angry, but also embarrassed by the presence of Alex Johnson, a satisfied leer on his face as he dismissed her anger and concerns. With one hand on Sinclair's shoulder, Alex had looked up lazily as she entered, shrugged and leered.

"*As we were walking down on the road to Portadown,*
Our Lambeg drums did rattle and did thunder...."

Sinclair sang, his voice slurring, the tempo erratic, oblivious to Dorothy's entrance on the scene.

"Has he been drinking?" Dorothy asked, needlessly. "Sinclair, have you strong drink taken?"

She moved to the table as Alex withdrew his hand and she shook Sinclair roughly.

"Och, hold off, daughter," Alex slurred. "He only had a wee sup."

"Sup, is it? Sure, he's roaring drunk. Anybody can see it."

Sinclair roused himself and pulled up from the table, unsteadily trying to find his balance. His eyes opened in two slits, the head tilted back. He saw and recognised his wife.

"What's the matter? Och, Dorothy darling, there you are. Looked all over the field, but couldn't find you anywhere."

His head slumped forward as he placed his elbows on the table and caught his face with his hands.

"I can see the looking you did. Through the bottom of Alex Johnson's whiskey bottle, judging by the state of you."

Alex rose to his feet. Dorothy was surprised how steady he seemed, although it was quite obvious that he had been drinking heavily too. He approached Dorothy and she sidled over to the other side of the table, placing her hand on Sinclair's shoulder now. He didn't respond.

"Och, he was only celebrating the Twelfth," said Alex, "and the shelling of the Four Courts in Dublin."

He had moved up on the other side of Sinclair now and placed his hand on Sinclair's other shoulder, his fingers extended. Dorothy could sense his hand close to hers. She withdrew. Alex laughed, "Wants us to take the next train down and join in the fighting."

Sinclair roused himself momentarily, shouting out, "Aye, c'mon boys. Sure, the men of the Ulster Special Constabulary'd red out the whole lot of them in a lock of hours."

"You'll come on home where you belong," said Dorothy, noting with annoyance how her voice faltered in her uneasiness with Alex's proximity. "That's the only place you'll go to."

"Och, go easy on the lad. It's only high spirits."

"Aye, Bushmills spirits is more like it," Dorothy responded, annoyed at how forced her attempt at a rejoinder sounded now as she said it. She knew she was too anxious to face down this man who now stood there with a proprietorial hand on the shoulder of her husband. She felt young and inadequate in his presence and he did everything he could to add to her insecurity, talking to her as you might to a child. His tone of indulgent patience only added to her feeling of inadequacy.

"Sure, it's the first time he's enjoyed himself since he came here," said Alex, pausing before he added, "Bar the wedding, of course."

"Surprised you'd even mention that," said Dorothy. "Thought it would be too dry for you."

Alex laughed and produced a pewter flask from a pocket of his trousers. He held it towards her, over Sinclair's head. "Sure, you know me. Always carry a wee spare drop."

Sinclair stirred again. "Quit the stalling, men. Let's join Collins and his Howitzer guns. Come on, we can take Drum on our way." He removed his hands to gesture and slumped forward, his face now resting on the table as he rolled onto his left cheek facing Dorothy, who used her hands firmly to prevent him slumping to the floor.

Alex noticed that, as she bent to steady her husband, the top buttons of Dorothy's blouse slipped their moorings. He could see deep into her cleavage and the soft mounds of flesh which formed it. He felt a twitching of renewed desire in his scrotum as he angled himself for a clearer view. There was no doubt about it, he thought, Dorothy is a right wee cracker. Her face was flushed with embarrassment as she called, "Sinclair, Sinclair, are you all right?" Imagining the source of her rising colour as desire, Alex felt his penis stiffen.

"He's out like a light, lass," he said. "Come on, I'll get you home to bed."

"That's decent of you, Alex Johnson," her voice faltering from the effort of holding Sinclair from falling, unable to register the sarcasm he knew she intended. "Seeing it was you got him in this state."

Alex grasped Sinclair, deliberately running his hand over Dorothy's as he did so, "Can't you see?" he asked her as her eyes came up to meet his. "It was coming and it's a relief. Sure, Sinclair's living in the same fear as the rest of us .... waiting for an ambush every time he goes out, expecting a blast any minute. He needed to get it out of his system and that's happened now. The whiskey and the fighting down in Dublin took care of it. Couldn't bottle it up any more."

Dorothy's eyes registered interest in what he was saying. "What makes you so sure the fighting is over here?"

"Sure, they're too busy going for each other down south to bother about us now. They'll do the job for us by taking care of each other. The Six Counties is safe and solid. We can rest and maybe, before too long, they'll send us home out of here."

Dorothy looked back down at Sinclair, his breath now bubbling as a stream of moisture flowed from his mouth. "But tell me, Alex, where's Sinclair's home now but here with me?"

Alex registered in his mind the way her summer dress flowed from her narrow waist over the haunches of her full hips. Her feet spread to bear the weight of her husband as she tried to raise him and the dress clung to her legs. Alex sucked in his breath and shook his head slightly.

"Aye, maybe it's only the drink talking," he said. "Come on now, love. We'll shift this boy and take Drum while we're at it. Maybe they won't notice in all the excitement."

Moses Planted Aaron's Rod

Noah planted the first garden,
Moses planted Aaron's rod.
He smote the waters of the Egyptians
And turned the Jordan into blood.

For we are the true-born Sons of Levi,
None on earth can with us compare;
We are the root and branch of David,
The bright and glorious Morning Star.

Set apart, we were the first-born of Aaron, the priests of Samuel's line in the House of David, walking forever before the anointed. We dwelt in the cities that God set apart for us - forty eight in number. In a land flowing with milk and honey, we kept His laws. Virtue guarded our lines and vigilance was ever the price of our liberty. Saved in the blood of the lamb, we refuted the gainsaying of the whore of Babylon. We put our faith in the King of kings and fought our battles beneath the shadow of his wings. We scattered our enemies and cut down the trees that bore no fruit. For with our enemy is an arm of flesh; but with us is the Lord our God to help us. And we rested ourselves upon the words of Hedekiah king of Judah.

****

Another commandeered outpost, its front wall bolstered by sandbags and the back yard sealed off. Ahead, a sweep of country road and hills beyond - the border. Sinclair peered through a rifle porthole and squinted as he looked off into the distance. Nothing changed, or about to change, he thought, surveying the hills of Monaghan cascading off into the horizon. He swept his rifle around, checking the trajectory, looking for signs of life. In the bright sunlight of a Spring morning, there was not even the sound of a breeze wafting through the leaves which were still only threatening to burst from their new buds. The only sounds came from inside the outpost, a sturdy farmhouse, its upper-storey dormer windows poking through the front of the roof line. From there, the sounds of early morning activity as men's voices demanded attention over the clatter of breakfast dishes. Sinclair wondered about the house's owners. Protestants, he was told, they fled as soon as the frontier line was drawn. The sergeant had told him they were living up around Lisbellaw now, the wife's home place and the land hereabouts had been set to Roman Catholic neighbours. For a steal, Sinclair surmised, sympathising naturally with the family which had fled.

Sinclair's group had arrived yesterday in a great flurry of activity, holding on to the back of the Crossley tender as it careened down small, twising roads on the southerly reaches of Upper Lough Erne. Their present position, he knew, was Derrykerrib Island. Although he could see no lake water, he knew it was just beyond a dip over there. A rickety bridge ahead was Monaghan, or maybe Cavan. He wasn't exactly sure, but slightly to the left of his present view was the great Castle

Saunderson. Sinclair had been there once as a boy, when the family had attended a UVF parade. He would have been only about ten years old then, before the war and still during the great Home Rule Crisis. The old colonel had passed on by then, of course, but his legend permeated the loughside keep in stories about his prodigious strength and his challenges to guests to match him in after-dinner feats such as scaling the walls up the castle's main stairwell. It was said that he could lift the great dining room table with one arm and chin-up the castle doors with one hand tied behind his back. The founder of the Ulster Volunteer Force, Col. Edward Saunderson had been a hero to Ulster Protestants from the time he rallied them in defence of the Union. His political legacy lived on in his son, Maj. Somerset Saunderson, a leader in the county UVF and a war hero to boot. He had been there on the day of the fete. Seemed so long ago now. A lot of water under the bridge beyond. Erne water, sacred to the cause of Ulster loyalists, trickling and gliding over the memories held in its murky fastness, the memories of a great battle, the precursor of the Boyne when 6,000 Jacobite rebels were harried and driven into the stream by the 1,500 loyalists who had marched out from Enniskillen and engaged them at Newtownbutler. Caught in a loop of land at a bend of the river only a few hundred yards from here, the Jacobites had neither the wit nor the leaders to beg for quarter. They were drowned to a man here beneath the lofty grey towers of Castle Saunderson. Sinclair's father had told him of that great battle on the day of their visit and he had guarded its memory with his father's assurance that this signal victory caused the Duke of Berwick to lift his siege of Derry, rightly fearing his lines of retreat would be cut off. Of such proud lore and Protestant valour was he sprung. The words of *The Sash*,

It was worn at Derry Aughrim, Enniskillen and the Boyne...

were a living memory of the greatness of their cause. It seemed a long way from the present, however, the routine of guard duty at a border outpost, rifle trained on the very scene of such glorious memory.

Yet they all knew this was more than a routine posting. A general alert had been signalled and they were mustered back on duty, a full day ahead of schedule. An air of tension had gripped the barracks as assignments were called out. Then, with a final roll-call, they were on their way here, each member of the platoon using his rifle to sweep the hedges along the way. It was as if everybody expected an ambush at any moment. Finally, as the tender pulled into the front street of the farmhouse and they disembarked, Alex had turned to him.

"This is it now, Sinclair," he had announced.

"What? The invasion?"

Alex laughed, mockingly, "Not at all. They probably began to retreat back down to Dublin when they heard we were coming. It's your big chance to go and take Drum."

Drum, thought Sinclair, if it's still there. It had been more than a year since he had last been home, and not even to Drumkirk, but to the McConkey's. It was just too risky, he knew, even during the troubles down south. Since the IRA around Clones had sided with the Provisional Government in Dublin, almost to a man, there had been little enough trouble in the area as the south was engulfed in a civil war. But the vigilance had not lapsed, nor had the number of cross-border incidents as bored soldiers on the other side took frequent pot-shots at patrols or positions. Anyway, he had little enough time for traipsing across the border, even if he had a mind to. Marriage and duty took care of most of his time and the wee bit of recreation he got seemed to fly by before you would know it.

Sinclair took a final sweep of the landscape and turned again to crouch into the sentry position. He had just retracted his rifle when he heard a motor engine approaching at speed from the northern direction. He roused Alex and they both went to positions at the side and looked out. A black car was slowing down as it came to the outpost, a small Union Jack attached to the front bumper. Sinclair recognised the inspector from Newtown in the front, seated beside a driver in police uniform. The car swung into the front street and the driver emerged and swung open the back door. A tall, balding man in his mid-forties emerged with another police officer, a portly man with flushed cheeks. The tall man had a military bearing, accentuated by his pencil moustache and the swagger stick tucked carefully under his arm. Sinclair felt his sleeve tugged.

"Sir Basil Brooke himself, be God," Alex whispered. "Must be a full alert all right when they have the top brass out to man the barricades."

"Looks fishy if you ask me. If it was an invasion, I've no doubt but those boys would be directing the defence of the realm from the safety of Enniskillen Castle."

The sergeant had emerged from the farmhouse and was talking to Brooke and the others. He withdrew, facing back to the door and blew a whistle. Men came running out. The sergeant gestured to Sinclair and Alex, beckoning. As they walked over, the sergeant called out, "Right men, fall in for inspection. Come on now, on the double."

Much jostling as the men fell into their pre-assigned places. Some were still buttoning tunics and pulling caps down from the back of their heads. Sinclair slipped into position beside Alex at the head of the line. All the while, he watched Brooke, a former captain in the Inniskilling Dragoons, pacing to and fro, banging his swagger stick into the palm of his left hand. The shuffling stopped. On command from the sergeant, they all stood to attention. Brooke looked satisfied and moved into position, front and centre. He smiled, his moustache curling up into the folds of his pale cheeks, full jowlers accentuating hound-like weary eyes.

"Congratulations, men," he said, his accent public school English with no trace of his Fermanagh roots. "Jolly well done, one and all. At this point, I think I can tell you that the purpose of this exercise was to test our mobilisation in case of an invasion."

Brooke paused, looking from face to face along the parade line: "While that invasion, happily, has not taken place, you will be aware that we must prepare for such an emergency now that hostilities in the south are coming to an end ...."

Brooke moved to the other end of the line, where the sergeant and the other senior police officer stood. Sinclair poked Alex with his elbow: "Christ, now he tells us."

"Aye, a wee game of soldiers for the top brass," Alex whispered back.

"Having visited most of our positions already, I can tell you that our performance here in Fermanagh will hardly be matched along the entire frontier of Ulster. Within 15 minutes of the alert from Enniskillen, our B constables had every access road along our 83 miles of border sealed and you men of the A Constabulary were taking up your front-line positions. I think I can safely say that Fermanagh was secure and the people of this country can rest assured that they are well and truly protected ...." Brooke stood at the far end of the line still addressing the men. Sinclair, eyes straight, whispered to Alex from the side of his mouth, "If they decide to hop across now, we'll be too damned tired to stir out again."

"Aye, they'll not be fit to move any further for the sleeping protectors of Ulster lining the roads."

Brooke was winding up, already braced to get back into the car and off. "The mobilisation period is 24 hours, men, so it will be some hours more before you can return to your other duties or resume your leave. But again, well done and congratulations. You can all rest assured that Fermanagh and, indeed, all of Ulster is justly proud of you and your comrades in the constabulary."

With a brisk swivel on his heel, Brooke was heading back to the car where the driver was already swinging open the back door. The others in the inspection group hurried off in his wake. The sergeant stepped forward in front of the men, saying, "Right then, fall out. Return to you positions now."

The others drifted back into the farmhouse as Alex and Sinclair returned to their sandbag wall. The car had already started up and was pulling out of the yard when they got there, the sergeant standing to attention and saluting its departure. Within moments, the place seemed deserted again. Sinclair hunkered down and set aside his gun. Hugging his knees, he remarked bitterly, "Twenty four hours? That means another seven bloody hours of sitting about here getting cold and hungry."

Alex crouched down opposite him, looking off in the direction the car had gone, "Aye, thanks for nothing, Sir Basil. Enjoy your lunch."

Sinclair groaned, "My bloody stomach thinks my throat's cut."

He looked at the farmhouse, wondering how much longer it would be until they were relieved of sentry duty. Two hours at least.

Alex smiled, reached inside his tunic and brought forth a naggin bottle of Bushmills whiskey. "We'll maybe join him so," he said. "Fancy some luncheon, Constable Armstrong?"

Sinclair reached over and took the bottle, extracted the loosened cork with his teeth and spat it away. He raised the neck to his mouth, sipping gingerly at first, then allowing a long gulp to cascade down his throat.

"Bottoms up, as they used to say in the trenches," said Alex.

Sinclair sank back, allowing the whiskey to bathe his soul.

Members of the congregation were filing into the church as Albert and Sadie entered the gate. The last of the stragglers again, they were hurrying along when they saw Roy standing with his back to the wall of the porch, drawing deeply on a cigarette. Already organ music could be heard inside. Roy gripped the tiny cigarette between his thumb and middle finger, twisting his hand now to take a final few drags of the butt. As Sadie and Albert approached, they saw him shaking his hand violently as his fingers were burnt. Albert laughed and called out, "You're getting your value out of Gallaher's Tobacco Company these days, aren't you, Roy?"

The young man smiled and joined them as they filed through the door. A few people were blocking the entrance, taking off coats and putting away umbrellas. They whispered.

"Wouldn't want to miss the farewells," said Albert.

"Aye," Roy replied, "we'll be getting the Book of Exodus or the Last Supper, I doubt."

Sadie gave a sibilant warning through her teeth, "Wheesht, the pair of you. It's a bit of respect you should be showing."

Chastened, Albert said, "Aye, suppose we'll miss him about."

Roy winked, "What's that they say about deserting the sinking ship?"

The people ahead moved on, relieving the blockage at the door. They moved inside, noting immediately that the pews were almost totally filled. Sadie led the way to their usual seats at the front and Roy, unable to occupy his normal seat at the rear, joined them. Neighbours nodded greetings as they made space for them. The organ played, filling the small church with its sound, drowning out any chance of conversation as eyes turned now to the front side door where the Rev. Burns was emerging. The clergyman walked briskly to the centre carrying a heavy tome and swept his gaze over his congregation. Then standing under the stained glass window with its legend, "Redeemed," he waited as the organist finished with a flurry. A moment of absolute silence. Then, suddenly, Burns's voice filled the church:

"How doth the city sit solitary, that was full of people? How is she come as a widow? She that was great among the nations, and princess among the provinces, how is she become tributary. She weepeth sore in the night, and her tears are on her cheeks: among all her lovers she hath none to comfort her; all her friends have dealt treacherously with her, they are become her enemies.

"Judah is gone into captivity because of affliction, and because of great servitude; she dwelleth among the heathen, she findeth no rest; all her persecutors overtook her between the straits. The ways of Zion do mourn, because none come to the solemn feasts: all her gates are desolate: her priests sigh, her virgins are afflicted and she is in bitterness. Jeremiah I, 1-4."

As if daring anybody to answer his scriptural challenge, the clergyman glared around his congregation, first with a general sweep of his gaze, then picking out individuals. His eyes focused on Albert, who squirmed and lowered his own eyes in discomfort. When he raised them again, Burns had moved and was now taking up his position behind the lectern. He set down the tome, readjusted his pince-nez, paused. When he spoke again, his voice was gentler, kinder, almost with a touch of warmth.

"Kind friends," he began, "the theme of our service this morning is, sadly, leave-taking and change. For, as you all now know, I am going from among you, just as our Lord and Saviour Jesus Christ had to forsake those he loved on this Earth."

The analogy irked Albert. If Burns were not already leaving, he would raise his concerns with the other elders. The man was verging on the blasphemous in comparing himself to the Lord Himself, he would say. Albert's devotion was leavened with enough non-conformist antecedents to make such allusions jar. He wondered how Sadie, a Presbyterian also since birth, could have assumed such deference to the cloth since their marriage. Maybe it was just as well that Burns was going now, he thought. Such grandeur did not sit easily with the Presbyterian worshippers of Drum. But, man a dear, he could certainly raise the thunder when he wanted to. Albert relaxed and focused his attention again on the opening address.

"In going, I will always remember the kindness of the people of Drum. During my time among you, I have had many valued friendships. Of these, I prize most the brotherhood we cherish in the glorious Orange Institution and in the Royal Black Preceptory. I have stood on many platforms here in Co. Monaghan, advocating the cause of Protestantism, Unionism, temperance and preaching the Gospel of Jesus Christ. I will never forget the happy times I have spent in Drum and I deeply regret that my departure means the beginning of days of trial for you. 'Say unto them that are of a fearful heart, be strong, fear not: behold, your God will come with vengeance, even God with a recompence; he will come and save you. Isaiah 35, 4.' "

The reminder, yet again, of their predicament sent a shiver through the congregation. Albert joined in the shuffling, remembering the others who were leaving now, unprepared to face an uncertain future. He knew it was worse in the towns and villages. Those with skills and trades were among the first to go, followed by the labourers and clerks who had relied on them for work. The shopkeepers, merchants and professional people still clung to their places, as did the farmers who were probably most rooted in the soil of Monaghan. But slowly, the area was changing. Albert wondered how long it would take until the local community here resembled more the Protestant middle- and upper-class communities of the south. The sense of all-encompassing Ulster Protestantism would be eroded and the links would be broken as fewer and fewer remained.

"Apart from all else," Burns resumed, "the question of amalgamation will now have to be settled, now that the Protestant community is rapidly diminishing in this new Free State in which you so regrettably and treacherously find yourselves placed. But perhaps the most pressing problem, and certainly the most distressing trial ahead, will be the continuing attacks on your very lives and homes. By now we've witnessed a terrifying list of cruel atrocities against our community and ourselves. Through them, your loyalty to our Sovereign King and your Protestant faith has brought you comfort, but little tangible reward."

"Who is left among you that saw this house in her full glory? And how do ye see it now? Is it not in your eyes in comparison of it as nothing? Haggai, 2, verse 3."

"But you are rightly a proud people and steadfast in your adherence to the principles forged by your forefathers here in this forgotten corner of Ulster. And while you are now passing through perilous times, you must place your faith the more fully in God above all else. For He is just and His will be done."

Burns paused again as a collective tremor went through the congregation. He reached under his lectern and brought out a hymnal, flicking open the pages with the bookmark ribbon. Albert reached for his hymnal and could hear the shuffle of pages as others searched for the number posted on the bulletin board to the side of the lectern. Burns harumphed for silence.

"So, to begin our worship here this morning, I want you all to rise with me now and sing in His praise, the 124th Psalm, *Unless the Lord His Arm of Power*. I feel it must express our feelings now and for the perilous times to come."

The congregation rose as the organist struck up the chorus. Albert flicked through the pages, as voices began to sing out around him.

"Unless the Lord His Arm of power,
Had o'er our heads extended -
Unless the Lord in Peril's hour,
His chosen had defended -
When fierce enkindling rage and pride,
Up rose the foe around us,
Deep plunged beneath their swelling tide,
Their waves of wrath had drowned us."

When Albert found the right page and joined in, he was a half beat behind the others. The organist paused before beginning the second verse as Albert finished the final phrase. He looked up and Burns was glowering in his direction. Distracted momentarily as the congregation prepared to begin the second verse, he thought he detected in the distance, the sound of a heavy engine.

Beyond the church grounds, a lorry was depositing a group of Free State soldiers in the village. They hopped down from the tailgate, formed single files on both sides of the road and began to patrol the quiet village street. A door slammed shut. Drum seemed to be deserted, yet the defiant voices rang out from the Presbyterian chapel:

"Wake, Israel, wake, this grateful strain,
His praise be sung and spoken;
For thee the snare is laid in vain,
The fowler's net is broken.
Hosanna, Bless the living Lord,
Each heart to fear a stranger,
The triumph of his name record,
Our stay in ev'ry danger."

Sinclair would have moped about the place for ever if he hadn't started to take a drink. Aye, and by God did he ever take to the same drink? Got so that the people in the village crossed the street rather than talk to him, except down at the pub, of course. Many's the night's fun we had down there and Sinclair at the centre of it all, singing and regaling us with stories.

I wound him up, of course. Better than have him sitting around with a face on him like a long wet Sunday in Ballymena. And it hadn't got so bad that we couldn't do the job. Sure, half the others were the same and, in the times that were in it, it was better to have a wee drop on you when you went out on patrol. Took the edge of it all, the feeling that you could be shot or blew up at any time.

Soon as the patrol was over though, Sinclair would say, "Right, Alex, your round." Then, off to the pub and a few before he went home. Well, most of the time he went home. There were nights when the sport was a wee bit too good and nobody better than Sinclair to stick it out.

Brought him home one night, worse for wear. We had to bang on the door for a good while with no stir at all inside. I thought Dorothy might be away home to her mother. But, after a while, you could see the lamp lighting up from inside the window and then the voice, "Who's there?" Who did she expect?

"Your lord and master," Sinclair roars back, drunk as a fool. I knew from there out that there would be trouble, worse trouble than usual. The bolt shot back, she opened the door and I hauled the bould Sinclair inside. The fire was dampened down for the night, but there was the man of the house's supper still sitting on the table.

Dorothy looked cracker though, face flushed with sleep and anger, hair tousled a wee bit and she was wearing a heavy dressing gown. Couldn't help wondering what she wore underneath. Well, I'm only a healthy male with natural desires.

"Look at the state of you, Sinclair Armstrong," she said. You always know a women's temper from her use of the surname.

"I thought I'd better get him home," I started to explain, your man hanging off my shoulder, near asleep.

"Like this?" she snapped back, "Get out, Alex Johnson. You're not welcome here."

There was hardly any call for that, was there? I could have left him back in the pub, or hauled him up to the barracks for the night to sleep it off on the bench. But here I'd taken the trouble to near carry him through the street and home.

"Only doing a favour by ...." I started to say, when she cut in. "Getting him drunk again," she screamed. "That's a favour that happens too often and I don't appreciate it. Now get out."

Then it happened, best part of the whole night. Sinclair was roused by the screaming and he lurched forward to quieten her down, I suppose. Saying, "Dorothy darling," he stumbled, of course, once he was out of my grip and he reached out for support from Dorothy, grabbing a hold of her dressing gown and ripping the whole front of it open and even her night-dress underneath as he fell to the ground.

She began to cover herself quickly, but I got a good look. Gorgeous they were, full and ripe and firm, the nipples erect, probably from her anger. She caught me looking, of course, as she made herself decent again.

Well, what was a man to do? I had to catch a hold of myself to stop from reaching out for a feel of one of them. As she glowered at me, she couldn't but notice how interested I was too. It was sticking out for anybody to see - my interest, I mean. But, in the circumstances, I knew I couldn't really say anything. She took care of that.

"You can go right now," she said coldly. "Go on, get out."

She pointed to the door, still lying wide open and her man lying there on the ground. I could have helped put him to bed. But women, what can you do? Can't live with them, can't shoot them. Well, not our own side anyway, as I was telling the same Sinclair the other day.

Head throbbing, bones aching, Sinclair knew he needed a cure to face the day ahead. Sitting in the dayroom, he poked idly at the fire. It was something to do to stop the tremors that surged occasionally through his body. Keep his mind off it. That morning, she had laid into him again with a tongue-lashing. It had got so that she was on about it all the time. You would think he was the only one took a drink now and again. And it wasn't just the drink, was it? He enjoyed the camaraderie down in the pub. Made him feel like he belonged here. A unit that didn't get on well off-duty was a dangerous unit to be in. Bonds of friendship counted when you were out there on patrol.

Sinclair was trying to explain this to Alex, him being a man of the world. Hadn't he been at the front in the war, going overseas after the Somme when others would have run the other way after what happened to the men of Ulster. Alex was like his brother Eric. They'd have been about the same age if Eric had lived. Whatever else about these days, Alex would see him right.

So, he was telling Alex how Dorothy never let up. Seems once a woman gets her hooks into you, she thinks she can change your ways. Trouble is, she didn't understand how it is in the Special Constabulary. Tough and dangerous work, relying on your comrades to watch your back, just as you watched out for them. But she thought he should do his duty and come home to sit by the fire. If you didn't do that every single day, it was nagging all the time when you did.

"Way I see it, Sinclair lad," Alex was saying. "You'll be hen-pecked anyway the longer you stay about this country. Sure, there she is, Dorothy like, the mother and all her cronies living around the corner. Matter a damn what you do, they'll be down on you along with herself."

He was right there, thought Sinclair. How often these days had he seen the looks from them when they'd be about the house, or worse, out on the street. They would sooner he wasn't about at all, or else living beyond at Gortraw with her mother where they could all nag him if he stepped out of line, even a wee bit.

"Way I see it is this," said Alex. "You have to get them to think a wee bit more about you, as a good provider like, and you don't do that by staying about here under their noses."

Made sense, that. What is it they say. Oh, yes.

"Familiarity breeds contempt, is that it?"

"Couldn't have put it better myself," said Alex. "Now where was I? Aye, with these transfers into Tyrone Division coming up, it wouldn't be as if you were walking out or anything. More like, just in the course of duty, you would be shifted out of Newtownbutler."

"Aye, well it wouldn't be that far."

"Now you're talking. And, sure, no harm just putting the name down. It might never happen, but you would be acting like your own man. Not just taking it as it comes."

****

From Clones town we sallied forth, not having fear or dread,
With noble Captain Madden, our Grand Master, at our head.
When we arrived at Hilton Park, after a pleasant march,
We found the gate surmounted by a most beautiful arch.

Upon that arch inscribed there as in characters so plain,
The Protestant Rights and Liberties we firmly will maintain,
While the motto on the inner side, heart cheering for to see,
Was the Glorious, the Pious and the Immortal Memory.

****

On April Fool's Day, 1923, the customs barriers went up. They were a joke from the outset. How could they not be along a 300-mile land frontier with almost 400 crossing points? Nobody knew quite what to do, especially not the Free State authorities down in Dublin which, in their wisdom, dispatched customs and excise officers up to the border - no doubt hoping they could find it. Never before had there been a land frontier to patrol for customs and excise duties. Even if there had been, the problem often was in deciding where the county lines ran and which of these comprised the new international frontier. As for the customs officers, they had no uniforms to identify themselves as government officials. A few did, however, equip themselves with officious looking belts and peaked caps for the job. Someone observed that they looked like train drivers who had been thrown from their engines. They erected wooden customs huts on the main routes, but they were short-lived. Before the officers arrived, indignant locals stuffed them full of straw and set them alight. It became a local pastime. More often than not, the customs authorities conducted their business under the shelter of accommodating trees on the roadside.

At Clones Railway Station, an official had chalked a notice and arrows on the flagstones of the platform, pointing off to the third-class waiting room which had been taken over for the purpose, leaving the passengers to fend for themselves. With 50 trains a day leaving the Ulster and West Yards, it was an important post and the customs officials had to cope with not only the lack of proper facilities, but the general scepticism of passengers.

Dorothy had noticed as much when returning from the town with her messages. Standing in a queue of bemused passengers waiting for inspection, she had heard a customs officer instruct Hughie Maguire, the railway worker, to tell Col. Madden that he must report for inspection. "And risk my good job," said Maguire, "You must take me for the right April Fool." Eventually the customs officer went off himself and hauled back the colonel, but not without a good bit of bother.

Dorothy laughed as she told Sinclair about it that evening. They were seated at the table, having dinner. Dorothy had decided to tell the story because there was a strained atmosphere between them these days. She couldn't help but notice it, but she doubted Sinclair was even aware of the damage he was inflicting on her. The loneliness when he was out on patrol was bad enough but, for days on end, she barely saw him now. Maybe if they talked more, he would want to be at home here. Anyway, it was a good story that needed telling.

"So, Col. Madden had to come the whole way back down the platform and the wee customs man scurrying along beside him giving orders."

"Did he get into the queue?"

"Och, not at all. Things is not that changed. But he went on past us like a bull and straight into the Third Class waiting room."

"First time for him in there, I doubt."

"Aye, seemed like it. Huffing and puffing on the way out."

"Like to see some of the big shots about here having to do the same. Sir Basil maybe."

It was good to see him laugh again. More like the old Sinclair, she thought. That man she had married. What was it? Less than a year ago still. Maybe though, it was just what they call a phase he had to go through, what with all that's happening hereabouts. Could hardly blame him for being unsettled, I suppose, and him not even able to go over to see his own people beyond in Drumkirk. But now maybe, with the border set up and working, it would settle down. They had to think of the future, though. He wasn't cut out to be a policeman. Not with the way he was fooled and abused by that Alex Johnson character. And then there was all the talk hereabouts. His drinking and so on. Now would be maybe a good time to talk about it, about the future. She would say nothing about the past wee while. Now that he was in a good humour.

"So you'll be held on a bit longer, I suppose, in the police??

"Course I will. Sure, we're the first line of defence ....You look disappointed."

She hadn't been aware that her smile had gone. It wasn't what she wanted to hear. Well, he already knew why.

"But I never see you for days at a time. It's no life for us, Sinclair. We should be settled down by now."

He was becoming angry, she could see. But what right had he? She was the one who had to carry on and act normal among her own people, while he was acting up all the time. He might not care about what people were saying, but she did. What right had he to rear up on her? She wasn't the one out drinking and carrying on.

"Och, are you bringing all that up again?" he said. Sure, she hadn't said a word, had she? Not a blessed word, but it would serve him right if she did. Now he was rearing up on her.

"Sure, I have to. Even on your days off, you're always off with thon Alex Johnson. He's no fit companion for a married man."

"Alex is a good friend of mine. I'll not have you bad-mouthing him again."

"But I'm your wife, Sinclair. Or have you forgotten that as well?"

"Och, give my head peace. You're always on about that."

"But people are talking about you hereabouts."

"Crowd of bloody begrudgers, that's all they are. I'm a grown man and I can take a wee drop when I want. Aye, and you'd do better to stick up for your own husband than go listening to all the ould gossips you meet about here."

"But they're my friends and neighbours, Sinclair. They'd be your own friends too, if you'd only let them be."

"They want it every way, don't they?," he shouted. "They need us in the barracks to keep down the Fenians. Yet they'd stab us in the back quick as look at us. Your own mother too, if the truth ...."

"Don't say that, Sinclair. You know these people and the decent neighbours they are. It's all this drinking."

"Don't give me that. The same ones were damned glad to be included in the Six Counties. More than my own people got, and we're a majority about Drum. Yet here I am in Fenian country, defending those that sold us out when it came to the bit. Aye, then they think we're a gang of robbers or something, just because we take a drink."

How could he be so blinded? Even the dogs on the street knew the way some of them constables were carrying on. Weren't the police investigating their own men all the time these days. It had gone well beyond sticking up for your own side. The truth must be told.

"Sure, you've seen yourself where it got some of your own comrades. That man was shot, for instance, when he tried to raid the public house on the Broad Road down by Wattle Bridge."

"I'll not hear that ...."

"Shot by his own in the cross-fire because he was too drunk to lie low when they were caught in the act."

"That's bloody Fenian lies."

"It's the truth and you know it plain as the nose on your face. Och, if you weren't so blinded by thon reprobate Alex Johnson and ...."

"Och, just shut up," he said, pushing the chair back as he rose to his feet. The chair clattered to the floor. "I'm going out."

Even though she had expected this, of course, Dorothy's heart sank. Another night of worrying, of seething anger, wondering when and if he would return home. Just when she had thought he could be saved from it all. She pleaded then, pleaded for his life and her happiness.

"No Sinclair, not drinking again. Sure, you're half distracted with it already. Leave it out for the one night. Stay with me."

But he was already taking his coat from the rack and hauling it on.

"And listen to more of your bloody lies and running down my friends? I gave you your wages, so leave me alone."

"Please, Sinclair, one night. Please, Sinclair love."

His hand on the door, pulling it open. He was colder and calmer now, his voice more sneering than angry.

"Och, quit you whinging. I'll be back in a wee while."

He was already pulling the door behind him.

"That's what you said other nights. But you know ...."

He was gone, the door slammed shut behind him. Dorothy felt a great well of despair engulfing her mind.

She buried her head in her hands, sitting there among the dirty dishes, and cried.

Boy, Sinclair needed a drink after that onslaught. Came from nowhere again, one minute sitting there talking and having the dinner and then it started. Hadn't even planned to go out, not until pay-day again. But she couldn't leave well enough alone. Maybe Alex is right. She's too well used to her own ways about here. Maybe it would be better if he got that posting away to hell out of it. At least then, she wouldn't have her friends watch his every move.

Sinclair pushed through the door of the Royal Arch bar, immediately turning right and into the snug. He knew Alex would be in there, holding court for the company beyond, lined up along the bar counter. Before he got a word in, the signal to the barman and there they were, a bottle of stout, an empty glass and a small whiskey. Sinclair didn't need to say a word, but he did. His version of the night poured out - the rumours she threw at him, the way she wanted to tie him to her apron-strings and so on. Couldn't even be a master in his own house. Alex said little, just let him talk on. Good thing about friends that, they let you have your say.

"Never you mind, Sinclair. She'll be well over it by now."

"Don't think so. She's always on at me these days."

Alex learned closer, "That's where you're making your mistake. See my wife. Her at home in Dungannon. Saw her near two years ago when she saw me off to the training in Newtownards. Her and the two wains."

He never talked about his home life. Sinclair knew he was married, but children too. He had no idea.

"Doesn't she mind? Your wife like?"

"Of course she does. So do I," said Alex laughing. "That's why I take a wee drop to comfort myself .... Well, that's my excuse and I'm sticking by it."

"But you can go home? It's not far ...."

"Why would I? Bad mistake from the beginning." he said, serious again. "You see, when I come home from the trenches, there was any God's amount of comfort for the taking. Young widow women everywhere with their needs crying out for a man like me. If you know what I mean," he winked. "Protestant lassies, aye even Fenians too. Didn't matter a damn. But you see, you can only spread your net so far. They were closing in and I had to take my pick .... Never got over it."

Alex watched the reaction in his young friend. That would get him thinking, for sure. Shouldn't have said that about children though. No need to bring up that stuff. But what could you do? If he had Dorothy at home, he wouldn't be standing here now. No indeed.

Look at him now calling for another round. He'll be here for the night now, no doubt about it. Might get a chance to nip out myself. Go around by the cottage, like a few nights ago when Sinclair was off on a patrol detail. Alex had been walking down that way when he spotted the cottage and the light dimming at the front and lighting up the bedroom. Up to the window. Sure, what else could a man do? And there she was through the sheer curtains, setting the lamp down on a side table. Alex had stood there, outside looking in, while she began to undress - the blouse and skirt, standing there for a moment, facing the other way. Bending forward now to pick up something - fine shape of a woman. Then sitting on the side of the bed and raising the slip to peel off her stockings. Now if a sight like thon didn't heat up a man's blood .... But a dog barked and he slunk off, with only the memory. It still stirred him. Maybe a few more drinks here and off. Sure, Sinclair was settling in for the night. Lots of others about too. He'd not be missed.

Albert was engrossed in *The Northern Standard* and its coverage of the moves to set up the long-awaited, but hardly expected, Boundary Commission. The end of the civil war down south had focused attention on the border again, and on the terms of the treaty. Article 12 promised to redress any injustices along the new boundary between Northern Ireland and the Free State by establishing the wishes of the inhabitants, insofar as they might be compatible with economic, social and cultural conditions. The Dublin government was now pressing for movement on the commission, but Albert remained sceptical. Sure hadn't they more loopholes in there than anything else. Dublin hadn't shown much interest in Ulster, even during the heated debates over the Treaty. The civil war was fought on what they called the externals - the relationship with the Crown and the Westminster government. Sir James Craig had made very clear his lack of interest in the loyalists of Cavan, Monaghan and Donegal. The division of spoils was already there to be seen. And with the frontier well sealed on both sides, there would be little enough give on either side, even if it came to a crunch.

Yet Albert devoured the news. There was little other source of hope for a change that might restore some sanity to the whole business of cutting off people from one another, from their own. He didn't even notice anybody around until he got a playful slap on the back.

"Good man, Albert. Nothing to bate the wee bit of learning."

"Och, Roy, just catching up on the news."

"What has you in?"

"Och, waiting on Sadie to do her messages."

"Any word from Sinclair?"

"Not a squeak this good while. Must be working fierce hard."

"Doubt they'll not run him off his feet, same boy. Don't think Dorothy would take too kindly to that."

"Aye, bid to be you're right. But mind you, there's been little enough sight of the same lassie."

"Dorothy?"

"Aye, used to come by the odd time, just to keep in touch like. For Sinclair would find it a danger maybe."

"Maybe they've no time for anybody now. Them just a year married like. Know what I mean?"

"Aye, but it'll not be too long till you're hitched up yourself."

"Och, lock of weeks yet. Eileen can't wait to make an honest man of me."

"You need have no complaints in that quarter. She's a grand wee lassie," said Albert, noting that things change so much and yet they don't change in the same way. Time was, Roy and Sinclair would be about all the time. Two years ago, Roy would have known a lot more about Sinclair's doings than either he or Sadie. They were always great with one another. Aye, maybe if Sinclair wasn't away, he would only be thinking of getting married now, same as Roy. Hadn't they been courting about the same time. Things move slower in the country maybe, and getting married is something that has to be worked in over time.

"Take it you'll be staying on at home after the big day?"

"Aye indeed, we talked maybe about building a wee house down by the lower meadow if you know it. The old house needs a lot of work on it and the boss is thinking of pulling back a wee bit and giving me my own hand at the place."

"Robert James is a lucky man has you to hand over to."

"Sure Sinclair will be back before you know it."

"Aye, Roy, and forgotten everything he ever knew about the running of the place, I doubt."

"Hay saved yet?"

"Not at all, she's near all lapped, but there's no drying the year, much less a wee bit of sun."

"We've near done. I could come over and lend you a hand maybe?"

"That's good of you, Roy. Maybe I'll give you a shout in a few days,"

"Aye surely, no harm to help out other now and again, Albert."

"Aye, indeed. I've wee Willie Houston about the place for now. But sure, he's a railway man and near more trouble nor he's worth if the truth was told."

"I know what you mean. So, anything in the paper?"

"Aye, well there's all about the Twelfth out at Analore. But sure you know all about that. And there's this Boundary Commission thing."

"Is she going ahead so?"

"Bid to be, but then it's only Dublin's looking for it."

"That adds up. I suppose the cute boys is waiting in the wings too. See they've set fire to those new customs huts."

"Aye, but it's a lot quieter forby what it was. We got walking the year anyway."

"Aye, only parade in the Free State."

"But with divil a much to celebrate. Not even the weather," said Albert glumly. 'Och, but I suppose we have to keep the presence up."

Roy laughed, "You're sounding more like Attorney Knight by the day, Albert. Which reminds me, I was to meet someone outside his office. Better be off."

Roy was already hurrying off across The Diamond, looking up at the clock on the Church of Ireland steeple which showed almost three o'clock. Albert called out in his wake, "Eileen is it? Sure you'll be seeing enough of her before too long, ye boy ye."

Roy paused briefly and waved back. Albert was laughing.

Roy hurried on, aware that Eileen might be waiting for him. But when he arrived she wasn't there and he settled down to wait, sitting on the low wall which formed a barricade between the steps of Knight's house and a drop of about six feet to the footpath in front of the post office next door. He looked off towards Fermanagh Street to see if she was coming, but there were few people around and she was not among them. Women, he thought, if he had been late he would have heard all about it. But they can dawdle along all they want and you dare not say a word.

Voices emerging from the post office. Roy shifted position. Rising from the wall, he sat down on the steps themselves. He caught a glimpse of Hughie Maguire and Jemmy Reilly. They spoke loudly, unaware of his near presence.

"Whole talk out about Newtown, Jemmy. He'll come to a bad end."

"Hard to think it's the same quiet wee cub that Packie McMahon near chased back across the border that time out by Lackey Bridge."

Roy strained closer to hear, suddenly realising the subject of their exchange. He did not know this man McMahon, but realised now that the incident they were referring to somehow involved Sinclair.

"Changed boy by all accounts, Jemmy. Drinking heavy and taunting all round him. Just spoiling for it."

"Uniforms and drink never got on. Him ever a quiet wee lad and his people along with him."

"You mind his uncle, Bob Sinclair, worked along with me at the railway. Mind he was shot?"

"Mind him surely. Thought it was yer man himself."

"Aye, Bob like, he took a wee drop every now and again. Like maybe about the Twelfth. But a decent God-fearing man at the back of it."

"Och, you never know what going on inside of their heads though."

"Or even when a lock of them get together in private maybe, down at the Orange hall or something ...."

"Aye, maybe drink's only taking out of that young lad what they all think and don't say open to your face."

"That's my way of thinking, anyway Jemmy. But sure the drink's a curse for them as can't handle it."

"Doubt you'd handle one yourself, Hughie. Time for a quick one?"

"Aye, maybe I could choke one down about now."

Roy peeped over the wall and saw the pair heading into the pub next door. And in the near distance, he could see Eileen approaching. He stood up to greet her.

****

As the head of the Orange organisation in this county - an organisation which includes none but loyal men amongst its members, I would ask how long the Government will allow this terrible state of things to continue? Must we wait until blood has been shed, and civil war has broken out, before an end is put to meetings which stir the blood of Ulstermen, and which, whatever the pretence may be, are simply disloyal from beginning to end? If the Parnellite party were not certain of police protection they would not dare to hold a single meeting within the bounds of our loyal province. I have now cleared my own conscience, and the onus of what is certain to occur - unless immediate steps be taken - must fall upon the shoulders of those responsible for the peace of the country.

Lord Rossmore, Monaghan, 20 October, 1883

****

It was an immense relief to talk about it, even though her first reaction had been panic-stricken alarm when Roy suddenly arrived at the cottage that evening. For weeks and months, she had wrestled with the fear and panic induced by Sinclair's behaviour. Unable to say anything to her mother, or even to her friends in the village, she was fully conscious that they were aware of it all. God knows, you could hardly miss it. She felt somehow to blame. Had she not loved him enough, done enough to make their marriage work? Was she too hard on him maybe? She had scolded him, pleaded with him and begged him to change his ways. The more she did, the worse he became. For the past month, she had simply ignored it as best she could, retiring early, leaving his supper on the table and likely as not finding it still there when she rose. Mornings were nearly the worst now, especially when he had to report for duty. He was almost incoherent when she would wake him and go out to prepare a breakfast she knew he wouldn't eat anyway. By the time he emerged, looked ragged and hungover, he would lurch about the place in silence. On those mornings when he broke the pattern and talked volubly about the barracks, she suspected that he had a bottle hidden somewhere and her suspicions were strengthened by the odour of whiskey which pervaded the air as soon as he walked in.

Yet, whether it was the silent treatment or the other, she worked hard to create a semblance of normality, telling him of her plans for the day and what she planned for dinner, and praying fervently that he would just go now. By the time he did leave, either to the barracks or off to join his cronies, she was exhausted, collapsing onto the sofa and crying. Her mother had called one day and found her like that. She had made some feeble excuse about her "time of the month" and no more had been said. Yet she knew that they all knew. She could hear their voices in her mind - you made your bed, now lie in it.

Roy was different though. He had come straight to the point and, as she got over his blunt approach, she realised that her burden was lighter suddenly, just from sharing it with somebody else who cared for Sinclair. She told him all, the words gushing out of her in a great dam-burst of release. He listened, his face grave yet kind, his hand at one stage clasping hers in his strong grasp. As she faltered to a conclusion, his voice was gentle and concerned.

"You mean it's as bad as all that?"

"Aye, Roy, worse even betimes. Hard to tell it all."

"And this man Johnson's at the back of it all you say?"

"Well, he's hanging about with him all the time. But Sinclair's different from even you knew him, Roy. We argue and fight all the time about him going off on his drinking sprees with these so-called friends of his."

"He won't heed you then?"

"Och, sure he won't even listen now and I've just stopped saying anything at all."

"Doesn't sound like Sinclair, but I'm not doubting your word, Dorothy. Things has changed so much this past while, and none for the better either."

"I can't talk to anybody about here. They think he's gone to the bad for good and all."

"Well, thanks for telling me. I didn't know what to think when I overheard that yesterday, as I told you. Had to check it out for myself."

"You didn't say anything at home?"

"Albert and Sadie? Och, no. They're worried enough about him as is."

"Someone has to help him," said Dorothy, breaking now into loud sobs from which her words escaped in gasps. "He won't listen to me and I'll lose my reason if he goes on like this. I just can't take it, Roy".

Roy embraced her awkwardly, yet it felt good to have a man's arms holding her once more. It had been so long since she and Sinclair had made love, she had almost forgotten the sense of security it induced, the warmth of human contact and love, the tactile sensation of just being held. Her sobs subsided as they sat in silence. Momentarily she wondered what would happen if Sinclair came in now. How would he react? Would he be jealous of Roy, his friend? She imagined the scene, but the only one she could conjure up was of Sinclair lurching drunkenly though the door, oblivious to her or anybody else here.

"You're a good friend to him, Roy," she said, extricating herself reluctantly from his arms. "And to me as well."

Roy smiled encouragingly, "Aye, well I'll be a good friend all right, even if I have to use my fists to knock some sense into him."

Sinclair felt strangely detached from the entire business. He was more concerned with the cold sweat he could feel trickling from his armpits and sending another tremor of shivers through his entire body. He gripped the handlebars tightly, but relaxed them again as he felt the pressure throughout his aching bones. All the while, a dull headache throbbed and he thought again how much he needed a drink to settle himself. He had tried to park the bicycle by leaning it against the wall at the side of the cottage, but had been unable to find its balance and, rather than allow it to clatter to the ground as he would normally do, he held onto it now as Roy went on and on.

Sinclair focused his attention on the bicycle and remembered how he had got it. The order had come from county command to seize all bicycles which might be used by the IRA gunmen still carrying out sporadic attacks against the security forces. The Newtownbutler detachment and, in particular, the B platoon had thrown themselves into the task with a level of commitment that Sir James Craig would envy. This bicycle had come from a farmhouse at Derrykerrib and Sinclair remembered the old man pleading for it. "Sure, I have no truckle with the IRA," he had said. They had ignored this, of course, knowing the area was a nest of sedition. As Sinclair held the bicycle on the back of the departing lorry, the old man had stood shaking his fist and shouting defiantly, "God's curse on ye, ye black bastard, ye'll not have a day's luck with it ...."

Was this the curse, he wondered, this annoying tirade from a man who was supposed to be his friend. It was quite clear how Roy had been dragged into this though, and Sinclair fought the well of resentment building up in him. Damn it, if he could only get a drink he would cope better with this. But he knew that there was little chance of that until his pay-packet arrived tomorrow. He had already borrowed and cadged drinks from everybody he knew down at the pub. He had searched the house that morning before going to work, suspecting that Dorothy kept a little money hidden from him that earned it in the first place. But he had been unable to find anything and he had been forced to spend his entire day fighting the effects of this cursed hangover. Now all he wanted was to go to bed and sleep if he could. But Roy just wouldn't let up.

"Sure, it's obvious she'll not take much more."

"She told you that, did she?" Sinclair asked, anxious now to pin down the source of this Judas betrayal. Damn it all, if she had been going off telling Roy, who else might she have told? He was rightly sick of her constant whinging.

"Any fool with half a mind could see it, Sinclair. You've the look of a drinker about you. Look at yourself, trembling so much you can hardly look me in the eye."

Sinclair turned his head to stare defiantly into Roy's eyes. "I can see that treacherous Delilah has you talked over," he said bitterly. "You're suppose to be a friend of mind, remember?"

"I am your friend. Sure, haven't we been companions from we were no height - went to school, fished together and run about? We even courted together. But you're different now and you wouldn't be calling Dorothy names if you were in your right mind, Sinclair."

So that was it, then. If she made him out to be insane, it would excuse her own unreasonable attitude. All these months of nagging and trying to make him into something he didn't want to be and couldn't be. Damn it all, she didn't know the half of what he had been through. How could she? How could anybody? The daily fear of ambush, the sight of comrades being shot, blown up and all the rest. Knowing that you were it - the front line. If we weren't ruthless in our job, then for sure they would all be finished. But the truth is hard to handle for those who didn't have to live with it at every waking moment.

"So, I'm some sort of madman now, am I?" Sinclair said, anxious to set this right and get rid of him. "Damn it, it's not as bad as she's making out. All right, I take a drop now and again with the boys at the barracks. But if you took a drink yourself, you'd know it's not the great demon it's made out. She's not left short or anything."

"That's not the way I hear it. Told me she had to ask her mother for money a few times, just to keep a bit of food in the house."

"Once, twice maybe, I went on my spree a wee bit too much. But her mother was paid back. I saw to that."

"But don't you realise that the wee girl just can't take it?" Roy said, changing his tack again like the bloody eel you can't get a good grip of and cast away. "She's distracted with the worry of it all."

Sinclair was tired of banging his head against this stupid argument that had nothing to do with bloody Roy in the first place.

"Damn it, what does she want? A hermit?"

"No, she only wants her husband back. That's all."

"You're near as bad as she is with stupid spakes like thon."

"All's I'm saying is that you should make it up till her."

"Make up what?"

"Tell her you'll change and mean it, Sinclair."

Damn, he would have to get rid of him. It was none of his bloody business anyway. This was a private matter and she had no right bringing in somebody from outside.

"Listen," he said, mustering all the indignation he could manage, "she made her bed with me and she'll lie in it. Now get off, Roy."

"Can you not even go that far?"

"Och, I can see you've taken her side ...."

"Not a matter ...."

"No point me talking. Just let me get on with my own life here."

"But she is part of your life, Sinclair. A big part."

Sinclair let go of the bicycle at last, his fists clenching in frustration. It fell against the wall and slid down into a heap on the ground, tumbling in a spine-chilling clatter of scrapes and crashes. The noise seemed to punctuate a new coldness in Sinclair, a resolution that superseded even his throbbing body and mind. Suddenly he was flooded with a lucidity that had escaped him for so long, a realisation that he could explain his behaviour in a way that Roy might understand.

"Listen here till I tell you something, Roy," he said, fixing the other with a cold stare. "I'm not accepted here, only for the boys at the barracks. I'm an outsider."

"Sure, you're from about ...."

"Och, they know me all right, and all belonging to me, many of them. But I'm an embarrassment, a reminder of what they threw overboard. They went for their Six Counties and left me and mine, aye and you too, outside of it. Every time they look at me here, here in their first line of defence, they know they did us wrong at the Ulster Hall when they sided with the Belfast crowd. I can't feel part of them for that ...."

"Och, Sinclair, you're going a bit far now, sure ...."

"I'd go further too and I'd still be telling the truth. Och sure, they make a great play of holding true to us. But the height of it is, they only want to look after themselves and they want me to do that for them."

"I didn't know you'd be so bitter."

"We've all a right to be ...."

"We'll get by on our side, even if it is the outside."

"Och, talk sense, Roy. You've been got by."

Roy was taken aback by the resolution in Sinclair's voice, the conviction with which he suddenly spoke. He had no answer for that.

"So you drink to forget the betrayal, is that it?"

"No, Roy, I drink to remember it."

****

You are no obscure person; your title and position, if not your person, are known to all men of standing in the three kingdoms; and if they will not now stand up for one of the few men of their class who had the honesty and courage to meet their natural enemy in the open (just because a radical government, on the report of bigoted Roman Catholic magistrates, chose to condemn you), then indeed I will begin to think that all hope for our country is gone. As to your humble Protestant friends in Ireland, there is but one opinion amongst them - to a man they are prepared to follow you to the end of the world.

George Knight, Clones, to Lord Rossmore, 29 November 1883.

****

Dorothy's hope for a release from the nightmare her marriage had become died after Roy's intervention failed. She had watched him leaving, without even a word of farewell. Yet she knew he would not have gone like that had he not been afraid of Sinclair's reaction. She felt dejected and defeated, hoping somehow that Sinclair would relent at the last minute. But when Roy was gone, he had simply come inside and went silently to their bedroom and slept. She spent the night on the sofa and suffered the same coldness from him the following day. He arose himself before she had stirred and made tea while she went to the bedroom to dress. By the time she came back, he was gone.

Nothing had been said, and that was even worse. If he had shouted at her for talking to Roy, at least she could comfort herself with the knowledge that his friend's intervention had some effect. Maybe after an initial outburst he would begin to think it over and come to the realisation that he was killing them both and their love. But this was much worse. His moodiness hung around the cottage, stifling any chance of happiness. She sobbed for hours when he had gone to work and dreaded his homecoming, whenever that would be. She knew it was his pay day. She wondered if she should go to her mother's and dismissed the notion. It would be worse for her mother if Dorothy was seen to have abandoned her own husband. Although they all knew what was happening, formal recognition of her failing marriage would only compound her sin.

Now she lay in bed and waited for his homecoming, her body tense and coiled like a spring for any noise. The cottage was quiet, with only the steady ticking of the clock. From a distance, she heard a dog bark, its howls carried on the wind. She tried to imagine the time. Seldom had he been so late unless he had collapsed in the pub and been taken back to the barracks to sleep it off. She hoped fervently that this was what had happened, yet she knew from the tension in her own body that it was not so. He would be home, drunk and probably angry with her. She only hoped that he would vent his anger and fall asleep. Then she could maybe drift off, on the sofa, for she hated the acrid smell of stale beer that permeated the bedroom when he was drunk and snoring.

When the sound of the latch came, she was shocked however. She had expected to hear the sound of his bicycle falling outside, or a lorry pulling up and taking off again before he would stumble in, left home by his cronies again. But he was inside now, slamming the door shut and calling out, his voice drunk, loud, but somehow controlled, "Dorothy? Ye'in there, Dorothy?"

She leapt from the bed, grabbed the empty chamber pot from underneath and crouched in the corner as he entered the bedroom, a shadow moving in the doorway.

"Keep away from me. Don't touch me. I'm warning you."

"Och, have a titter of wit, will you. It's only me."

He was walking towards her, footsteps unsteady.

"I know. Now stay away."

"Och, is the wee wife annoyed again? Sure, I've big news that'll be the end of all your worries, haven't I now?"

She rose, half standing now, the chamber pot raised to defend herself. She was terrified more by his soft voice than if he had simply vented his fury and passed out. She noticed the pale light from the window, and knew too late that he could see her, the arm raised. He moved closer.

"What's that you've got? Put it down."

"No, I'll ...." she screamed, lunging at him. Even in his drunkenness, his hand sprang forward and grabbed her wrist, twisting it suddenly. The chamber pot crashed to the floor and shattered. Caught in his vice-like grip now, she braced herself just as she noticed his free hand rising. She felt a slap across her face, stinging, her eye gushing tears, her brain jolted, her spirit broken. She staggered back to the wall and slid down.

"Wee bitch going behind my back to spread stories to the likes of Roy McConkey and anybody else who'll listen."

She felt a hysteria grip her, the shock, the fear that he would strike again. The coldness of his voice, the hissing venom in his words. She whimpered, "You hit me, you bastard. I don't believe this is happening."

"Shut up, or you'll get more than a slap in the gob, you treacherous wee bitch."

Silence now as he slumped back onto the bed. He sat there, while she cowered. She felt revulsion now. Never had he raised his hand to her. Not even on the worst nights of recent months. She could handle it though. It had broken the threads of their pretence. She suddenly realised that she pitied him more than she pitied herself. His slide was complete and what a precipitous slide it had been.

"Look at yourself," she said now, the words clipped and commanding as she raised herself to a sitting position. His shadow loomed over her. She didn't care. "You're not such a big man anymore, are you?"

Silence again. He sat there staring at the window, the pale moonlight waning beyond, the darkness engulfing the room. Moments passed, full minutes, he sat on and she waited. Soon he would tire of it, fall back and sleep. She would leave.

From the darkness, his voice, calm. As if nothing had happened.

"I've been moved, transferred to Cookstown. I'll send you money, but you'll have to stay here for now."

She didn't answer, weighing it up. If he went, she would stay. Peace at last. He might not come back. Other women had managed, living alone after their husbands had gone off. She could too. It would be an escape from the nightmare; not perfect, but safe at least.

"Do you hear me? I'm moved to Cookstown this weekend, but there's only single quarters there."

Unless she answered, he would just sit there, talking, pretending that nothing had happened tonight. She drew in her breath and said, as calmly as him now, "Go then. Thank God, go then."

He roused himself, standing up. She drew in her feet as he moved to the end of the bed, not looking back.

"Right then. If that's the way you want it. There's a wee bit of a do back in the barracks. I was coming to take you over ...."

She couldn't believe what he was saying. She was affronted by his presumption that she would go anywhere with him now.

"I wouldn't go the barracks if I was arrested and taken there."

He opened the door, his shoulders slumped, the fight gone out of him, defeated by her at last.

"Och, calm down, for Christ's sake. Stay here then. I'll see you later."

He went through the door. It closed in his wake. She heard the latch on the front door, the slam and silence again. She climbed onto the bed, drew her knees up to her chest, hugged herself and cried. Before she slept, she would barricade the door. Drag over the bed against it. She would manage. She wondered how long until he left. This weekend, he had said. Tomorrow was Friday.

Sinclair's anger dissipated as he cycled to the barracks. In its place hung a great emptiness. He remembered striking her, vaguely conscious of his hand having done so automatically. He remembered the coldness of her voice after the blow, the pleading gone. It had been replaced by a resolute strength. He was frightened by what he had done, what he had become. But the urge to go back was secondary to the urge to have a drink and think it over. Clear his mind. He needed to think. He needed to weigh up his life again. He needed to think of Dorothy, not the woman who cowered and shrank, not the woman he could barely abide for her nagging these past months, but the Dorothy he loved. Maybe he could go back now. He wondered, torn by the shame and the need. The need to belong, the need to have a drink. He rounded a bend and heard voices, shouting, men running onto the road.

"That's the black bastard now."

His bicycle came to a sudden jarring stop. Sinclair was thrown over the handlebars and onto the road. Feet kicking, a blow from a cudgel to his shoulder, numbing

"Not such a big mouth now, are you Constable Armstrong?"

Feet again, boots. The sound of an engine, footsteps running off, screech of brakes. His body numb all over. He checked his face, no blood that he could feel. He felt winded though, his breath heaving. Unable to speak as he heard new voices. Alex Johnson's.

"Jesus, it's Sinclair, the party boy himself. Give us a hand, Sammy."

"Is he dead?"

"No, just kicked about a wee bit. He'll be right as rain when we get him to the barracks and a wee drop of whiskey into him. Right, Sinclair lad?"

He grunted, still too winded.

"Maybe we should take him home."

Hands grabbing him now, raising him. Alex again. "Somehow I don't reckon he'd be too welcome. Anyway, Sammy, his home is away down in the Free State. If only he'd accept that."

He didn't want to speak now. Hands helping him over to the tender. It was starting to rain as he fell into the back.

Crossing Over Jordan

As Joshua and I crossed over Jordan
We did twelve stones bear along.
'Twas the High Priest and our Grand Master
That moved the ark of God along.

For we are the true-born Sons of Levi,
None on earth can with us compare;
We are the root and branch of David,
The bright and glorious Morning Star.

Should he deal with our sister, Dinah, as with a harlot and make me stink among the Canaanites and the Perizzites? I, being few in numbers, they shall gather themselves together against me and slay me and I shall be destroyed, I and my house. For Jerusalem has been taken from us, the houses rifled and the women ravished and half of the city sent forth into captivity and the residue of the people cut off. But we, sons of Aaron and his sons Eleazar and Ithamar, shall not uncover our heads; neither shall we rend our clothes, lest we die and lest wrath come upon all the people who bewail the burning that the Lord hath kindled. For without are dogs and sorcerers, and whoremongers, and murderers, and idolators and whosoever loveth and maketh a lie. By the sword of Gideon, we shall go forth against those nations who went a whoring after Ballim and made Baalberith their god. We shall raise a great altar to God on Mount Gerizim in defiance of the accursed of Shechem and Abimelech and their moon god Ur.

****

A stranger in a strange land, Sinclair thought it would not matter. He hardened his heart against the insecurity of being an outsider and he turned his gaze from his own forlorn people. Yet, even here in Cookstown, they asked him where he was from and they knew. For even his detachment and his speech betrayed him to those who had eyes to see and ears to hear. He kept to his own company a lot, even in the sleeping quarters of the barracks. In the midst of others, he sought out loneliness. As he heard the cheers below and the stampede of footsteps on the stairs, he pulled the blankets over his head. The door burst open; rough hands shook him. He did not want to be bothered. He feigned sleep, but it was no use, the shaking was persistent. A voice, Ronnie McCoubrey.

"Wake up, Armstrong. Come on, shake a leg."

"What's the matter?" Sinclair asked at last, opening his eyes a crack.

"Results are announced."

"Who won?"

"We did, of course. Even in Fermanagh and Tyrone. Nearly 4,000 votes to spare. They won't shift us now."

"Who won't shift us?"

"Not you, us. The Boundary Commission won't shift us"

"That nice for you. Now can I go back to sleep?"

"Christ Armstrong. Sleep, drink and duty. That all you ever think about?"

"Aye, now give my head peace."

"Not even women."

"Married, amn't I?"

"Och, aye. We've never seen her."

"Hardly see her myself."

"Doesn't bother your sleeping too much."

"It's none of your business. Stick to your elections. Much good they'll do you anyway. If they take a mind to ditch Tyrone, Fermanagh or anywhere else though, they'll just do it."

"Och, listen to the lost soul from the lost counties. Away on back to sleep, Armstrong. For you'd only lie there begrudging anyway."

Sinclair pulled the blanket back over his head and sought sleep.

Dorothy wasn't sure that she had heard a knock on the door. The wind was howling outside and the flames flickered in the grate as she worked at stitching a piece of crochet lace, the needle hook beating a faint tattoo on her thumbnail as she wound the fine white Manloves linen thread in, through and out. Another knock, this time she was sure of it. Setting aside the lace and hook carefully, she rose and went to the little side window. A uniformed figure hunched into a greatcoat. She unbolted and opened the door to see Alex Johnson standing there. He was wet, beads of moisture clinging to his face.

"Sorry to disturb you, Mrs Armstrong," he said. Formal. Could he be here on police business? Had something happened Sinclair maybe?

"What has you here?"

"Just called to see how you were, you being all alone and that. You are alone?"

"Aye, you know I am. Well, I'm fine and dandy. That all?

"Well no. But could I step in a wee minute? It'd perish a body out here."

"Well, if you must, I suppose."

She stood aside as Alex entered and pulled off his cap. He closed the door, removed his coat and she returned to the sofa. He placed his coat and cap on the table, walked over an sat beside her, stretching his hands out to the fire to warm them. He's making himself at home here, she thought, feeling strange to have a man in the house again. Sinclair had been gone two months now, and had only been back once since. It was a difficult visit, full of silence. She knew he was still drinking, could smell it off him. She suspected he had a bottle of whiskey in his bag, but he didn't produce it when she was around. He did not go out to the pub during the two days and the single night he spent there. Just sat brooding. She had gone to bed early and next morning found him sleeping on the sofa, still in his clothes. It had been a relief when he set off for the station.

Around the village, little was said. Even her own mother made only cursory references to the husband who was absent. Her mother's visits were brief anyway. Most of the time, Dorothy was alone. She had been making a lot of lace. On her infrequent ventures out, she had gone with a list, done her business quickly and returned home. None of her former friends called to the cottage either.

She looked at Alex now, rubbing his strong hands together in the warmth of the fire and almost felt glad of his company. God knows, she had little regard for the man, but what had happened seemed so long ago now. She could hardly find it in herself to blame him for what Sinclair had become. Yet, when she spoke to him, she was curt.

"Suppose you'll have a wee drop of tea, now you're here?"

"Och no, I'll do rightly. But go ahead yourself," he said, settling back in the sofa, knees apart and the legs of his trousers raised a fraction to preserve the crease. His right arm, nearest her, rose lazily and grasped the back of the sofa. She leaned forward a fraction.

"Aye, well it's near that time. But I'll wait a minute."

"That's a grand fire you have going there. I can feel my blood circulating again," he smiled at her, his teeth regular and bright. She felt a fluttering in her stomach, her breath short.

"I don't suppose it was to talk about the fire you came here. What's your business, Alex?"

"Aye, well Dorothy .... suppose I can call you Dorothy," he smiled again, looking at her for a reaction. She looked away, determined not to respond.

"Aye, well," he began again. "It was just that ...." He paused and she looked back at him. His smile gone, serious expression, concerned. "You don't like me much, do you?"

"That a question?" she asked, dreading the answer if there was one, her mind a jumble of conflicting sensations. His arm on the back of the sofa, his voice gentle but strong. His presence filled the room. She waited.

"I suppose you don't have to answer."

She could feel a ghost of the old anger she had always felt in his presence. His presumption of knowing her mind.

"What do you want, Alex Johnson?" she asked now, her voice sounding hollow, almost frightened. "Admiration? Respect? After what you did to Sinclair?"

He smiled, leaning closer to her now, his arm sliding along until it was directly behind her back. His voice, still low, caressing almost.

"Sinclair didn't need a push from me. He was going there anyway. He was like a trap waiting to be sprung."

"You just provided the bait? That it?"

"No, this whole situation was bait enough. He feels he's outside and he wants to get inside. But he went too far."

"Where? To Cookstown?"

"No, into himself. He's purging himself for the sins done to his people."

"You make him sound like some sort of penitential lamb."

"He is in a way. He didn't fit. But you're being sacrificed along with him."

"Was that why he was transferred?"

"He wasn't transferred. He asked to be moved."

She felt her mind jolt. She looked at Alex. His face composed, no hint of his usual cruel humour. She knew he was telling the truth. It made sense to her at last. The suddenness of his departure, the silence of his return. He had deserted her.

"Do you see him?"

"Once, about a month ago. For the weekend."

"But it's not the same, is it? As before you married, or for a while after?"

He knew it all anyway. More than her, she knew now. Sinclair must have talked it all over with him before he put in for the move. God knows, he spent more time with him, on duty and off.

"No, it's not," she sighed, almost relieved to know this part of the truth. "I don't know why I'm telling you this. I haven't told anybody else. But we're not living like .... like man and wife, even those couple of days he was back."

His arm on her shoulder now. Holding her. She had not been aware of it before. She felt strangely comforted by it. Anxious to talk, to tell somebody.

"You needn't say more."

"Yes, I have to. I want to tell. God knows, I don't like you Alex Johnson. But that actually makes it easier. To tell you. We sleep separate, Sinclair and me."

His hand moving, his body closer. She felt herself relaxing, enjoying the sensation of being held by somebody stronger. His voice soft, gentle, coaxing her.

"You blame yourself too much. But you're a victim of it too, not the cause."

"What do you mean?"

"Well, as I say, I didn't make Sinclair drink. I only offered him a way to distraction when he needed it. He has to find himself. His true self. His place. He thinks that by doing so, he'll find his people. He sees himself as deserted and deserting, put upon, deprived of his heritage with the 75,000 Ulster loyalists he's always going on about. He can't find his place in the new Ulster, because he's not really a part of it. He can't find contentment with you, because he sees you as part of the betrayal. He wants to be able to belong, but he can't. That's why he took to drink and that's why he left."

"What's to become of him .... of us?"

"He'll find his way eventually. We all do. But don't forget that you are being sacrificed as well."

"And how do I purge myself? With drink too maybe?"

"No, not drink. But you'll find your own weakness and wrestle with it. I can help there too."

"My own weakness? What do you mean?" His right hand caressing her shoulders, her neck. She could feel her tension going, yielding to his touch.

"Dorothy, you're an attractive women. A young woman. You've been deprived of admiration and attention to your intimate needs." His voice caressing her too, soft yet forceful. His left hand was now on her thigh, caressing, her skirt inching up. She could not stop him. "You didn't have to let me in here tonight. But you did. I think you can work the rest out for yourself."

Dorothy made a half-hearted attempt to stop him. Her hand on his left hand, holding it back as her thigh was fully exposed, the bare skin above the top of her stocking. His hand was firm though. She tried to wriggle from his embrace.

"No, you mustn't ...."

"But you must," he insisted. "You need this and you know it."

"Why are you so sure of yourself?" she asked now, her hand still on his, holding it back.

"I was in the trenches, remember. I learned to read people's emotions? Had to, to survive."

"You say you can read my mind," she faltered, her hand relaxing again allowing him to resume caressing, his right hand now finding and cupping her breasts. She yielded fully to the touch, her body yearning.

"Well, can't I?"

She fell into his embrace, his legs now straddling her. She could feel his desire, hard against her thigh, his eyes burning into hers. She felt a well of passion rising in her, a need to feel him in her arms and she in his.

"Oh damn you," she whispered, her voice urgent, willing him to take her. "Yes, yes ...."

****

O strengthen me, that, while I stand
Firm on the rock, and strong in Thee,
I may stretch out a loving hand
To wrestlers with the troubled sea.

O teach me, Lord, that I may teach
The precious things Thou dost impart.
And wing my words, that they may reach
The hidden depths of many a heart.

****

There was a bit of a hoopla all right, on the day the Boundary Commission came to town, surging up the Monaghan Brae in a fleet of cars with military escort. Crowds milled around the courthouse on Whitehall Street where the commissioners sat to hear evidence. Groups filed in and out, petitioning for changes to and fro across the new frontier. For once there was a general consensus. When asked where the border should be situated, everyone agreed that it should be as far away as possible from them.

In Co. Monaghan, several groups representing the Protestant communities petitioned to be transferred north and reunited with their co-religionists. The Protestant Sanhedrin, however, was much more circumspect. If the resurgent organisation of Protestants was to have any impact on public affairs in the county, it could not countenance even the nip and tuck approach of the most trepidatious. As Ulster had come together at Belfast City Hall a decade earlier to maintain the union, so the Orange Institution had come together at the Twelfth of July field in Kilacoona, near Analore Bridge, to maintain Co. Monaghan. There, at the behest of Grand Master M.E. Knight, they opted for strength in unity. "We are Ulster men and Protestants and we should constantly remind ourselves, and those who would do us wrong, of that irrefutable fact," Knight declared to loud cheering.

But now, on the first day of the hearings in Clones, Albert met Robert James McConkey. They stood on the periphery of the activity around the courthouse, regarding with the cynical detachment of country people the general hubbub. Amidst the cheers and party slogans, they huddled.

"Think will it make a blind bit of differ, Robert James?"

"Thon boys or the petitions?"

"The both, I suppose."

"Well, suppose anything's worth a try now, for them that has a chance of being taken in by the Belfast crowd."

"Attorney Knight's agin it, of course."

"Aye, Albert, but you heard the Clough men saying there's others getting up petitions as well."

"Doubt it's aisy enough for the Clough men, within spitting distance of the border. There's a lot more of us, though, out our way."

Silence now as the two men reflected on the patchwork of communities on both sides of the frontier. Each group trying to leapfrog over another to stake their claim for inclusion on this side or that. The whole business was an almighty mess, they agreed. Albert spoke of the court case he had read about, here in Clones it was. Attorney Knight had been suing on behalf of his client, Mervyn Armitage, who was seeking compensation from a man called Seamus Connolly. Armitage lived in the townland of Ballyhoe in Co. Fermanagh, Connolly in the townland of Drumaveale in Co. Monaghan.

"Anyway, one day Armitage sees your man digging the sheough on the marches of the two farms, widening it like," said Albert. "The judge asks whether he was digging in Fermanagh or Monaghan and Mr

Knight's to have said it was on the boundary line of the two townlands. Like, on the border itself. But then he stumps them by saying, since it's a mathematical certainty that a line has length but no width, then the four-foot ditch was actually taking from Armitage's farm as well."

"What did the judge say to that?"

"Well," said Albert, "he's to have said that it appeared Connolly was doing more nor the Boundary Commissioners. While they only talk, he's out there with his shovel taking part of Fermanagh into the Free State."

The two men laughed, causing several heads to turn in the crowd.

"If it wasn't so ridiculous, this whole thing would be funny," said Robert James at last.

"Right enough, even when the whole thing's settled, there'll be stories going the rounds for years about here."

"So what's the story on young Sinclair these days?"

"Och, divil the word and we haven't seen hide nor hair of him this good while," said Albert, his smile gone now. "His mother's fierce worried. Thinks he might be hurted."

"Och, sure you'd hear if he was."

"Bid to be, but it's fierce what a body would be inclined to think for not hearing to the contrary."

"Sure there's that much coming and going with this Boundary Commission now, maybe there's more duty. Doubt you'll hear before too long."

"Aye, well, I hope so," said Albert, now preparing to move off. "Best go and look for the same Sadie. Bad enough one member of the family gone missing without her fretting over me as well."

Sinclair could not control the slight tremble in his hand. He raised the shaving brush and soaped the bristles again, but when he tried to apply the razor, the shaking was there again. His head throbbed with a dull pain, his body sore and lethargic. He regarded himself in the small shaving mirror and concentrated on the task. The razor sliced off a section of foam again, without drawing blood. The exposed skin was flushed and raw. He concentrated again and began on the other side. It was a slow job, taking tiny swipes of the razor, but eventually it was done. He lifted the hand towel and began to dry himself off. A voice, mocking and insistent, "You'll cut your throat with that thing less you're careful."

Sinclair buried his face in the towel now, his breath registering his annoyance with McCoubrey who never missed a chance to pass some remark. With the sanctimonious certainty of the teetotaller, McCoubrey availed of every chance to lecture about the evils of drink and the folly of those who indulged. He took perverse pleasure, it seemed to Sinclair, in those who suffered from over-indulgence, laughing at their hangovers and provoking their wrath. And while Sinclair was drinking less now that he did not have the company of Alex and the others, his steady consumption was the sole relief he had from his tormentor. Until the next morning, that is. He wondered if, as usual, he should just ignore him, but McCoubrey was already jostling his way into the washing area of the sleeping quarters.

"Och, away and give my head peace," said Sinclair, his voice registering his annoyance.

McCoubrey laughed, "You're not giving it too much peace yourself, are you?"

"What's it to you?"

McCoubrey faced him now, his look registering disdain for drink and those who indulged in it. Sinclair tried to avoid his eye by starting to gather his few belongings from the sink and the shelf.

"I'll tell you what it is to me. Any man's protecting my back out there, I want to know he's able to shoot straight."

"You needn't worry on that score."

"Wish I could believe you."

"Well, why don't you ask for a transfer then?"

"Thought you might do that yourself."

"I've no plans."

McCoubrey now grasped his elbow, holding it in a tight grip. Sinclair recoiled, but didn't react beyond that, unable to decide whether to simply drop his razor and other belongings and wrestle free. McCoubrey's face was serious, almost angry. Sinclair was trapped.

"Listen, I've nothing against you Armstrong, bar your drinking and whinging. Maybe it's not your own fault, but surely to God you'd be fit to do something about it."

"Or what?"

"Well, you know there's been complaints."

"To where?"

"County command in Omagh. You'd want to catch yourself on."

McCoubrey released his elbow and Sinclair backed off to the lockers beside the bunk beds. The other man had already poured water from a large ewer on the shelf and was starting to soap up his shaving brush. Sinclair could almost feel his eyes in the mirror regarding him. Complaints? He knew he wasn't popular, but he could see now that others, and McCoubrey especially, wanted him out of here. He suddenly felt as if he had nowhere left to go.

When she heard the firm knock on the door, Dorothy didn't even bother to peer out the little side window. She threw off the bolt and, without looking back, moved away as the latch was released and the door pushed open. Her back to the entrance, she walked to the bedroom, almost in a daze. She undressed as she did so, her clothes scattered along the floor in a trail leading towards the bed. He did not speak either as he followed her lead in their twice weekly dance. Both knew the steps and where they led. She could feel the physical need, had felt it for hours as the time approached and she worried that he might not show up. Even as she had tried to work on some lace earlier, her entire body trembled as she felt her desire peak, building up to a crescendo from sensations that had begun almost since his last departure.

She imagined again his hands on her body, rough and demanding, callused hands passing over her breasts and gripping her hips as he forced himself inside her, hard, penetrating, satisfying. Only then would she relax, she knew, glancing again at the clock as she counted off the minutes. Once tasted, their adultery had become an intoxicant she craved, shutting out all doubts as her body demanded it.

The first few times, she still harboured the feelings of guilt and shame afterwards, but that had only added to the excitement as she felt her body ravished. Her revulsion for the act, and also for the man with whom she acted, consumed her with a wave of desire as she felt herself debased and depraved, yet released. They had done it that first night, there on the sofa and afterwards in the bed. When he left immediately after his passion was sated, she had cried bitterly, the male smell of his spent passion still noticeable on the bed and on her own body. The sticky residue now congealing on her stomach where he had pulled out at the last minute even as she writhed beneath him and tried to hold in his stiffness with her threshing hands squeezed between their sweating bodies. He had ignored her needs as he rolled sideways, grunted then and paused only momentarily as she wondered what she would do if he attempted to caress her now, or kiss her. She was spared that indignity, as he dressed casually and headed off, but not the feeling that she would surrender again if he returned.

He had, three days later, this time not even bothering to indulge in the pretence of courtship. She had let him in and was immediately forced back to the kitchen table as he strode towards her, his right hand already unbuttoning his trousers quickly and then ripping open her housecoat. With both hands he pulled up her petticoat and, pushing aside her drawers, he was suddenly inside her again, pumping roughly and relentlessly, releasing his passion and hers as she felt her body gripping his member and luxuriating in its assault on her very being. She had moved in tandem with him, matching his thrusts, her legs closing around his penis, eager to intensify her pleasure. His thrusts began to enter her slowly, so slowly that she could feel every muscle, every ripple and contour of his member. Then once firmly inside, he would retreat again, leaving her engorged and dripping. Gradually, he had increased his thrusts, her body responding as she flailed against the table, now pushed over against the wall, the chairs straining on their hind legs. She writhed against his pelvic thrusts and felt her very being shuddering from its core. She screamed with pleasure and release, her voice rising to a pitch above his gasps and groans as she felt him pulling out, his body shuddering too as he came to his peak with a deep, almost frightened moan. When he had spent, this time on her petticoat, he tried to kiss her, but her hand covered her mouth and he did not press it. He started to say something, but she turned away in shame. She did not want to talk about it, or them. She wanted no more from him than she had been given. He had buttoned up his trousers and left in silence.

By the next time, again three days later, a tour of patrol duty completed, she knew what to expect of him. So began her retreat to the bedroom and her silent compliance in the ritual. She worried about his withdrawal and always bathed carefully afterwards, washing out what might be left of his ejaculated sperm, wondering what she would do if any had escaped before he jerked out of her, free from her body's demands. But she no longer seemed capable of caring that what she was doing was wrong. It only mattered that he came and took her in the way he did. It was a relationship based on lust and loathing. That actually made it easier to cope and to wait out the days until his return.

****

Blest are they in Thy house that dwell,
They ever give Thee praise,
Blest is the man whose strength Thou art,
In whose heart are Thy ways:
Who as they pass through Baca's vale
Make it a place of springs;
Also the rain that falleth down
Rich blessing to it brings.
So they from strength unwearied go
Still forward unto strength,
Until in Zion they appear
Before the Lord at length.

****

A hoar frost blanketed the graves and a puddle on the path was speckled with broken shards of thin ice where footsteps had scrunched their way to service on Christmas morning. Now as the congregation emerged, exchanging seasonal greetings and tidings in voices tinged with a note of excitement and anticipation, the air of goodwill was palpable in the wafts of steam exhaled with each breath. Here and there, men clapped their hands together and rubbed them vigorously. Some exhaled warm breath into their cupped fists, while women pulled on gloves and readjusted hats and shawls. As she emerged, Sadie noticed Roy helping Eileen with her warm shawl. It covered her shoulders but not the expanse of stomach now bloated with pregnancy. How long left, she wondered, filled with motherly concern for the younger woman who stepped gingerly from the porch onto the gravel, worried that she might lose her balance. But Roy's steadying hand was there at her elbow, she saw. Beside her, Albert was already calling out in greeting, "Happy Christmas to you all now."

Roy and Robert James, standing to the side, responded in kind and Sadie added, "And all the joys of the same."

She could feel the bite of the easterly wind now, whipping up the hillside from the small lake below. The high stone walls of the churchyard offered little protection against its swirls and gusts. She took Albert's arm to steady herself along the gravel to where the McConkeys stood. As they drew into a huddle, Roy had already pulled out his packet of Park Drive cigarettes and was offering them to the other men. They bent and drew in the flame from the match that Robert James cupped in his hand, and inhaled deeply. When they exhaled, the smoke came in a great waft from their mouths, multiplied by the winter steam of their breath. Sadie knew they were settling in for a chat. Her expectation was confirmed by Roy, who said to Eileen, "Why don't you tip on over to see your mother there. I'll be along in a wee minute."

Eileen said, "Aye, Happy Christmas then," and complied. Sadie could see that she was going to join a group of women at the church gate, among them Mrs Anderson and several of the older women. Albert was already laughing as he said, "Good man, Roy. You have her well in hand and I see you're doing your wee bit to keep up the congregation here."

Sadie tut-tutted his coarseness, here in the very church grounds itself. "Stop you that ould nonsense, Albert Armstrong. Leave the lad alone, why don't you? While I go over and see the women."

The men were guffawing now as she wheeled around. She knew rightly that Albert was just having a wee bit of fun with Roy, and even Robert James enjoyed the banter. It was hard come by too, she realised, in the times that were in it. She knew Albert envied his friend having his son at home, while missing Sinclair himself. She felt another pang of concern, wondering why he hadn't been in touch. The thought of another Christmas dinner with just Albert and herself filled her with a forlorn loneliness. But she had to keep up appearances, and even pretence for Albert's sake. Before she had gone too far along the path, she turned and called back, "Now don't be standing there chattering for too long. I've to get back home, for that goose is in the oven for the dinner."

Albert nodded, even as he heard Roy's voice now whispering loudly, "Fraid your own goose is rightly cooked there, Albert." They laughed and lapsed into silence. Albert was too acutely conscious that the others were aware of how he missed his own son who would have been here with him now, completing the circle. Robert James coughed and then said, "Talking about the goose, see there was powerful prices going for the turkeys the year. Ten bob and more maybe for a good big hen."

They were content to move onto the familiar ground of farming. Albert could hold his own here and more maybe.

"Aye, Sadie had a few."

"Saw you in with them at the market in Clones the other day. Did she get her price all right?"

"Did surely. All gone. Not even a one left for ourselves."

"Do you say?"

"Aye, but you know, I've half a notion to bring on a few for next year myself. With the prices going, it's more than what they'd call pin money these times."

"Deed it is," said Roy, "and with the year that's been in it, you'd want something like that to tide you over."

They reflected on the year, the dreadful weather and the sense of gloom it had cast over the whole country. When winter had begun its frosty grip a few weeks ago, it was almost a welcome relief. The winds and squalls had continued almost unabated since the summer, if you could even call it summer - a few weeks of respite in July and August, when the rain fell only intermittently. It had been a disaster for the farming community here and throughout the entire countryside.

"Never in my whole life saw worse," said Robert James, as Albert glanced off into the pale sunshine from the brow of a hill beyond the church where the village sat. "It's a quare bad sign of it when you get snowdrifts in June."

"Aye, it is in soul," said Albert. "We should have known. Have you fodder enough to last out, do you think?"

"Just about, I'd say," said Roy. "Deed, you'd be even better off with a few loads of hay to sell than with a lock of gobbling turkeys."

"Hear tell it's very bad out beyond Roslea," said Robert James, now looking in the direction of the low mountain to the north. All three were aware of the recent reports of famine and deprivation on what were known as the College Lands, the small tenant holdings leased from Trinity College which owned a great swathe of that Fermanagh countryside.

"Aye, and nearer maybe," said Albert, his voice registering the realisation that, whatever his own troubles, some were a lot worse off. "Not much of a Christmas for them the year. Suppose we should count our blessings here."

Roy seized his chance, "Any word from Sinclair and Dorothy, Albert?"

"Aye, a card, a Christmas card like, from Dorothy day before yesterday. She says Sinclair was on duty right up to today and, sure, with the border closed down for the holidays, they can't get over. They'll be spending the day in Newtownbutler. Doubt we'll not see them this time."

Robert James was sympathetic, "Bit much at Christmas that they couldn't see their way to allowing him get home. Och, but I don't suppose they'd be bothered too much about the border being shut down."

"Hoped I might see him," said Roy.

"Didn't we all," Albert said, his voice hollow again. "Besides all else, I wanted to talk to him about thon petition the Clough men's got up for transfers across the border. He should sign it himself, so he should, for he'll have the running of the place before too long."

Albert sensed that the others were aware of how his hopes for Sinclair's return might be dashed. It had been so long now since he had gone off, more than three years, they wondered if he would return at all. Albert would not allow himself to wonder the same, clinging to the words of his son on the day he had told him that this place was still his home. He would be back, he thought. He had to come home.

"It's a holy terra," Robert James was saying. "Thought with that curfew lifted in Belfast and all, they would all be off for the Christmas, near enough."

"Aye, well," said Albert, "the old folks will just have to make do alone again the year."

Roy laughed, "Aye, you'll be poisoned with goose, Albert. You'll have to ate that much of it."

Goose, thought Albert, we might even have to eat crow if he never comes back.

Alex Johnson was taking a perverse and immense pleasure in this Christmas dinner. Seated at the table between Sinclair and Dorothy, he revelled in their discomfort with each other and, especially, in Dorothy's discomfort with his own presence. He had anticipated it with relish after only momentary misgivings when Sinclair had sent a message to invite him. It had taken him only moments to realise that the invitation would not have come if Sinclair had any inkling of what was going on. For Sinclair, he knew, his presence would be a foil, a means of avoiding having to endure his wife's questions and recriminations. For Dorothy, his presence would be a tribulation, yet one in keeping with the course of their relationship. Throughout their regular trysts, she had allowed, even initiated, her further debasement as they found sexual release together. There was no question of anything other than copulation, fornication, adultery. She had made that clear when she had spurned his gestures of endearment on the first couple of occasions. But it was enough for him. He eschewed any pretence that this was anything more than satisfying coupling. He did not want to become emotionally entangled and was fully satisfied that she didn't either. For his part, he could afford to be relaxed. He knew there was little danger of Dorothy saying anything that might reveal their recently begun relationship. However she might dislike him, even hate him, she needed him and she had so much more to lose if it became public knowledge.

So he had accepted her husband's invitation and even brought a small gift for her, a needlepoint picture - Home, Sweet Home. When he had presented it to her, she almost dropped it to the floor. He caught it in time, setting the precedent for her subsequent fumblings as she prepared and served the dinner. Alex was aware that Sinclair attributed them to no more than her discomfort with being in the company of somebody she blamed for his errant ways. As the dinner progressed, he basked in his sense of control, his knowledge that Sinclair was as incapable of deducing his wife's involvement with his friend as she was incapable of revealing it. With a perverse cruelty that approached sexual foreplay, he loaded his effusive conversation with innuendo and watched Dorothy wince as he did so.

The dinner over now, they sat at the table, the men sated from eating. Alex raised his beer glass in a mock toast.

"Would you look at the cut of us. Like one wee happy family," he said. Then, looking earnestly at Sinclair, he added, "Very good of your wee woman here to have me, Sinclair."

Sinclair brushed aside the remark, "Aye, well, I knew you'd be no bother."

"Maybe Dorothy's the one should say if I'm a bother."

She was curt, "Sure, I had to cook the dinner for two anyway."

He looked at her now, the colour rising in her face again, her breasts heaving and straining against the white blouse whose high neckline and ruffled collar only accentuated the swell of her bosom.

"Aye, well I hope I'm not, like, squeezing you too much, Dorothy."

"I said it's no bother."

Alex leaned back in his chair, raised his arms and cupped the back of his head with clasped hands. He looked at Dorothy as he said, "Well, it's just I feel betimes I'm butting in between the pair of you a wee bit."

Dorothy looked away, towards the fireplace and then to Sinclair. His eyes were downcast, almost avoiding her but she saw no inkling of him realising what was happening. She spoke to him urgently, anxious to fill the silence since Alex had spoken, "Would you see about a few more sods for thon fire, before she goes out on us?"

"Aye, right back," said Sinclair, relieved to have an excuse to rise from the table, if only momentarily. He went out the cottage door, to the turf stack in the lean-to shed. Dorothy turned to Alex and, in a rushed, angry voice, said, "Will you quit that?"

"What?"

"Poking fun like that."

He laughed, released his hands, brought them onto the table and leaned towards her.

"You had no complaints about my poking last night, nor all those other nights before that either."

Dorothy's eyes darted towards the door, "Wheesht. Do you want him to hear? Bad enough he asked you over here."

"Well, if he wasn't about, I'd be here anyway, wouldn't I, pet? But there would be more fun to that and less talk of turf on the fire to keep us warm."

He reached with his right hand, under the table and onto Dorothy's knee, forcing his hand between her legs, easing them apart. She panicked and, glancing guiltily towards the door again, pushed his hand away. "Quit that and shut up, for Christ's sake. Here he comes."

Almost immediately, the latch lifted and Sinclair entered with an armful of turf sods which he off-loaded into a big basket beside the range. He threw a few sods into the blazing fire.

"Here he comes now," said Alex. "Always said you're a great man to stoke a fire up, Sinclair. Best I ever come across."

Sinclair rose to the compliment, "Aye, times you'd sit in that dayroom beyond and the fire near out."

"Aye, well that's a fact. But I keep the heat up now, so I do. Isn't that right, Dorothy?"

She looked at him nervously. He could see the fear in her eyes. She was totally in his control. He knew he would have her before the day was out, her final submission to his wants and her needs. He just had to twist it a little more and she would agree at the first opportunity, frantic lest he simply say it straight out. He could see she knew he would, as she snapped, "How would I know?"

He smiled at her, then at Sinclair, "Anytime you'd come across me, in the barracks like, you'd not be cold would you?"

She seized the escape, "Not that I noticed, but it's not too often I'd be in the barracks now."

He could see Sinclair trying to make some sense of their exchange, wondering if his months of near solitude had rendered him incapable of table chat maybe. "Freeze you betimes in Cookstown, too ...." Sinclair's voice trailed off.

Alex paused, smiled. "Aye, well there wouldn't be a whole lot to keep a man warm up about the lough shore. Not like here."

Silence now, an uneasy silence from them, a deliberate interlude on Alex's part. He wondered when and where he could ravish Dorothy. It wouldn't take long, he knew, feeling his excitement building with each moment of her ordeal. He knew it would happen and he took his eyes reluctantly from her breasts to look at her husband. Sinclair was passing the time by gulping from his beer glass. Already he had consumed three bottles of his own and had even taken Dorothy's untouched glass, seemingly without knowing it.

"Well, as I was saying, Sinclair. Me and Dorothy's more friendly these times, but I can tell she misses a man about the house."

Dorothy began to rise from the table, lifting her plate as if to clear off, "Do any of you want a wee bit more of anything?"

"No," said Sinclair, "I'm rightly."

"I've my fill here too. Grand bit of stuffing you make, Dorothy, and a lovely dinner, too."

Sinclair rose, "Anyone want another bottle of beer?"

"Och no," said Alex, watching as they were both suspended in mid-air, rising from the table while he sat. Dorothy slumped back into her chair. He resumed, "I wouldn't want to make a glutton of myself, not with the way I'm being looked after in this house. But you go ahead yourself, Sinclair."

He was already standing, moving away from the table, "Aye, then, I'll just bring in a few more bottles from the other room."

Sinclair had barely gone out of the room when Dorothy turned and hissed at Alex, "Shut you up your filthy hints. He'll know."

Alex laughed indulgently, "Not a bother, but we could be doing it here right fornenst his nose and he'd not know. But I'll not ruin your good dinner."

Sinclair, returning with several bottles, had heard the final words spoken by Alex in a carelessly loud voice. "What's that?" he asked, as he sat and grabbed the corkscrew.

"Just saying that was a good dinner. Aye, indeed, a great one."

"Right, tell us Alex," Sinclair said, as he poured from the beer bottle. "Are you boys about here out after the poteen stills, like we are?"

He took a long steady gulp from the frothing glass.

Alex laughed again, "Aye surely. We're like excise men out after the quare stuff. Water rats, they call us hereabouts. But, as I always say, you can't beat the Special Constabulary for finding drink if there's any about."

An almost oppressive heat hung in the air. Both men had long ago discarded jackets and pullovers and were seated, slumped, in their shirtsleeves. Sinclair had kicked off his boots and was reclining now in the armchair with his feet on Dorothy's sewing box, his hands clutching a whiskey tumbler to his chest. Alex sat beside her on the sofa, attempting every so often to nestle closer. Each time, she got up and went about the kitchen on some pretext or other. She wondered how she had managed to get through this dreadful day.

From the outset, she had known she faced a dreadful ordeal. It had begun a few days earlier when her mother had come by to say that she would be spending Christmas with her sister in Lisnaskea. Dorothy knew that this was deliberate, a way of avoiding being in the company of Sinclair. She had noticed that her mother pointedly never mentioned him now. Then Sinclair had come home late on Christmas Eve, only hours after Alex had been there, to announce that Alex would be having his Christmas dinner with them. The conniving bastard had not even mentioned the invitation as he had ravished her twice that evening. The second time, he had been lying on his back on the bed after he had spent. She waited for him to leave, as he had always done. She waited, but he did not move. She eventually stirred, turning around anxiously in case he might have fallen asleep and with Sinclair due home at any time. But, as she turned in the bed to see, she felt his hand grasp her hair roughly, her face pushed down upon his penis, stiffening again now, growing rigid as he forced it into her mouth. "This one's for Christmas," he laughed as he began to thrust his pelvis and she began to respond, even as she gagged. She shuddered now at the memory.

Then the constant jibes and innuendo during the dinner had been bad enough, the occasional attempts at groping had caused her to panic, but now as Sinclair got drunker and drunker, he had given up any pretence at decorum and tried to touch her any time she came near. She was horrified by his cruel taunting, his implied threats that he did not care in the least if Sinclair realised what was happening. She felt a renewed revulsion for Alex, yet watched with disgust also how Sinclair sank into an alcoholic haze, totally oblivious to her predicament. At one point, her anger had become so acute she almost decided to tell him straight out what was happening, but she was dragged back from that brink by the constant awareness that she would be disgraced.

Sinclair slurred his words now, his eyelids heavy as he addressed Alex. "Way I see it, there's nothing natural about drudgery. Mean to say like, if that was the attitude people took years ago, then we'd still be out hoking at the ground with our fingers, wouldn't we?"

Alex was sober, not having consumed much all day as Sinclair took to the bottle with a vengeance. He regarded his host now with the indulgent nonchalance the sober reserve for the pestering drunk.

"Do you tell me now, Sinclair?"

It was quite obvious to Dorothy that he had not been listening, nor could she blame him for that as Sinclair waved around his hand to emphasise his point.

"Well, this single horse plough they have now takes the back-breaking drudgery out of it. Yet there's them would say it's not the traditional way and they want us all to stick with the spade or the three-horse swing plough."

"Well, maybe they have a point," said Alex, clearly winding up Sinclair, even as he looked at Dorothy, his eyes roving over her. She felt the onset of another panic attack.

"Divil a bit," Sinclair said, his voice replete with drunken indignation. "Let them stick with it and not be passing judgement on those wants to get on. Them that wants to get the ploughing done without spending weeks or months maybe before they can sow a few acres of oats. I seen men in ...."

"Well, I wouldn't know one end of a plough, nor a spade even, from the other," said Alex, clearly signalling that he wanted this topic of conversation ended. "I wasn't reared on a farm like yourself, Sinclair."

Dorothy seized the chance to end the night and get Alex out of the house as quickly as possible. "Anyone want a wee drop of tea for the road?" she asked hopefully.

But Sinclair was already attempting to rise from the armchair, gulping down the remains of his whiskey as he protested, "No, no, howl on with the tay. We'll have another wee drop of thon whiskey before winding up." As he attempted to lever himself off the arm of the chair into a standing position, his elbow gave way and Sinclair slumped back into the cushions. His eyelids drooped and closed and almost immediately, a wheezing snore filled the room. Alex regarded the prostrate body now. Dorothy could sense the air of contempt as he spoke. "Doubt it's tea he needs, all right. That's him gone now, out like a light."

She felt devastated, as much by the fact that any restraint on Alex's behaviour was now removed, as by the drunken state of her husband. Damn, she thought, I knew this would happen soon as I saw him going for that bottle he had hidden away.

Alex began to sidle across the sofa, grabbing her arm before she could rise and escape his clutches, "Well, maybe we can do something more than drink tea while he's out, eh?" She wrestled with him, trying to push him away, but his grip on her arm was firm. She could feel the anger and contempt that had been building all day come to the surface now, also freed of the restraint she had felt earlier.

"Quit that ould pawing, will ye?" she demanded, looking him in the eye for the first time and realising as she said it that the fear had gone, replaced now with cold anger and determination to end this torment. "Stop it, now," she screamed. "I'm warning you."

He released his grip and sat back, amused almost by her outburst. His expression fuelled her anger.

"What's the matter? Afraid he'll wake up?"

She felt calmer now, her voice steady, "No, I don't want to. I don't feel like it."

Alex laughed, and began to move towards her, his face betraying his certainty that he was in control, not her. "I do, come on."

She slapped him then, the sound ringing around the room like the crack of a rifle shot as she landed her open palm with all the force she could muster on the side of his face. He recoiled, shocked perhaps, but still determined. His left cheek reddened and tears began to form in his eye. She leaped to her feet and stood there, close, facing him down. Her voice, when she spoke, was calm, steady, mustering her anger and contempt in her deliberation, "No, not any more. I want you to leave, Alex, and not come back."

"Why? Because of earlier on?" he asked, the tear beginning to slide down the side of his nose now. He raised his hand and rubbed it away with the ball of his wrist.

"No ....Yes, that and more," she began. "I don't want you calling here again. Never. Do you heed me now?"

"Well ....," he began, but she cut him off, impatient now to end this as quickly as possible, before he regained the upper hand. "I'm not going to argue about it. I want you to leave."

She took a step back, a single pace to allow him to rise, but she fixed him with her stare. He rose uncertainly, feigning casual indifference.

"Makes no odds to me. You're the woman of the house, Dorothy."

She watched him as he looked over at Sinclair and said, "But maybe you'll change your mind before too long."

"Don't count on it," she said, her voice full of resolution and determination as she found renewed strength in his grudging acquiescence. "If you want the truth, I'll give it to you now. You make me sick, Alex. You always have. God knows how or why I put up with you for so long. But every time you touched me, even when I wanted you to, I could feel my skin crawling."

"That's only natural," he smiled, his face again a leering mask.

She did not want to hear him. "Shut up," she ordered him. "You're a smug bastard and a cruel one at that, Alex Johnson."

She looked over at Sinclair, lying there, asleep and felt a rush of tenderness for him, "God knows, he's not up to much these times, but behind it all he's decent, even when he's slobbering drunk like now. But you," she look him in the eye again, "You're so full of yourself, it's hard to believe ...."

"All right," he cut her off, "All right, I'm going."

She stood there resolutely as he fetched his overcoat and put it on. He went to the door and paused before leaving. She turned away from him to look at the fire, hearing him say, laughing again, smug, "Well, suppose I had a good innings here, anyway. Take care of yourself, Dorothy, and him for what he's worth ...."

She snapped back, "Don't even think the like ...." But he was already gone, the door lying open in his wake, a gush of cold air now blowing through the cottage. She paused, buried her face in her hands and sobbed for a moment, her body wracked with shame and relief. Purged at last. She then went over, closed the door, bolted it firmly and walked over to Sinclair. He was snoring softly in the chair, for all the world as calm as any other sleeping person. She lowered herself to her knees and grasped his hand which had fallen off the arm, clutching it tenderly now. Her voice was calm, soft, pleading. "Och Sinclair, how did it ever come to this?" She shook her head slowly, perplexed, "Both of us ...."

Outside, Alex had gone only a few paces, crunching through the frosty residue on the road when he heard the door slam and the bolt shot. He stopped abruptly and looked back - only a chink of light escaped from the side window and he remembered the warmth inside. He gathered his coat around him against the cold swirling wind which bit into his face, the left side still warm, however, from her slap. His surprise at her reaction had gone, replaced with a deep resentment. He felt his angry indignation rising, his loss of control rankling as he thought of the freezing tramp back to the barracks. Then a cold calculation filled his mind. He turned and muttered darkly, spitting the words out under his breath, "Wee bitch. I'll show you. You're not finished with me, not by a long chalk, Mrs Armstrong."

****

Brethren, I ask you, as Ulstermen, are you going to allow this great and prosperous province to be governed by men who take every opportunity to declare their determination, not only to have Home Rule, but complete separation from the great Empire to which we belong? As you know, Mr Redmond has said, if he believed armed rebellion would be successful, he would advise it. He has also said, when speaking up here in Ulster - 'If necessary the minority must be overcome by the strong hand.' Brethren, may I say to Mr Redmond on your behalf today, we fear not his threats and refuse to be governed by him and his friends.

J. C. W. Madden, Clones, at Belfast Twelfth in Ligoniel, 1908.

****

From where he lay, reclined on the top bunk bed but fully dressed, Sinclair could see out through the window of the sleeping quarters to a patch of garden beyond. A cluster of snowdrops around the trunk of a leafless tree basked in the chilly February sunshine. Beside them, the stems of daffodils carried green bulbs with just a hint of yellow inside. Sinclair reflected on these early signs of spring and wondered about all the farm tasks that would soon be underway in preparation for ploughing and seeding. He missed the country, the perennial certainties of farm life, the routine tasks, the satisfaction of preparing for and anticipating the harvest it would bring. He took an imaginary stroll around the farm at Drumkirk, the land soggy and the grass yellowing after the winter. He surveyed hedges that would need to be repaired to stop livestock breaking through and wandering, the sheoughs that would need to be shored up, the grassland that would need to be fenced off for hay pastures. He wondered how Albert was faring with only Wee Willie Houston to help. Other farms, he knew, had suffered badly because of the dreadful weather of the previous summer. But he was buoyed by the knowledge that those who had managed to take in a harvest had benefitted from higher prices in the scarcity. The industrious farmers of Drum, his father among them, would have fared all right in the end, he was confident.

Farming occupied more and more of his thoughts these days, cut off as he was from the others in the barracks, drinking alone during off-duty hours at a pub in the town. While the isolation here did not bother him as much as he might have expected, allowing him to be absorbed in his own thoughts and sort them out, he missed acutely the familiar comfort of home and the land.

Police work, on the other hand, had become a bore - an endless cycle of patrols and arrests, broken only occasionally by other duties with the regular policemen. The A Specials were a paramilitary police force, he knew, but there was little call now for the units that were administered and run like army platoons. It was hardly clear that they made a difference now that hostilities had lapsed into only occasional outbreaks of violence. Yet the Belfast government was insistent that it would maintain its armed camp, particularly in the vulnerable areas of Tyrone, Fermanagh and elsewhere that were the subject of so much speculation in terms of the Boundary Commission to which the Dublin and London governments were so committed. When Craig's administration tried to ignore the appointment of the southern and British nominees to the commission, London appointed Joseph Fisher, editor of the Belfast newspaper *The Northern Whig,* to be the Northern Ireland representative.

Since his return from Newtownbutler, Sinclair had found little satisfaction in the constabulary. Other personal concerns occupied his thoughts. After the tension of his arrival home and the strange atmosphere of Christmas Day itself, when he had got drunk, he had niggling recollections that surfaced from time to time. Nothing clear or definite, of course, just memories of looks exchanged, remarks brushed aside. The next day, he had been surprised by Dorothy's attitude. When he had woken up, a blanket had been wrapped around him where he lay in the armchair and he found her more gentle, more caring. Nothing was said, of course. It was just a general atmosphere that pervaded the cottage. He felt a bit subdued himself, guilty over his heavy drinking on the previous day and nursing a mild hangover as a result, but at least there had not been an argument. He carefully avoided taking a drink that day and, though it was quiet in the cottage, he did not feel on edge as he usually did. He had not gone up to the barracks to see his former comrades and, when he left for the train back to Cookstown, he even thought that she seemed a little sad to see him go. He felt it too, the keen regret of parting. After other visits, when he had been simply relieved to get away from the constant arguments and accusations, he had looked forward to the loneliness of Cookstown. Now he wondered if he and Dorothy could ever again be reconciled enough to capture something of the joy they had before, the comfort and excitement of each other's company, the sense of belonging and being wanted and loved.

What he missed most was the quiet and serene comfort of waking up beside her, feeling her head resting in the crook of his arm, knowing that she would be there again the next morning and every morning after that.

He was thinking of Dorothy now as he lay alone on his bed, while around him others were busy shining boots and buckles and brushing down their uniforms. Divorced as he was from barracks life, he ignored the air of resentment with which McCoubrey worked around him. But as the general hubbub died down, he heard McCoubrey addressing him, "You not getting yourself ready, Armstrong?"

Without looking up or stirring, Sinclair mumbled, "I've done."

"Must have been while the rest of us were asleep last night then."

"She'll do rightly."

McCoubrey came around the bunk and looked at him, blocking the view of the window and the garden beyond.

"Och, well you know they'll be expecting all spit and polish for Sir James and all. As the sergeant's never done saying, a unit's only as good as every man in it."

Sinclair flipped his body around to look in the other direction, away from McCoubrey. "Sure, who'll notice? They're clean enough from all the other inspection parades."

McCoubrey walked off a few paces, as if to leave, then returned, still at Sinclair's back. "By the way, Armstrong, know a man called Johnson do you?"

Sinclair flipped around again, this time raising his head to rest it on his open palm and elbow. "Aye, Alex Johnson is it?"

"That's him," McCoubrey was smiling, smugly it seemed to Sinclair.

"Sure, me and him's great from the time we were posted together."

"Bit of a ladies' man, I hear tell."

"Och, all ould blather if you ask me. Alex is a wee bit inclined to let his imagination run away with him betimes, same boy. But he's dead on for that."

"Wonder if it's all ould blather from the stories that's going the rounds down in Fermanagh Division."

"What stories?"

"Well, I haven't got it all mind you. But the way I hear it, seems he's had this nice wee arrangement going for him."

"What arrangement?"

"Right next to the barracks and all."

"In Newtown?"

"Aye, Newtownbutler. Seems there's this wee woman ...."

Sinclair shut his eyes and ears, refusing to hear any more. But he knew. His mind a jumble - the looks, the remarks the strange behaviour on Christmas day. Sinclair's heart sank like a stone. How could she do it? How could she betray him? And with Alex? His own Dorothy? A great emptiness seized his brain and grew, worse than ever before.

Roy had fixed a centre pole at the end of the field and taken three long strides from it on each end where he fixed twigs into the ground. From there, he had marked off the field in both directions. He had then gone back to the house and shackled up the horse to the new plough and led it out to the field, lowered the coulter by unloosening the square-head bolts to release the shaft of the big wheel so that it matched the small wheel and tightened the pins at either side to keep it steady. He was now ready to plough the three acres of southern facing hillside. He check again to make sure the apparatus was in order, unfurled the traces and "hupped" Sam, flicking the traces to signal the off.

The horse set off to the side, unused to not being led down the field. Roy ran around and drew him back into position, wondering if he should go and call his father to help, but hesitating because he wanted to prove that one ploughman could do the job. Robert James had been unconvinced, of course, preferring to rely on the more common three-horse swing plough used in these parts, the animals brought together by neighbours. That was the traditional practice of "morrowing" or "neighbour-dealing," when clusters of farmers would help out each other at the main tasks of the year. That was all right for hay-making or pulling flax in the months of July and August, or even at the threshing in October, Roy thought. That was when farm life was a hive of social activity centring on the neighbourly help and convivial atmosphere of the milder weather. Ploughing was a necessary chore, and the easier it could be accomplished, the quicker completed, the better it would be.

The horse now back in place and the traces taut enough to keep his head, Roy grabbed the wee handle and main handle of the plough and urged the horse forward again. This time Sam went in a straight line and Roy set his long ploughman's gait to the job, looking down as the blade cut through the dark, cloying earth, heavy with the rains of winter and early spring. It opened in a slice of maybe five inches deep, the mould bar pushing it out on either side to create a uniform furrow. No stones so far, apart from the usual pebbles in the dark grey soil Roy regarded it with satisfaction. He inhaled deeply, savouring the rich smell that burst forth from the freshly turned earth, the dark musty scent of wet saturated soil now exposed to the light. It was the odour of Spring and a beginning of new life. He might have this job done before the dinner, even if he took it at a slower steady pace to get accustomed to the new plough.

As he passed the mid-point of the field, he looked ahead at the pole and then back to make sure the furrow was straight. It was, he decided, watching as flocks of birds, starlings, crows and finches, swooped down on the broken earth to grub for worms and insects. He looked ahead again and felt himself relax into the ploughman's gait he had set. He steadied the traces in his hands and waited for the end of the field when he would begin the return. The steel plough cut through the soil almost effortlessly. Roy thought of the old wooden plough they had used before and how a third man would be needed to walk alongside with a strong stick bearing down on the beam to keep the coulter in the ground. Even then, the ruts and lumps left behind after the ploughing would require a group of men to go out with a mallet each, known locally as a mell, to break up the clumps and fill the holes with spades before sowing to save the seed from being lost and wasted.

At the end of the field, Roy paused and, walking back a part of the way, he regarded with satisfaction his work, a clean crisp furrow with the soil powdering off on its two banks. He heard a voice calling, "Roy, Roy," and looked around in the direction of the road which cut through the valley formed by this hill field and the one opposite. The road was deserted, as was the lane. Finally, his gaze focused on a figure at the top of the field, standing beside the centre pole, almost invisible against the hedge beyond. It was a woman, but not Eileen. He peered closely and then began to walk up in her direction. He had traversed most of the field before he could hear the voice calling out again and see the woman who stood there with a bicycle resting against her hips.

"Roy, Roy," she called, "It's me, Dorothy."

He smiled broadly in welcome and called out, "Och, Dorothy, it's yourself. Have you come over to lend a hand with the ploughing?"

Her face was grave, serious, worried. "No Roy, it's ...."

But her voice had dropped as he got nearer, and he hadn't heard.

"On your way over to the Armstrongs, is it?" he was saying as he drew alongside her, noticing her grave expression. "Nothing the matter is there?"

"Aye, I think there is," she said, her voice almost inaudible. She seemed reticent, he thought. "But not here. It's Sinclair ...."

Roy became anxious, "Sinclair? Has he been hurt?"

"Well, not that way, I ...."

"What do you mean? Is he shot, blew up in an ambush or something?" Roy asked, fearing the worst for his friend, the friend he had left behind in Newtownards when he had come home from the constabulary training depot.

"No," said Dorothy, hesitating. "He's not come home. He was to come to Newtown three days ago on leave. But he never arrived and ...."

"Och, I wouldn't worry," said Roy, relieved almost. "Maybe he's just been given extra duty or something he couldn't get out of. Hear tell it's happened before."

"No," she said, her voice sounding empty, forlorn. "I don't think he'll be coming home again. I think he has heard something."

"What? What has he heard?"

Dorothy lowered her head, whispering now, "About me. I think he heard something about me and ...." She broke down in tear, great sobs heaving her body, her face now buried in her hands. Roy felt awkward, yet concerned enough to go over and put his arms around her, hugging her and patting her back with his strong hands as she went limp in his embrace.

"There, there, Dorothy. It can't be all that bad."

She sobbed violently again, then caught her breath and steadied herself as she said, "Oh God, Roy, it's worse than bad. And it was all my fault ...."

"Shh, Dorothy," he comforted her, too conscious now that they were standing here on the edge of the field in full view of anybody who passed. He waited until she was calmer.

"Take it easy now, girl. Take it easy."

"What have I done?" she asked, her head still resting on his chest. "How can I tell anybody? Oh God ...."

He steadied her as he withdrew, taking her arm in his, "Listen, come on up to the house. Eileen's away up to the village to see her mother. You can tell me what it's about if you want. I'm sure we can work something out."

She pulled a handkerchief from her coat pocket, dried off her tears and blew her nose. She seemed more composed now, yet still heartbroken. She nodded, and they set off for the house. "What am I to do?" she wailed softly as they went. "You're the only one I can think to tell, Roy. But it's so rotten and bad ...."

A single furrow in the earth behind them, the horse still shackled to the plough grazing along the hedge at the far side, the work forgotten for now. Roy knew that it would take all his best resources and more to comfort his friend's wife, the broken young woman who leaned on his arm.

****

Gentlemen, we must stand firm, the times demand it. Ulster must not cool down, for Ulster still holds the key of the situation. We have a united, organised, passionate Unionism that has been struggling for years within the Constitution to defeat the baneful policy of Home Rule, and I believe it will do it. What we object to is a Romish Parliament in Dublin with a responsible Executive controlled from the Vatican. Then ascendancy and intolerance would come, education would be denominationalised, agricultural and commercial progress would be paralysed, exorbitant taxation would end in bankruptcy, our civil freedom and religious liberty would be imperilled, and finally no doubt civil war and bloodshed would accrue. No wonder we protest against Home Rule when we think of the awful consequences.

Rev. William Armstrong, Drum, 1912.

****

On her return from the village, Sadie found Albert seated on a kitchen chair with two big baskets in front of him. He was hunched over one of the baskets, his back to the door. The kitchen table had been shoved into the side against the wall. Sadie saw he was engrossed in his work, hardly noticing as she came in and peered over his shoulder. He had a potato in his hand and a knife. As she watched, he examined the potato, cut it diagonally and then into smaller sections, each of which he tossed into the big basket on the other side. Sadie sighed, went over to the table, put her shopping basket on it and began to remove her hat and coat.

"Albert, Albert," she said fussily. "What are you doing in the house?"

"What?" he replied, not even bothering to lift his head and look at her. She went and placed her coat and hat on the rack beside the door.

"Declare to heaven, what're you doing with them two big baskets in the house?"

"Och, can't you see what I'm at?" he said, irritably. "Getting these seeds ready for putting down. Roy says he'll be able to come by, maybe the morrow, with that new plough of his and I want to get an early crop in."

"Could you not do it outside?"

"Och, too cold. It's no bother in here. Man of my age ...."

"You were fit enough to drag them in here," she scolded, trying to negotiate her way around the baskets to put on the kettle. "You're not on your last legs yet."

He raised his head at last and pulled the lighter basket aside to allow her passage, "Aye, well I'll be done in a wee bit. Maybe you'd give me a hand with them."

"I've more to be doing," she said, wondering again at how the men folk presume that they are the only ones with important work to do. If she didn't get the tea on soon, the day would be over and he'd be complaining of the hunger. She noticed now that he had stalled in his work, the knife sitting idly in his hand.

"Well, maybe when Roy comes around ...."

She could see it now, the two baskets shoved to the side until he felt like resuming the task, or until he had to get back at it when the ploughing was done. She sighed in exasperation, "Oh no. You're not leaving them here till God knows when. Taking up half the place. I've little enough room as it is."

Albert bent back to the task, lifting another potato and studying it. He seemed fascinated by the tiny eyes of the tubers, examining the most effective way of maximising their potential. He had certainly slowed up at the work, she realised. Time was when he would be flicking bits of potato off the knife as if he wasn't even bothering to look. Yes, and he'd be out in the barn where they belonged, not hugging the heat of the range here in the kitchen and getting in her way.

She wondered was he going odd with age, maybe a wee bit soft in the head, but she dismissed the thought. He just didn't seem to have the will to go on, not like when Sinclair was about the place learning to take over. Then Albert had been a committed teacher who imparted his fascination with the cycles of farm life, his store of lore and skills and, above all, his passionate love of these fields in Drumkirk. There had been no soft options then, no let up in the toil as Albert set out to prove that he was every bit as good and able a man as he'd ever been. His son's interest was whetted on his father's need to show that Drumkirk was where they belonged, the Armstrongs, just as they had belonged for generations stretching back 300 years and more maybe. Would Sinclair come home, she wondered again, each period of absence removing him further and further from his roots here. And, if he didn't, what would become of the place? His father would not continue to work the land. Would he set it out, to Roy or somebody else maybe, a young farmer in the community who wanted to expand his holding? It would break his heart, Sadie knew. For now, he was still counting on Sinclair returning.

Thoughts of her son prompted a memory for Sadie, really more of a hint, a sensation that she had brushed from her mind after it had flitted through in a fleeting second. Now she remembered it. She paused again in her meal preparations.

"Funny thing happened there in the village ...."

"That's nothing new. Sure wasn't ...." Albert began. But she would not let him interrupt, not now while she had it fresh in her mind again.

"No, wheesht a wee minute. I thought I saw Dorothy."

"Dorothy? What Dorothy?"

"Our Dorothy. I was coming out of Mrs Anderson's and I thought I saw her cycling off down by Pump Brae. Away out of the village like."

"Sure what would Dorothy be doing ....?"

"Well, it was the cut of her. Tell ye, if it wasn't Dorothy I saw, then it was certainly the spit of her."

Albert looked up from the basket.

"Down Pump Brae?"

"Aye, she wasn't up here, was she?"

"No, sure wouldn't I have told you soon as you come in?"

"That's strange. Mind you, I could be wrong. Might have imagined it.

It was only for a wee second, maybe not even."

"Aye, tell you what, your head was turned with all the ould gossip you heard in Anderson's shop and ...."

"Sure, it couldn't have been then. Dorothy wouldn't have been about Drum and not called."

Sadie resumed her meal preparation, taking a soda farl from the porcelain bread bin and cutting it into thick slices.

"Then again, maybe she was coming over and she remembered something and had to rush back home."

"Go on out of that. Sure it would only be the likes of you would think that. Rushing about, fussing over this ...."

Albert's remark was cut short by the sound of a motor engine pulling up outside. Albert wheeled in the chair and Sadie rushed over to the window to look out. A car door slammed shut. She turned immediately and began to gesture at Albert, her voice panicking, "Holy full goodness Albert, get those out of sight quick. We've callers."

"Who is it?"

"It's Robert James McConkey and someone, I can't see ...."

"Sure, Robert James'll pass no remarks about ...."

Sadie looked out the window again at the figures coming towards the back door.

"Wheesht, aye, it is," she said, recognising the other man at last. "It's Attorney Knight along with him."

Now it was Albert's turn to panic, flinging the knife into the basket and rising from the chair. He pulled both baskets off to the side of the range and started pulling out the kitchen table. "Let them in, let them in," he urged, "but hold on just a wee minute."

Sadie looked in the mirror and brushed down her hair with her hand. She then moved to the door and opened it, just as the two men stepped up to it. Both men, she noted immediately, were formally dressed, Robert James in his good Sunday suit and Knight in his usual dark suit, butterfly collar shirt and black tie.

"Och, good day to you both," Sadie greeted them warmly. "Come on inside. You'll have to forgive the state of the house. It's Albert here, I'm afraid, doing his wee bit of work where he shouldn't."

They greeted her and stepped inside, where Albert was still straightening things up, bending now to recover a lump of raw seed potato from the floor. He rose as they entered and smiled in greeting. Robert James laughed at him, "Good man, Albert. Hard at it, I see."

"Aye, well," said Albert, somewhat embarrassed now, "Good afternoon, Mr Knight. What has you about Drum?"

"Good day, Mrs Armstrong, Albert," said Knight, removing his hat now. Sadie took it from him and gestured. "Here, sit up by the range there, why don't you? Albert, pull out a few chairs again. It's cold out there. You'll have a wee drop of tea and a little something to eat maybe."

Knight began to protest, even as he accepted the chair that Albert brought over, "Well, we have other calls to make ...."

Sadie would hear none of it, moving towards the range herself now after placing Knight's hat on the rack, "Och, a wee drop in your hand, as they say. The kettle's just off the boil. Sure, it'll see you right."

Sadie was already fussing about with cups, saucers, plates and tins, Albert could see, even as Knight said, "Now, no more than a simple cup please, Mrs Armstrong."

He would get more than he bargained for there, thought Albert, arranging the chairs back over near the table. The three men sat.

"We're here about the elections, Albert," Robert James began.

"Och aye, heard they were coming up shortly," he replied, waiting for Knight to take up the subject, as he knew he would.

"About two months time, I should think," said Knight. "But there is a lot to be done before then."

"We'll be counting on your vote, of course," said Robert James.

"Och certainly. We'll both be out, you can be sure."

Albert noted that Knight was settling back, allowing Robert James to speak, "We were wondering as well if you would help out a bit in the organisation work," he said. "And maybe help to man a polling station on the day."

"It would only be for a few hours," said Knight. "We want to get as many as possible involved. To build for the future."

"Of course, anything I can do to help. You need only ask."

Knight was pleased, "Good man, we've had a very good response so far."

Albert could see that Robert James was already immersed in the political work, now more than willing to take credit for the strength of the support in the area. "Och, we're safe about here, anyway," he said. But Albert was still a little doubtful about what could be achieved. He had been puzzling over the way that the local party organisation had been so adamant in opposing any requests for transfers of loyalist communities into Northern Ireland. It seemed to be a complete shift from the foundation on which they had fought for years as Ulster Unionists. Why would anybody oppose them seeking what had been guaranteed to them as their right under the Covenant?

"Tell me, Attorney," he began, "I was reading in *The Northern Standard* a while back where you won't be standing as Unionists any more. What is that all about?"

The solicitor pulled out a white handkerchief, removed his glasses and began to clean the lenses. He paused briefly before he spoke. "Well, that is a matter of authenticity and convenience, if you understand me. We have seven candidates going for the county council - Col. Madden, Mr Beattie and myself here in the Clones Electoral Division. Then in the Monaghan division there's Sam Nixon, John Holdcroft and Sharman Ross. We'll have another candidate running in the Mullyash area for the Castleblayney Division. But we want seats in those divisions where we're still strong - here in Clones and in Monaghan. We want a good showing to get all the candidates in ...."

Sadie was still busy with the tea preparations, Albert could see, but she had clearly been listening closely to the conversation. She interrupted now, "But if you're not Unionists, then what are you?"

Robert James turned around to her, "Protestants, Sadie. Protestants and Orangemen ...."

Knight resumed, "Well, I suppose that's right. But since we're no longer in the Ulster Unionist Council, we've formed ourselves in a new association here in the county. We're on our own now, as it were, so we've set up a Protestant Protection Association."

"What is it going to protect us from though?" Albert asked.

"Och, Albert," said Robert James, slightly impatient now. "You know rightly what we stand for."

Knight was more patient, even more circumspect than his local aide, "Right, you've seen our motto in *The Northern Standard*, I take it," he said. "We stand for Economy and Efficiency, as it says. We're out to protect the ratepayers and farmers and, indeed, anybody of our persuasion here in the county."

"Aye," said Robert James, "we'll be looking after our own. The other side's doing it, so why shouldn't we? This compulsory Irish language thing, for instance. All that rubbish they're getting into the schools and government jobs and all ...."

He had touched a raw nerve for Albert who had been scouring any newspaper he got for news on what changes were coming, his indignation rising every time he saw another erosion of the way of life he had long cherished as his heritage, the heritage he wanted to pass on if he could.

"Aye," he said, "beats me how they're allowed to get away with it. You would think they would do something over in Westminster ...."

Knight clearly did not want to get embroiled in all the issues before he had finished explaining the organisational changes. "Yes, but as I was saying, we'll protect Protestant interest. But we also have to widen the net for votes. Our numbers are sliding, even about here."

Sadie joined in again, "That's right. Mrs Anderson was saying where the Nixons of over by Newbliss is moving across ...."

Trust her to start quoting Mrs Anderson, thought Albert. The solicitor would think them right fools. He interjected, "I'm sure these men know as much as Mrs Anderson, Sadie."

"Well, Mr Knight, I doubt you need have no fears about here," said Robert James. "The Armstrongs will be out and working. Isn't that right, Albert?"

"Surely, count us in. And you can put my name down for the polling booth work."

Knight was pleased, "Good, good. What about your lad, Sinclair? Any chance of him coming home to help out. It's important we get the young men involved too."

"Wish to God he would," said Albert, as Sadie added. "Och, you'd never know. It's a possibility, I suppose."

Robert James was reminded of something. "By the way, Albert, Roy told me to pass on word he won't be able to come over the morrow with the plough. He's got to run a wee errand or something."

"It's not Eileen, is it?" asked Sadie, excitedly. "She's not come into her time."

Robert James laughed. He was pleased, it seemed to Albert, at the good fortune of his family. Albert did not begrudge him. He could only wish for the same.

"No, not yet," said Robert James. "But any day now I expect. Roy says he'll be over in a day or two."

Knight chortled. "Well, good to see that it's not all sliding Protestant numbers about here, eh?"

Albert laughed, "Aye indeed. Doubt they'll not hold back the elections though till the child's of age."

"Aye," said Sadie, now carrying over a stacked tray of tea and buttered scones and settling it on the table, "maybe it'll be your own successor for the seat, Mr Knight."

"You would never know," said Knight, as the three men moved closer still to the table.

The reflection in the mirror said it all, Roy thought as he hesitated before approaching Sinclair. The uniform unkempt, as if he had been wearing it for days on end, hair uncombed and several days' beard growth. Roy noted how he sat there on the stool, staring vacantly into the large mirror behind the bar. Before him, a bottle of beer and a tumbler of whiskey, a cigarette burning away as he held it awkwardly at the very base of his middle fingers, the fingers themselves stained a dark mahogany brown from the smoke. The barman was busy at the far end with a couple of customers and, when he exited through a side door, Roy approached Sinclair and sat up into the stool next to him. Sinclair barely turned, still regarding the reflection in the mirror as Roy said, "Was told I'd find you here."

"Aye, what has you up?" Sinclair said to the reflection, his voice vacant, deliberate but barely interested in an answer.

"I came to see you, Sinclair. We were worried."

"About what? And who's we?"

"Dorothy came to see me. She told me about it."

"Told you, huh? Well, welcome to the club for the last to know .... the damned Jezebel."

Roy was taken aback by the venom, "Sinclair, take it easy, boy."

"Easy? Take it easy, is it? Everybody's taken from me easy."

"Damn it, listen a wee minute. I think it can be worked out."

Sinclair turned at last on the stool and looked at him, his eyes now registering hurt, despair almost. "How? Tell me how, Roy? What makes you so damn sure anything can be worked out any more? Because I don't think it can."

"Don't get angry with me. I'm trying to help, for God's sake, help you as well as her."

"Jesus, has she fooled you too? Along with that conniving little bastard, that snake in the grass Alex Johnson?"

Roy put a hand on Sinclair's shoulder, staring into his face.

"Look, it's me Sinclair. It's Roy. I know how you must feel. I'd feel the same. But you can't let it ruin your life."

"What then? Should I just forget it? Turn my head maybe when they all laugh and point? For that's what they're doing. There's Constable Armstrong, fooled again. Boys a dear, Roy, but we're easy taken."

"Is it all one way though, Sinclair?"

"What the hell are you talking about? I didn't fornicate behind anybody's back. That's what it is, Roy - fornication, adultery, lust, sins of the flesh and lies and more filthy lies ...."

"Aye, but she's distracted with blaming herself," said Roy, his voice lowered, trying to quell his friend's anger. "Dorothy knows she did terrible and sinful wrong and she'll have to answer to her Maker on that. But is that all the story?"

"What do you mean? You got the story from her?"

"Well, tell me your own side then. Are you without blame?"

"You know I am."

"But, Sinclair, look at yourself. You're wasted, hardly fit to dress yourself, a week's growth on your face, eyes red and raw from the drink. I hear tell it's been bad."

Sinclair stubbed out his cigarette and looked back into the mirror.

"Och, Christ, now my taking a drink is to blame for it all."

"Not it all, or anything like it. But some."

"How?"

"You didn't come home hardly and when you did, you ignored her. Did you beat her too? She didn't say, but I guessed from what she did say that it wasn't going well between you."

"Damned right it wasn't going well. Nagging constantly and ...."

"Did you hit her though?"

"Yes, yes, yes. All right, I hit her once, only once. She went on and on. But if I'd known she'd become a whore for that little rat .... Och shite."

Sinclair broke down, slumped to the bar counter and rested his head on his wrists, the heaves of his body signalling despair.

Roy grabbed both his shoulder in his hands. "Easy, boy, easy. It'll be all right.You'll work it out, but give it a chance to come right. God damn it, you've both done each other enough harm. But work at it now. Don't just climb into a bottle."

Sinclair sobbed, "What can I do? What?"

"What do you want?"

Sinclair gulped, holding back the sobs and started to pull himself upright again. "I want it back the way it was ...." He pointed at his uniform, the bar, towards the street outside, a gesture encompassing everything in his world, ".... before all this."

"But we all do, Sinclair. It's just we've got to live with all this and make do with what we have."

"What I mean is .... I want Dorothy as she was and I was before all this began. Before we lost out and I, we, all of us from our side, were rejected, thrown out and forgot about. God, Roy, there's not a day goes by but I don't think of that betrayal. Not a day. But we've been forgot already. You can see that. Maybe that's what's wrong. Maybe that's why I drink. Maybe that's why I hit her. I don't know. Maybe that's why I lost her. Maybe ...."

"But you haven't lost her, if you want her back."

"Och, what's the point, Roy? It'd be the same all over again."

"Not if you don't want it to be. I know Dorothy doesn't."

Sinclair turned, his eyes now reflecting a glimmer of hope, "You believe that? Well, maybe you're right. But what ...?"

"I am right and you'll see it for yourself. She came here with me."

"What? Dorothy? To Cookstown here?"

"Aye she's over in the hotel. Want to come over?"

Sinclair turned back to the mirror, stared into it for a few seconds, debating the question with himself. Then, without looking, he lifted his drinks, leaned over the bar and poured them both into the sink directly below the counter. He straightened up, adjusted his jacket and finger-combed his hair, before turning back to Roy.

"Aye, why not? Not much else I can do, is there?"

They began to climb off the stools.

"Just don't expect it to be easy," Roy cautioned.

"Is anything any more?"

They barman was just re-entering as they walked down the bar and exited. He nodded as they left. Then outside on the street, the sun shining brightly, Sinclair rubbed his eyes to adjust them to the light. He grasped Roy's elbow, halting him for a moment. "Maybe I should tidy myself up or something?"

"Aye, if you want to go back to the barracks to change and shave first."

"I'd be as well, I think. It'd give me time to think of what I'll say."

Roy laughed, "Aye, suppose you're out courting again."

Dorothy felt a mixture of panic and relief when she saw them entering the hotel, Roy leading as walked across the lobby. She had been waiting anxiously for more than an hour, unaccustomed to hotels and feeling embarrassed every time one of the staff approached to see if they could get her anything. Only moments before, she had decided to order tea, but when she told the waitress, she had been confused again when asked if she wanted high tea or just a cup. She said the cup would do and now wondered if Roy and Sinclair came back would she have to order more. The lobby was quiet, just a few commercial travellers sitting at the far side, having a drink. They hadn't approached her, but each time she looked over, one of them, a well-dressed middle-aged man in a suit and with a moustache and receding hairline smiled at her and then said something to his companion. She had been embarrassed. Could they tell? Was she a scarlet woman now for all to see? She assiduously avoided looking back that way and kept her eyes fixed firmly on the door, willing them to come. But now as they approached, she felt all the fear and nervousness crowding in again. Roy was smiling, she saw. How would she have managed today if not for him? She felt a surge of gratitude, and then looked at Sinclair as they drew up. He was wearing civilian clothes, the suit he had worn at their wedding, and he was shaved and clean looking, his hair combed. But around his eyes she could see the tell-tale signs - dark patches, the eyes themselves blood-shot. He looked older than she remembered. Maybe she had just not been looking this past while. His face, more firm set, leaner than she remembered, bore the lines of his experiences.

As she had sat and waited, she had relived those experiences in her own memory, trying to establish where it had all started to go wrong for them. She thought of his excited nervousness during their courtship, his incredible tenderness, the way she had teased him, his earnest pledges of love for her. She had thought of his hurt at the political developments, his decision to join the constabulary and how excited and independent he had become, how Roy had left him in Newtownards, their visits in Belfast, his passionate care for her. Then the day of the railway murders, the horror, the fear, the self-loathing almost that he had survived. She had to take care of him after that.

Even as they got married he seemed incapable of taking charge. He was easy bait for Alex Johnson, the very name revolting her as it flitted through her mind. Then the drinking, the despair, the way he seemed incapable of seeing the damage he was doing to them both. The night he had hit her, the shock and fear robbing her of the last vestiges of her capacity to save them both. It had all been downhill, to this, she thought. Now here, in Cookstown, in a strange place she did not know. She prayed silently, admitting again her own sins, pleading for forgiveness from God, from him, from anybody who could forgive her.

They waited, Roy standing as Sinclair sank into a chair opposite, a slight tremor in his arm as he lowered himself. Roy, too consciously trying to act normally as he said, "I'll leave you then. Will you be all right?"

Sinclair spoke, "Aye, I think so.

She paused briefly, then, "Aye, thanks Roy."

Roy walked off towards the hotel door and, before exiting, Dorothy saw him stop, glancing back in their direction. She smiled and raised a hand in farewell. It was shaking, too. She clasped it into her other hand as the door closed behind Roy and nervously turned back to Sinclair. He was sitting there, avoiding her eyes. Silence, then they spoke simultaneously, he saying, "He said you ...." and her "I'm sorry ...." They broke off and she noted that the first words she spoke were an apology. This would be difficult, she knew, more difficult maybe than she had dared to hope as Roy talked to her incessantly on the train journey up. She took a deep breath and began again, "Thanks for coming over. God, I know it's my fault, all of this. You had to hear sooner or later. I suppose I knew that."

He said nothing, his eyes downcast. There was so much she wanted to say, so that he would know. Know it all if he had to, if that was what it would take, a full confession, a repentance, forgiveness, reconciliation or at least freedom from the terrible secrecy and horror of it all. He said nothing though. She wondered if he would listen. She began again, "But it had no real importance, not really.You know, what I did, I felt nothing, nothing that mattered in a real sense ...." Her voice faltered, she couldn't find the words. "How can I tell you?

He looked up, his expression composed, his eyes softer, searching too for the words. "Don't, don't .... not for now anyway. Best we wait a wee while ...."

Suddenly she felt an immense surge of relief. Wait a while, he had said. It wasn't the end. It was a new beginning. She would wait, as long as it would take, with him, together. A wave of love flooded her very being. Sinclair, sitting there opposite now, willing to wait, willing to hear, willing to forgive. She would forgive too. It would be all right, after all. She smiled, a smile conveying all she hoped for them both. She felt like crying suddenly. She composed herself, aware of their surroundings.

"I've ordered tea. Will you have some?"

"Aye, tea would be good ...."

Gilgal's Resting Quarters

Where seven trumpets of rams' horns
Sounded along before the Ark,
Gilgal was our resting quarter,
There we left our holy mark.

For we are the true-born Sons of Levi,
None on earth can with us compare;
We are the root and branch of David,
The bright and glorious Morning Star.

The tabernacle of David is fallen, its branches closed up, but the Lord will raise up its ruins and build it as in the days of old. Then the sons of Aaron, brothers of Nadab and Abihu who were devoured in the sacrificial fire of the Lord, brothers of Eleazar and Ithamar who were anointed in His blood, will inherit the remnant of Edom. And their enemies, the descendants of Esau will be cut off forever from their rock city of Sela. Then will the Lord roll away the reproach of Egypt from the tribe of Levi and call them into the resting place of Gilgal. In the plains of Jericho they will eat the old corn of the land. Then the walls will fall to the blast of their trumpets and the great shout of the people and the manna will cease and they shall eat of the fruit of the land of Canaan.

****

Sadie knew she was prattling on, but she couldn't help herself. It was good to have somebody you could talk to, somebody who would listen and know what you meant. God knows, Albert tried his best, but he couldn't understand the way another woman could. And now, here at last, she was sitting in her own kitchen with Dorothy. How long had it been? Best part of a year maybe. No, not that much, but it seemed like it, the days dragging out with only the odd wee trip down to the village to talk to Mrs Anderson. Goodness knows, it was her did the talking. Albert was right there, sure enough. All Sadie did was listen and get the odd wee word in, when she wouldn't be interrupted by another customer coming in, or one of the family maybe. A woman needs to talk, she knew, and to other women. The men had their own ways of going about things. They could sit quiet enough most of the time, even with other men.

She often wondered how much Albert listened when she told him things. Maybe about half the time. Maybe not even that. How often had she asked him something, what he thought of this or that, and he stared back at her, not a clue in his head what she was going on about? It only made her feel foolish. But Dorothy was listening now. She could see it in her, yes, drinking it all in as they sat and sipped their tea here at the kitchen table in Drumkirk. Maybe she thinks I'm scolding a bit much, about Albert like, but sure, she knows rightly it's only my way, a woman's way. It was just coming out, a stream of it. Och, and sure wasn't it something different, something to cheer us all up.

"Morning, noon and night," said Sadie, "it's all the same these days. Gone to his head completely if you ask me. There he is drawing up big lists of names and townlands, ticking them off and then starting all over again. Then there's the meetings, near every night either here or up in Robert James McConkey's. And the calling on people. Get us a bad name, if you want my opinion. The whole place here has gone to rack and ruin from he put down those spuds. Hardly a hand's turn done since. You'd swear he was running himself for the House of Commons over in London."

Dorothy was smiling warmly, indulging her, she knew, but interested all the same. "Good he has the interest," Dorothy said. "These local elections are important about here. What with the Boundary Commission ...."

"Och, there's that all right. And sure, it's a bit of life about the place, too. You know ... it's been quiet this good while. Nobody only Robert James or Roy maybe calling. Eileen used to come by the odd time, but she's near her time now and sure, it's too far. Not the same..."

"Aye, I doubt so. You need a bit of ...."

Sadie grasped Dorothy's hand, squeezing it. She could feel the sobs coming on, the tears, again. "God, Dorothy, it's good to see you again. I've missed you something fierce this good while. Near as much, no every bit as much as I miss Sinclair. Fretting that much I couldn't sleep for it, daughter. It's the ..."

Dorothy squeezed her hand back, "Aye Sadie, I know. God knows, I've missed you too. But, sure, it'll be better for us all from here out, I hope."

"You're sure about this move to Cookstown? With no house or anything like?"

"Aye, we'll make do in the married quarters. We'll get two rooms. But sure, it's only temporary. Sinclair will only wait till this Boundary Commission report, I think."

"Aye, well maybe. But, you know, I'm not from about this country here myself. No indeed, I come from over Ballinode direction. Haven't been back there this good many years, nobody left now. But sure this is where I belong, here in Drumkirk. With my man ...." she laughed, "and his politics and all."

"Aye well, it's like they say, home is where you hang your hat."

"Well, I hope to God you've space enough for that anyway up in Cookstown."

It was good to have a woman to talk to. Somebody who would listen.

****

Now I would like to remind those who imagine that Unionists exist only in the four counties comprising the North-East of Ireland that in Monaghan alone 5,000 men signed the Covenant, in Cavan 4,200 signed it, and in Donegal 8,300 signed it. These figures are alone sufficient to show the falsehood of such an assertion. In point of fact, Home Rule becomes the more detestable the more you are brought into close contact with the great ascendancy which is attempted to be set up over you. That was the reason Lord Dartrey, when in the House of Commons, moved an amendment to the Home Rule Bill with reference to Ulster, in order, as I stated that we might avoid civil commotion - which I believe we certainly will have if the bill is put on the Statute Book. I moved that you should leave out the whole province of Ulster, and let the whole province stand together.

Sir Edward Carson to UVF parade in Newbliss, August 6 1913.

****

Clones station, another train. Dorothy marched along the platform with Hughie Maguire, the porter, who was wheeling a push cart on which her travelling trunk rested. She remembered him and his slighting remarks, but she really didn't care any more. By tea-time she would be with Sinclair again and that was all that mattered.

"Now you've got that?" asked Maguire. "You change at Portadown and take the Dungannon line and on for Cookstown. It's on up a bit..."

"Aye, I know," said Dorothy as they came to the carriage door and stopped. Maguire though wasn't to be shut up. He began to haul the trunk on board, pulling it after him as he held the door with his shoulder and wrestling it inside.

"You might have a wee bit of a wait in Portadown," he said. "It's the two o'clock Omagh train from Belfast you'll be getting ..."

His voice died off as the door swung to after him. Dorothy held it before it slammed shut and was about to board when she heard another voice in the background, calling her name. She turned back towards the station building and heard the voice again, "Dorothy, Dorothy, wait a wee minute."

A figure coming running down towards her - Roy. She greeted him warmly, glad to see him. It had been 10 days since they had taken the same journey. So much had happened in between. Before leaving Cookstown that day, she and Sinclair had agreed that she should move up to Cookstown to be with him. They needed each other now more than ever. The other business would be sorted out in time, they both knew. After she had gone, he applied for married quarters and got them. Not much, but it would do. She had the telegram two days later and began the preparations for going. Her mother had been relieved, she could see. They did not talk about the rumours, but she could read it in her eyes. Then she had gone over to Drumkirk, to tell Sadie and Albert. That had been like a homecoming. She stayed the night and most of the next day just talking to Sadie. There was so much she had never known about Sinclair's family, about Eric who was killed in the war, about the days of the Ulster Volunteers, about the depth of their sense of betrayal and loss when the Ulster Unionist Council went against them, about how they were now organising again, hoping to stop others from leaving them. She felt a warmth for them she had never really known before, especially for Roy who had stood by her and by Sinclair when others would have turned their backs.

He was panting, "Albert told me you were taking this train and, sure, I was coming into town anyway, so ...."

"Good of you to even think of coming down."

"Och, sure, couldn't have you going off and forgetting all about here."

"Not too much chance of that."

"Had to tell you anyway," he smiled broadly. "It's a girl."

Dorothy embraced him with delight and noticed several people on the platform nearby look disapprovingly. She didn't even know them.

"Congratulations, Roy. How's Eileen?"

"Och, grand, grand. You'd swear she was doing it all her life."

"When was it?"

"Yesterday evening, six or thereabouts. Grand wee lassie, though she takes after me, they say." Roy laughed, "Albert says its breeding stock for all the elections to come."

"Well done, the pair of you. That's just powerful altogether."

"We've decided to name her for you. Dorothy McConkey, eh?"

Dorothy felt flattered and overwhelmed almost by this gesture of acceptance and fidelity. She knew now where she truly belonged. "Och, thanks Roy. That is really great of you both."

Maguire was back out now from the carriage door. She had to step aside to let him by, noting that he was feigning great weariness as he announced, "She's all set up for you. I put her about half-way down where there's a bit of space between the seats ..." Dorothy handed him a coin and he moved off, looking at it in the palm of his hand. As he realised it was a two-shilling piece, he turned back, pleased. "That's very decent of you, mam," he said. "Safe journey and God speed now. She'll be taking off any minute."

Dorothy turned back to Roy, "Sinclair will be delighted for you both, I know."

"Maybe you'll have one of your own."

"Och, there's a few hurdles to cross before that, Roy. I'm afraid ...."

"Don't be. It can only be as good as you both make it. You've had a bad time, both of you, but it's over."

"Well, ending maybe, I hope. Doubt it'll not be over ...."

A shrill whistle interrupted her and the train engine let out a deafening blast of steam which now swirled down the platform in their direction. Roy shuffled about to help her on board. "You'd better get on. I don't want blamed for you missing the train."

Dorothy hugged him again, "You're too good to us both, Roy. Thank you for ...."

"Sure what's the good of us if we can't help other out. God knows we've enough to put up with," he said, holding her elbow as she boarded. He shut and door and she lowered the window, "Just remember us, write and come back when you can."

"We will, Roy. Love to Eileen and .... wee Dorothy. Take care now."

"Aye, bye for now. Keep believing in yourself, Dorothy. And believe in Sinclair, too. Don't let that go."

She could feel tears coming on. God, did she do much else these days only cry? She gulped them back. "I did before, Roy. But now ...." She smiled as the trains began to pull off slowly. She leaned out of the carriage and waved back at Roy, standing there waving on the platform.

Albert was in his element, scurrying around the hall as the election results were counted up. The ballot boxes had been opened, papers sorted in bundles and, as the votes were compiled in little stacks, they were bundled together and passed along to a central position where the returning officer sat and examined them, counting them up on his own notepad. Here and there, party representatives looked over shoulders, made notes and then conferred with each other. Several even passed outside party lines to confer with opponent's supporters. There was an air of tension, mixed with the smoke plumes from cigarettes, pipes and Col. Madden's plump cigar.

The first four seats had been announced. Knight was in, easily topping the poll. The other three had gone to two government party supporters and a labour representatives backed by the railway workers mostly. Three seats remained, the candidates had been whittled down to four and the tally men could not agree on how they would fall. Albert reckoned they could take one anyway on the spillover of Knight's support and transfers from the railway votes. They had worked hard to ensure a proper distribution of second and subsequent preference votes to maximise their impact on the slate of candidates. Having mastered, with much difficulty and painstaking instruction from others, the intricacies of the Proportional Representation (Single Transferable Vote) system, Albert had been working for weeks showing others how it would work to best advantage. The only doubtful factor was getting the vote out. With the Boundary Commission still at work, many were reticent to vote at all, thinking that by participating in this election they would be deemed active citizens of the Southern jurisdiction and ineligible for transfer. If certain areas had not voted in strength, however, valuable transfers would be lost and the new party could lose by default.

Albert went over the figures again on the small notepad and then went over to Robert James who was standing in a group with Knight and Madden. He was fairly sure now they could make the cut for one seat. The last was anybody's guess. Even as he reached the group though, he could see the returning officer ascending his small platform, leafing through some papers and then clearing his throat noisily. The throat rattle silenced the hubbub in the hall.

"Ladies and Gentlemen, the tenth count for the Clones Electoral Division of Monaghan County Council is now completed and I have the result."

Albert and the others strained forward, as did the entire assembly. Sadie had come up from the back of the hall to join them. From her cynicism of only a few weeks past, she had become infected by Albert's enthusiasm.

"No candidates have reached the quota," said the returning officer, to a general groan from the assembly. Would this go on all night, Albert wondered. But the returning officer continued, "and with only four candidates left for the three remaining vacant seats, I must now declare the top three duly elected. So I now deem Mr Beattie, Mr McGorman and Col. Madden to be duly elected for the Clones Electoral Division."

Albert led the cheer from the group as they realised what had happened. They had won. Against the odds of disaffection, apathy, hostility and a general exodus from the area, they had come through. He turned to Madden and joined in the congratulatory handshakes. Madden was clearly delighted, not having expected many Labour transfers from the railway yards. It was the Drum vote got him through in the end, Albert guessed. Behind him, Knight was ecstatic and Albert turned to hear what the party leader was saying.

"Three seats out of the seven in the division and with only three candidates in the field. We couldn't have done better."

"Aye," agreed Albert, "every one through. Maybe we should put up another candidate for the next time."

Robert James was more circumspect, "But it was tight at that. We only squeaked through in the end."

"Yes," Knight agreed, "and the word from Monaghan Division isn't promising. Only Sam Nixon managed to hold on. Mr Holdcroft is out and Sharman Ross didn't even figure."

"The back-up wasn't there then," said Albert, who now firmly believed that strong organisation and strategy was the key to success. "With that you can always get the vote out."

"Some doubts about whether it's there to be got out," said Robert James, "With all the people moving across the border, like."

Madden, flush with his victory, came over and joined the group, saying, "Just needs a bit of determination and drilling in the ranks, as we've shown here."

"The Protestants of the Clones area aren't finished yet. It was discipline that counted in the end right enough," said Robert James.

"Maybe even the Boundary Commission will sit up and take notice now," said Albert.

He noticed that his remark fell flat. Knight firmly opposed any fragmentation of the county with transfers of Protestant areas to Northern Ireland. Just as he and others in the "Lost Counties" had long argued that Ulster was a political entity that should never have been split, he was determined now to hold the county intact. That offered the best hope for the remaining loyalists there, he had argued. Transfers of strong communities would only leave others more vulnerable than they already were in the Free State. As it now stood, Clones Division would be the springboard for a resurgence of Protestant interests in the county and every vote would count.

"Your boy, Sinclair, will be pleased with the outcome," said Knight, obviously calculating voter numbers for the next election.

"Aye, indeed," said Albert, pleased that the solicitor should again mention his son. In the past few weeks, his relationship with Knight had changed. It was a mark of changing social relationships in the area where Protestants were finding that a common cause and isolation had created a real sense of community. "He'll be home in a few weeks for the Twelfth. Might stay on with a wee bit of luck."

"Well, I suppose at the very least him and Dorothy would make two extra votes, eh Albert?" said Robert James.

****

We meet, we Ulstermen have hied
From vale and mountain, garth and town:
From Antrim's glens and hills of Down;
From Derry, with her 'Gates' of pride;
Dungannon, with her camp of fame;
The barrier cliffs of Donegal,
Where the fierce western billows fall;
From grey Armagh of sainted name;
From fair Fermanagh's lough and street;
From Cavan and from Monaghan -
With march and mind as of one man
In Ulster's capital we meet.

We meet that Ulster's voice be heard
Beyond the blare of fife and drum,
From cot and castle, plough and loom,
To utter one determined word.
We speak not here in accents low;
We whisper not our thought today.
Traitors would us own their sway
Let England hear our answer - No!

****

The field was almost bowl-shaped, a natural amphitheatre in steep drumlin hills on the edge of Newbliss. With the crowds now ranged around the sides, it was a vast family picnic, a co-mingling of interests under the auspices of the Orange brotherhood. With more than 50 lodges in attendance, and more than half of those from within a six-mile radius of the village, a general feeling of security reigned for the first time in many years. The feeling was compounded by the results of the local elections and a determination to build on the seats won by the Protestant Protection Association. Grand Master Knight had speculated that the association could win as many as nine seats and hold the balance of power in the county as a result. From a beleaguered community, scorned by co-religionists in neighbouring counties, Monaghan Protestantism was flexing its new found resurgence. Indeed, the tenets of the new movement were vividly encapsulated in the banner which formed an arch over the speakers' platform now being dissembled in the hollow below where some young men were marking out a cricket pitch. The banner, moved to the side now, still proclaimed the words of Peter's First Epistle, 2, 17, "Honour all men. Love the Brotherhood. Fear God. Honour the King."

Sinclair read the words again, his gaze drinking in the atmosphere. He was almost overcome with the sense of belonging. For almost three years, he had felt constantly the loneliness of an outsider. Here among his own people was truly where he belonged. From the moment the train had pulled into Clones that morning, throughout the long wait for the connecting train to Newbliss when extra runs had to be put on to accommodate the throngs, he had felt at ease. Even a momentary recollection of the horror of his last time at the station did not dispel the general sense of comfort he felt.

Although he had barely thought of the words before, Sinclair found a strange solace and fortitude in the prayer that had closed the formal proceedings, a prayer he knew from the lodge meetings he had attended so faithfully before joining the constabulary: "O Almighty God, who art a strong tower of defence unto Thy servants against the face of their enemies, we humbly beseech Thee of Thy mercy, to deliver us from those great and imminent dangers by which we are now encompassed. O Lord, give us not up as a prey to our enemies; but continue to protect Thy true religion against the designs of those who seek to overthrow it, so that all the world may know that Thou art our saviour and mighty deliverer, through Jesus Christ our Lord, amen."

During the parade itself, he had shared the pride of his father as both he and Roy were elevated to the front ranks of the Sons of Levi lodge. He could feel it now in the animated conversation of his father as they lay on the grass, their heads propped up on elbows as the womenfolk dispensed the packed food and chatted among themselves.

"Sure it's got too big for us now," Albert was saying. "A smaller wee house, like the one just beyond the back meadow would do us rightly at our time of ...."

"Och, there's no need to go buying or moving, dad," Sinclair said, aware now that his father would do something rash to coax him home. He was fully determined to come home, he now realised, but he would do it in his own time. The likelihood was that with the Boundary Commission report expected any time now, the security build-up in the North would subside. That is, if there wasn't war first. The bonhomie displayed in front of him was not a universal phenomenon he knew too well. Better not plan for the immediate future.

"Well, I'm just saying, if you took a notion to come home ...."

"We will be coming home," Sinclair said again. "In a while though - not yet."

"We wouldn't want to be in the way, like. So we could ...."

"Och, no point in getting away ahead of yourself."

"Just planning. Like you'd have most of the running of the place to yourself and all that. Sure, it's your own now for the taking, if you had a mind."

"You see, I can't just walk out now. It's more a matter of waiting to see what happens."

"Sure, no matter what's decided, your place is back at home. You can't get away from it, son. For it's in the blood of ...."

"I know all that. Listen, dad, we'll let the hare sit a wee while on it. For now anyway."

Albert was clearly unwilling to end the conversation without a resolution. For days, he had been mustering all the arguments in anticipation of Sinclair's homecoming, determined to convince him to stay on. He had not seen him for so long and he was afraid that, once out of his own environment, he would simply fail to return. Hadn't he done it before.

"Aye, well, maybe we can talk later on."

Sinclair was relieved to see Roy advancing on them. It would spare him from this never-ending conversation, he hoped. As his friend approached, he called out, "Hey Roy, Eileen not feeding you or what?"

Roy came into the centre of their group and nodding to Sadie and Dorothy, squatted down beside the two men.

"When you're finished stuffing your face there, Sinclair, any chance you could help us make up the numbers for cricket?"

"Aye, surely. Who are we playing?"

"The Glaslough boys. Come on or we'll miss the start."

Albert piped up, "Hey Roy, any need of a fast bowler?"

Roy laughed, "Aye, indeed, Albert. Know any, do you?"

"My day I knew a fair few," said Albert.

Sinclair rose and turned to Dorothy. "Back in a wee while. Just playing some cricket with Roy here."

"Fine, best of luck. You too, Roy," she said as they moved off through the field. Sinclair wondered if he was making too obvious his need for Dorothy's approval of everything he did. Since that day in Cookstown, he had not had a drink and, after the first few days when his body revolted in a craving for alcohol, he had not really felt the need of one. During those days of withdrawal, he had still been alone, waiting for Dorothy to come and join him. She was spared his physical anguish, the tremors, the vomiting which caused him to take to his bed for a whole day. Most of his colleagues were of little help, McCoubrey in particular. They assumed he was still drinking and just suffering the effects of a bad hangover. As he writhed in his bed that second night, McCoubrey had even shaken him roughly, assuming he was having a drink-induced nightmare. There was no forgiveness in them, Sinclair decided. He said nothing.

Except for one man, a middle-aged police constable from Raphoe in Co. Donegal. He had recognised the truth and, in the quiet of the daytime, had come and spoken to Sinclair, admitting that he too had had a long destructive affair with alcohol. He brought soup he had made himself. Sinclair had not forgotten that kindness, but he had avoided Willie Baird after that also. When the older man tried to induce him into his born-again Christianity, Sinclair had recoiled, thinking it would merely be substituting one addictive fixation for another. He was determined to do his time in silence and win back what he had lost, not just in his relationship with his wife, but in his relationship with himself. He had to tackle the demons within himself - the source of his doubts and fears - not cast them out. He had to control them, for they would not go away.

His health began to come back when Dorothy arrived at last. He felt good again, although their relationship was strained by his refusal to talk of what had happened either of them. In the married quarters of the barracks, they kept to themselves as much as possible and, every moment off duty, Sinclair was in Dorothy's company. Yet he knew that she too was waging her own inner battle against what she had done.

Now as he walked through the field with Roy, Sinclair was acutely aware of groups of men here and there sharing drinks surreptitiously. He tried to avoid looking at them, but he knew that Roy noticed his deliberation in this.

"Good to have you back," said Roy at last. "Like old times."

"Aye, didn't think there would be as big a turn-out."

"Och, we're not all gone yet, you know. By the way, what's the word on the Boundary Commission up your way?"

"Hear there's a few moves about here for transfer."

"Aye, all directions."

"Dad was saying something about a petition he signed a while back."

"Och, we all did. He was wanting you to sign as well."

"Doubt it'll not get much of a hearing though."

"Well, word is they'll transfer from both sides - to balance up like."

"Aye, but the fear up north is they'll try to take a big slice out of Tyrone and Fermanagh into the Free State."

"How much?"

"Well, about here they're talking of Newtown and Roslea and all about there for a start. There's not much comfort on our side."

"Suppose it would put paid to any notions of transfer about here too. There wouldn't be anywhere to join on to."

"Och, it'll not be handed over too easy. Seems we're to be fully mobilised and the B and C men called out."

"But I wonder will it all come to anything, Sure they can't want to start another war, can they?"

"Doubt it looks different from over in London, or even from Dublin or Belfast."

"Aye, it's like a game of cards for them."

"What cards?" Sinclair laughed. "Beggar my neighbour?"

They had reached the bottom of the hill. Ahead of them lay the flat area, or as flat as they were likely to find in the locality. The stumps were already there and the teams lined out at the far side.

"Come on, though," said Sinclair, "it's cricket, not cards, we're playing now."

Roy grasped his arm, holding him back, "Houl up a wee minute.

Wanted to ask, how's things with you and Dorothy?"

"Well, better, I suppose."

"Never mind. It probably takes time to heal the wounds."

"Better anyway since she moved up to Cookstown."

"Aye, you'll not find till it's all forgot about."

"Accepted, yes, forgiven maybe, but I doubt it won't be forgotten."

The New Jerusalem

Come all ye Brethren and join with me
And bear the Ark as I have done.
Come enter into our High Temple
To this the New Jerusalem.

For we are the true-born Sons of Levi,
None on earth can with us compare;
We are the root and branch of David,
The bright and glorious Morning Star.

Now in the second year of their coming unto the house of God at Jerusalem, in the second month, began Zerubbabel the son of Shealtiel, and Jeshua the son of Jozadak, and the remnant of their brethren, the priests and the Levites, and all they that were come out of the captivity unto Jerusalem; and appointed the Levites from twenty years old and upward, to set forward the work of the house of the Lord. And when the builders laid the foundation of the temple of the Lord, they set the priests in their apparel with trumpets, and the Levites the sons of Asaph with cymbals, to praise the Lord, after the ordinance of David king of Israel. And they sang together by course in praising and giving thanks unto the Lord; because he is good, for his mercy endureth for ever toward Israel. And all the people shouted with a great shout, when they praised the Lord, because the foundation of the house of the Lord was laid. ***Ezra, III; 8, 10, 11***

****

Albert reclined against the side of his cart which was loaded high with full potato sacks. He sucked deeply on his pipe. Through the cloud of exhaled smoke he could see other men doing exactly the same. The Diamond was choc-a-bloc with farm vehicles of one shape or another, crowded around the imposing front of the market house building. All the carts were full, all guarded by men with too much time and too much produce on their hands. A group of children was flitting through the crowd, taking handfuls of potatoes here and there. Nobody seemed to notice or care. The lucky ones had managed to off-load their supplies hours earlier, taking the going rate. Albert, convinced it was too low, had held out for better. He now realised his mistake. He should have taken what he was offered then and gone home. Now it looked as if he might have to take the entire load back to Drumkirk.

He studied those at neighbouring carts and knew that they were thinking the same. But the banter of earlier hours had gone; there was little conversation now as they stood about dejectedly. Albert considered going over to the shop of Edward Brady, a local grocer, and offering him the load. He would get little for it, he knew, for the Cavan man had a reputation of hard dealing. If nothing else though, it would save him the ignominy of arriving home with what he had set out with that morning in the expectation of striking a good deal. But it was dinner-time now, so the shop would be closed. He looked up at the clock on the church tower, half past one. He would wait out the next half hour and, if nothing had happened by then, he would go over and see Brady. He now looked off in the direction of Brady's shop beside the Ulster Bank. In the passage between the stationary carts, he could see Roy approaching, a broad smile on his face as he called out, "Well, Albert, how's the spuds going?"

Albert waited until the young man had come up alongside him before replying, "Problem is, they're not, Roy. At least not quick enough. Too many about the year and no price for them worth taking."

"Och, wouldn't worry. You'll get rid of them yet."

"Aye, bid to be."

"Did I hear tell you've a whole dose of turkey pullets in for fattening?"

"Aye, and a good lock of day-olds from the Summer still thriving."

"There'll be not shortage of them either the year."

"Will you quit. Sadie's saying the same thing. But sure haven't I got to do what I can to get the place into some sort of order for passing on. You know, move with the times like."

He could see that Roy was thinking he just wasn't moving fast enough. Like a lot of others, Albert had rushed into extra potato acreage and poultry after the bonanza in prices for both the previous year. But so had a lot of others. There would be a glut on the market now, he could see. Roy, on the other hand, had anticipated the change. He had invested part of his profit on last year's potatoes in his new plough and, this year, he had sown extra acreage of barley and oats, both of which commanded top prices. Subdued by his own lack of success, Albert cast about for an excuse to change the subject of conversation. His gaze fell on a group of Free State soldiers lining up across the way.

"Fierce lot of military about the day, I see."

"Aye, seems a whole clatter of them come in on the last train from Dundalk the other night. Big build-up, it seems."

"About the border business, I suppose, with the report due and all."

"Aye, well, they're giving nothing away."

"Sure, it would be the quare soft dealing man would disclose his bottom price," said Albert, biting his tongue after he had said it in case Roy would take it as a cue back into a discussion on farm produce.

"Och, not much fear of that about this fair the day," said the younger man with a smile and a wink.

Albert jumped in, almost too quickly, "Sadie got a letter from Dorothy the other day. Says the same thing's happening all over the north. The B men's been called up for full-time patrolling and word is the C men's to come out too."

"What are they doing with themselves?"

"Sure, they've trenches dug all over the country, aye, and trees down blocking the roads and lanes. Out Newtown direction, they think they're likely to be handed over."

"So they're getting ready to fight?"

"Aye, doubt there'll be trouble over this yet."

"Best thing for us then would be to keep out heads down and wait it out."

"Aye, and say nothing," said Albert. "For tempers will be quare and aisy riz these days."

The group of soldiers opposite now moved off in formation, followed by the marauding children who had fallen in behind them, some with sticks they pretended to be guns. As they approached, Albert and Roy both turned silently and looked in the opposite direction. In the background, they heard a shout, "Up the Republic" followed by a few cheers. Albert was conscious of the tension, the level of exuberance that the military always generated with the threat of violence and reprisal just below the surface. While the civil war had long ended, the pro-Dublin camps were still sharply divided. The Free State side held sway in the border regions, but there was a growing support for the republican side. That disaffection was fed by the spillover from north of the border. Just as Protestants had been moving across the frontier from this area, others had been coming in from nationalist areas of the north. Albert had heard that many of the republicans released from internment in the Ballykinlar camp in Co. Down had been freed on condition that they did not remain in the North. Many of them had now settled in North Monaghan. If this Boundary Commission business blew up, as it had to in one way or another now, it was almost certain there would be serious confrontation in the area.

After the military patrol had passed by, Albert noticed a couple of men coming towards them, engrossed in a newspaper, *The Belfast Evening Telegraph.* He nudged Roy, "Early evening paper's in I see. It's getting on for going home."

"Aye, those boys seem to be getting their value out of it anyway."

"Might just nip over and get one myself."

"On you go."

"You'll look after this for me?" said Albert, nodding at the cart. Roy laughed, "Aye, I'll not let anybody steal them and if I happen to get a buyer, I'll haggle away for top price."

"Never you mind the haggling. If someone wants them, don't bother holding out," said Albert, setting off now through the crowd towards the newspaper kiosk. He met a steady flow of others, men in groups, pairs or alone scanning the newspapers as they walked or standing around in clusters reading over shoulders. Albert hurried along, more anxious now to see what was so engrossing. But there was a large crowd gathered around the kiosk, scrambling for the paper and he knew he had little chance of getting to the counter before they were all gone. He cast about for somebody he recognised with one and, just as he had decided he would join a group of strangers in his desperation to read the news, he saw Robert James emerging from the huddle, a paper grasped firmly in his hand. He rushed over to join him.

"Hey, Robert James, what's up?"

Robert James had pulled up at the stone bollards surrounding the pump and his head was already buried in the front page. He didn't look up as he muttered, "Tell you in a wee minute. Seems there's something in about the Boundary Commission report."

Albert stood beside him now, scanning the headline, in big bold type, "Boundary Report Disclosed." He scanned the page, more details, a map of Ulster, some areas shaded. He was trying to make sense of it all when Robert James whistled softly, "Declare to my God, Albert. What do you make of this? Part of Monaghan and Donegal to go to Northern Ireland."

Albert read quickly through the first few paragraphs, then cast his eye down the column for further details, hopping for some mention of his own area maybe. He glanced back at the map. "Och, wheesht will you? Do you see that? It's not us."

Robert James had read on, "Oh, aye, Mullyash district."

Albert drew back now, shaking his head, "No sense nor reason to it, if you ask me. Do you see there where it says it's all from a report in *The Morning Post* today."

"Aye, might not be a word of truth to any of it, I suppose."

They scanned the columns again for anything that would lend authenticity to the report, an attribution to one of the governments or their representatives. There was nothing. But as Albert read, he was conscious of a conversation, barely audible in the background where a couple of men were also reading the paper.

"The boys won't take too kindly to this."

"Aye, there'll be hell to pay if it's true. Bloody murder before the night's out, I'd say."

"What about the Free Staters?"

"Can't see even them wearing it. Wasn't this to be their big stepping stone?"

Albert nudged Robert James and whispered, nodding discreetly at the other men, "Time we were gone from about here, I doubt."

****

Our people look upon themselves as betrayed and deserted and the people of the Six Counties look upon themselves as shamed and dishonoured. It has gone far further and far deeper than you imagine. Any movement that comes must come from the Six Counties themselves. We only protest and resign from the Council. How can we remain members of a body that has plainly told us they don't want us and that we are an encumbrance to them and have broken a solemn Covenant in order to get rid of us."

Lord Farnham on quitting Ulster Unionist Council, 14 April, 1920.

****

In the nine months she had been there, Dorothy had transformed the small two-roomed flat in the married quarters of Cookstown barracks. She had sewn curtains which now framed the sparkling clean windows. There were matching cushions on the two armchairs, pads on the two kitchen chairs and a tea cosy and little matching place settings on the table. The walls were scrubbed clean and the linoleum on the floor was so polished and shined it threw back an almost perfect reflection of the interior. Inside in the bedroom, she had made a patchwork quilt for the bed and their clothes were neatly arranged in the small wardrobe. With such tiny accommodation quarters, Dorothy was always looking for ways to make them more homely and Sinclair marvelled at what she had accomplished. Coming off duty, he rushed to the flat and, every time he arrived, she had a meal prepared and just ready to go on the table. For much of the rest of the time, she busied herself with lace-making and her sewing box was almost bursting at the seams with motifs depicting the bunch of grapes, the rose, shamrock, thistle, whitewash brush, spade and many other traditional shapes. In the box she had an elaborate shawl of similar motifs which she had already stitched together with the distinctive Clones knot - the "wee teardrops," some lacemakers said, recalling the Great Hunger of 1847 when Cassandra Hand, wife of the rector of Clones, introduced the craft to the area. When she got back home, Dorothy knew, she would be able to sell her work to one of the agents for a tidy wee sum. It was a little nest-egg for Sinclair and herself.

The flat wasn't much in the way of living quarters, but Sinclair loved to be there. It was their special refuge, a place apart. Even with the noise from their neighbours, they could find sanctuary and comfort there. But as he stood just inside the doorway that morning, he felt crestfallen and very nervous. Only minutes before he had been in the dayroom where the inspector announced transfers for the group of about 10 men gathered there. The announcement was almost akin to a death sentence for Sinclair when the Inspector said, "Armstrong, you're for your old posting down in God's own country, Newtownbutler. You've been transferred back to Fermanagh Division while this lasts."

All of the others, he noted, were being moved to stations in the Clogher Valley, Aughnacloy and Caledon, still within Tyrone Division. McCoubrey was going to Augher and, as the inspector read on down through the list, he had turned to Sinclair and said, "Newtownbutler? Should bring back some happy memories." Sinclair tried to ignore the remark, but he noted several others sniggering in the background.

Then with only an hour before the lorry left for Dungannon, he had to gather the few belongings he would need and tell Dorothy. For some time, they had been expecting news of a transfer. The build-up of constabulary strength on the border had already depleted the local garrison and the moves continued into the areas that were considered especially vulnerable. In Cookstown and other areas further back from the border, the departing A Specials were being replaced by the B Specials who had been called in for full-time duty. An announcement that the C Specials were mobilised was imminent any day, they all knew. The entire North had become an armed camp again, especially since the disclosures in the press. Many talked openly of war to prevent any transfers of territory from the jurisdiction of Belfast.

As he told Dorothy of his transfer, Sinclair could see the look of concern on her face, yet she tried to conceal her worries by immediately talking about their moving arrangements. "I could join you there maybe the morrow or the day after. It's only a matter of packing the few belongings and getting the train."

"But I doubt the trains will be disrupted too in all this. That's why they're sending us by lorry to Dungannon. I'll get another on to Enniskillen and then back to Newtown."

"I can go by Omagh maybe, and get the train from there to Enniskillen."

"Maybe you'd best do that, but leave it for a few days till we get set up."

"We could stop over with my mother in Gortraw."

"I mightn't be too welcome."

"Och Sinclair, that's all forgot. You're not drinking now."

Sinclair had not been thinking of that and he could see that she read his thoughts from the expression on his face.

"You mean him?" she said nervously, eyes lowered, voice frightened. Sinclair moved on into the bedroom and, taking a kit bag from under the bed, began to sort through the few belongings he would need. He called back to Dorothy in the other room.

"He's still there."

"Aye, suppose so."

"Damn, why does it have to be Newtown?"

"Can you not get it changed?" she asked hopefully. She had come in behind him and started to help organise his kit bag. He let her do it.

"Tried. Spoke to the inspector, but he said it was up to Enniskillen. I couldn't say why though."

"Och, it might not be for long."

"A day's too long. Or even an hour."

"So where will you stay?"

"Barracks the night anyway."

Several moments of silence. Dorothy finished packing the bag, Sinclair watching as she methodically laid out each item, folded shirts and other clothes and then packed them neatly inside. He reached for his shaving kit and put that in on top. As she fastened the bag, he could see her hands tremble. He knew that this move would be even harder on her maybe, returning home and dreading it. But together they could see it through. He realised that her company was more important to him than what anybody thought or said of them. Even a couple of days absence from her would be more than he could bear. He wanted to reassure her of this.

"I'm sorry," he said at last, gathering her in his arms. "You're right. Come on down on the train soon as you can."

She brightened up visibly, "Aye, sure maybe we could get a cottage again. I'm sure there's plenty vacant with people moving out."

"Aye, I can ask about soon as I get there."

For the remainder of the hour, they lay on the bed in each others arms, caressing, drawing comfort from each other and gathering strength for the trial ahead. As the hour of departure drew nearer, they made love, urgently, passionately. Then, as the bell sounded the muster for departure, Sinclair slipped from the bed, rearranged his clothing and kissed her good-bye.

Five and a half hours later, that kiss still lingered on his lips as the transport lorry pulled up into the yard of Newtownbutler barracks. For most of the journey, he had sat in silence, reliving over and over again in his mind their lovemaking, shutting out his dread of what lay ahead. But now it had arrived and, as he jumped from the back of the lorry with four other constables, there were the familiar surroundings, sandbagged walls, wire fences on top. He thought it would hardly be a worse prospect if he was arriving in prison.

Pausing briefly before he entered, Sinclair looked around. There were many new faces among the uniformed constables who went to and fro, a patrol departing, several moving in to unload supplies from the lorry he had come in. Perhaps there would be few of the old crowd here. He comforted himself with the thought, knowing that the general mobilisation had seen many changes at every station. Maybe he would even be out in one of the outposts, he thought as he moved thorough the corridor towards the dayroom where he had to report for duty. But even as he pushed open the door, he knew that he was entering the lion's den. Like Daniel of old, he wondered if he would survive the ordeal.

When he saw him there, playing cards with a few others over beside the fireplace, Sinclair felt a slight jolt in his mind and his stomach tensed. But that was it, he decided, as he swung the kit bag from his shoulder and dropped it to the floor in front of the sergeant's desk where the other transfers were lined up to report also. Even as he heard Alex Johnson's sneering voice, he relaxed and knew he could do it. He could get through this.

"Well now, would you look what the cat dragged in," said Alex. "It's my old mate Sinclair himself. How are you Sinclair? We must have a few drinks later on to celebrate the prodigal's return."

The others at the card table laughed, but Sinclair ignored them all as he bent down now to sign the book on the sergeant's desk.

"Right, Armstrong, you can drop off your kit and report back here. Take it you know the way?"

Sinclair nodded, lifted his kit bag and moved off through the door into the barracks interior. As the door closed behind him, he could hear Alex Johnson laughing loudly.

****

We believed, no matter what the consequences might be, it was the duty of all who entered into that Covenant with us to support us, stand by us and stand by us through thick and thin. I will give those people the consideration that perhaps they were honest in their beliefs, but we now know that the Protestants of Donegal, Monaghan and Cavan must, no matter what eventuality takes place, rely upon ourselves and upon ourselves alone. I do not want to minimise the gravity of this situation. We know not what the future may hold for us, but, Brother Orangemen, let us trust in the God who has never forsaken us in the past.

Michael E. Knight, County Grand Master, at Clones Twelfth field 1920.

****

Albert had opened up the small door on the range to let some heat out into the kitchen and he was sitting now in an easy chair he had moved in from the drawing room. His armed outstretched, he held the weekly newspaper. It carried a detailed report of the county council meeting of the previous Monday, under the headline, Council Pledges To Resist Boundary Recommendations. He was engrossed in the article. At the kitchen table nearby, Sadie was kneading dough, her strong hands punching into it and folding it over on the scrubbed deal of a special baking board she kept for the purpose. When satisfied of its consistency, she reached into a big earthenware jar and took another handful of flour which she spread on the board, grabbed the rolling pin nearby and began to work the dough into a flat shape about an inch and a half thick. When she had it rolled out, she took up a knife and began to cut it into long triangular soda farl shapes. She dusted them with flour again, patted some of the irregular ones into more consistent shapes and then stacked these neatly on a baking tray which carried them over to the range. She had to turn sideways to get past Albert's chair and tut-tutted as she flicked the range door shut with her knee. Albert jostled around in his chair facing off now to the side as he said, "By God, but they're going to town all right on this one."

"What's that?" asked Sadie as she began to drop the dough shapes onto the top of the stove.

"The council meeting. They went to town on this Boundary Commission report."

"Aye, so I heard tell from Mrs Anderson the day," said Sadie, absent-mindedly almost, as she pulled a metal spatula from her apron pocket and flicked over each of the dough shapes in turn as they began to brown on the underside.

"Huh, maybe I could save the price of the paper here if you just reported back all you hear about Drum village."

Sadie looked around. "Aye, but you don't believe anything I say until you read it in print."

Albert pretended not to hear, his eyes still scanning the columns closely, his lips reading silently. After several moments, he said, "Did she tell you the words of the motion that come up then?"

"What's that?" Sadie flipped soda farls with the spatula, moving some of the centre ones out to the sides and bringing others in to the hottest part of the plate.

"The motion. Has it all here. Did Mrs Anderson not tell you?"

"What motion?"

"Wait till you hear this then," said Albert. He began to read with some hesitation, "We the county council of Monaghan, hereby pledge ourselves to resist to the last and to the utmost, the attempt if such be contemplated, to dismember our country as well as Donegal, and to bind in perpetual bondage in defiance of the wishes of the inhabitants, large areas of Down, Armagh, Tyrone, Fermanagh and Derry. We call upon the President and the Executive Council to take their stand with us and with the people and show the forces hostile to us and the people, that the government will never acquiesce in the refusal of the heart's desire of the people in the disregard of the economic interests and in the ignoring of the geographical realities."

Albert paused and looked up. Sadie, eyes furrowed, laughed, "There's a quare mouthful for you, eh?"

"Aye, but it was supported by all but our five men."

"Those of us that's held in perpetual bondage too?" said Sadie.

"Col. Madden tried to stop it being put to the vote by saying it's all only rumour."

"Is that all it is then?"

"Sure, there's been no word from any of the governments. It's only what was in the *Morning Post* the other day."

Sadie laughed, "See what I mean about believing all you read in the papers?"

"Suppose you know better than them from Mrs Anderson then?"

"Well, I might as a matter of fact. She says if it wasn't all true, they would be tripping over other to deny it. The governments like. But they're not, are they?"

Albert knew he had to concede the point: "True, and I suppose all this military build-up is sign enough as well."

As he returned to reading his newspaper, Sadie turned back to her bread, smiling now as she poked the thin end of the spatula into one of the farls and withdrew it again, noting a thin film of sticky dough on the tip. Only a few minutes more now, she thought, as she reached for the kettle at the side and set it onto the hot plate to boil up. She rearranged the farls again and then went over to clear off the table and set it, moving an earthenware dish of fresh churned butter to the centre. In a few moments they would sit down and slice open freshly baked bread and slather them with butter. Albert always complained afterwards that the hot bread gave him a touch of heartburn, but it would not stop him eating it with relish, she thought.

He tried to read the newspaper in a corner of the dayroom, but it was difficult. Alex Johnson hadn't let up all day, sneering and jibing from over at the card table with a few of his cronies. At first Sinclair had been tense and angry, but now he held himself in check and ignored the sneering tone of the voice that mocked him. He wondered what he had ever admired in the man's cruel way, his taunting and baiting. But he could see that the younger recruits now in his company were equally infatuated by the hard edge. They laughed at the taunts, currying favour with the taunter. Their time would probably come, too, Sinclair thought.

"Harmless wee crater, he was," said Alex now. "Just off the prison ship Argenta up in Larne harbour with the other long-term internees. But, be god, Sinclair there hauls him in for questioning anyway and not a bother to him. That right, Sinclair?"

Sinclair recalled the arrest just the day before, arriving at the small thatched cottage in Clontivrin, the turf fire blazing in the hearth where the young man sat in the smoky gloom of the place. The old woman pleading for her son. His own protests that he was just off the Argenta and had done nothing. But Sinclair had his orders, the arrest warrant he showed to them. Sean O'Neill was not the only suspect being hauled in for questioning at Newtownbutler barracks. A major sweep of the area had been ordered since the shooting resumed. Now with the Boundary Commission in disarray and the Free State member resigned, a major assault on the North was expected.

Sinclair had no time to argue with the old woman or her rebel son. He had a job to do and he did it, not with any great pleasure in the woman's distress, but with no sympathy for her son who would probably shoot him dead as quickly as he would look at him. Leaving the cottage, however, she had cursed him and the entire constabulary as a "shower of bastards," even as she knelt on the dirt floor, faced a Crucifix on the wall and took out her rosary beads. It was a nest of vipers and no mistake, Sinclair thought now.

"Aye, they just held him overnight and let him go," observed Alex in a fresh taunt. "Tell you, at this rate of going we'll have our work cut out for the next ten years hauling in Fenians right, left and centre."

Within one day, it had become obvious that no great attack was planned. The resignation of Eoin MacNeill, the Free State commissioner, had knocked the heart out of the rebels. They were in disarray, scrambling to win back some face. They had no will to take on the border garrison. The suspects had nearly all been released and the area was presumed secure. But the patrols and sweeps of the countryside continued. The show of force was considered vital to demonstrating that Ulster would still fight, according to the newspaper article that Sinclair was still trying to read over the taunts from the card table. If he was still staying in the barracks, he would simply go to the dormitory to sit out the period before the patrol, Sinclair thought. But since Dorothy had arrived two days ago, they had managed to get the loan of a cottage from her cousin who had moved with his family to Enniskillen to sit out the emergency. After this final patrol, his roster would be ended and he could go home. He only had to bear with Alex for a wee while longer.

The sergeant came in and moved over to the seat beside Sinclair as the card game resumed. Since his arrival back here, Sinclair had found a surprising well of sympathy from the sergeant who was from Cavan originally and, like Sinclair, considered a "Southerner" by Alex and his group. Sinclair knew that many remembered his drinking and they all seemed to be aware of his marital history, but already he could sense a small measure of respect for the way he had faced back to duty in Newtownbutler. Since Dorothy's arrival, there had even been a few nods and greetings from others at the barracks. The same Alex, Sinclair soon realised, had made more enemies than friends. The sergeant leaned over and spoke in a low voice, "Why do you put up with it, Armstrong? He never lets up on you."

"He wants me to rear up, all right. But he'll wait till hell freezes over before that'll happen."

"You could get another duty roster, you know?"

"That would be like hiding."

"Might make life easier for you."

"Och, I'll bide my time. Maybe next week."

"You're on the same patrol detail now. Want it changed?"

"No, leave it. I'll manage all right."

"It's up to you, then."

The sergeant rose and called out, "Right men. I'll have to break up your wee card party. It's time for the off."

Sinclair grabbed his rifle from the rack, buttoned on his great coat and went outside to the yard where the lorry engine was already turning over. Gradually the others joined him and soon they were sitting in the back, trundling towards their drop-off point at Kilturk on the Clones Road. They had already been assigned to a foot patrol from there up to Clontivrin cross-roads, just outside Clones, and from there over to Cloncallig near the Annies Bridge and back by Clontivrin to Kilturk. When he had been told of the patrol detail, Sinclair reflected that at Cloncallig and the Annies, they would only be about three miles from Drumkirk. The area also reminded him of his uncle Bob's murder. This patrol was a risky undertaking, all right, but in four hours he would be back in Newtownbutler and signing off duty.

The lorry now jolted along the potholed road. Because of the security alert, no repairs had been carried out for years on these cross-border roads. Traffic across the frontier had slowed to a trickle of its former volume. Deliveries were impeded, contact lost, partition copper-fastened by physical neglect and commercial fear. Now many of the potholes looked like deep craters, others sizeable ponds as the rainwater gathered. Vehicles moved back and forth along the routes, seeking the path of least resistance, causing these to soon deteriorate also. But vehicles traversing these roads were more likely to be impeded by felled trees or deliberate trenches dug for security or ambush. For that reason, all patrols were dropped off within a safe distance from the barracks to complete their missions on foot.

The lorry rounded a corner beside a small lake and came to a grinding halt at Kilturk Post Office. Alex and the nine other special constables jumped from the back, wondering why they had even bothered to take the lorry this short distance. Forming two lines, staggered on both sides of the road, they set off keeping near to the hedges for cover and protection. Sinclair noted that Alex had taken the rearguard position on the line opposite while he was the last of the formation on his side. Alex called over, a barely audible jibe about "keeping an eye" on his back. They marched along like this for about 10 minutes, eyes wary now as they skirted the border to their right and maintained a course that would take them up to it straight ahead before going off into the Clonagun salient towards Ballyhoe townland. Ahead of them a sharp corner with high hedges on both sides, a wood to the right where the townland of Coleman Island penetrated deep into Co. Fermanagh from the Drumully district of Monaghan.

Alex was whistling nonchalantly, as if he was out for a stroll. Their heavy boots tramping along the autumn roadway, a martial crunch aimed at deterring interference and maintaining morale. As Alex finished his tune, Sinclair became aware of an almost eerie silence. The formation had now opened up. As the road had curved to the right several times, there was now a gap of about fifty yards between him and Alex. He quickened his pace, aware that he would be alone and vulnerable if he did not make up lost ground. Alex began to negotiate the curve.

The others had already rounded the corner and disappeared from view. Suddenly a figure emerged from the hedge, raised a rifle and fired two shots at Alex's back. Alex slumped to the ground. Sinclair ran a few steps and then dropped to his knee to raise the rifle into firing position. The figure turned. It was Sean O'Neill, the man he had arrested yesterday. The sight of that familiar face threw him off guard momentarily. O'Neill stared back defiantly, then leaped for cover as Sinclair shot once, twice, again, now aware that the assailant was gone to ground, traversing the bushy terrain towards the copse beyond in all likelihood. Sinclair sprang to his feet then and started running, the shape of Alex's body now visible on the road ahead. He slowed to a walk, approaching gingerly, even as he heard the running footsteps of the others from around the corner in the road. Alex didn't move, lying there on the road, his face in a puddle, mouth and nose covered. A large bubble floated on the surface of the water. It popped - Alex's last breath. Sinclair looked down coldly, and then used the toe of his boot to raise Alex's face from the water, crooking it under the nose and edging it around. It looked up at him, eyes open, the sneering smile still on the lips. Sinclair recoiled in horror, the face slid back into the puddle of water.

Shouts now as the footsteps drew up: "Armstrong, what happened?"

Sinclair stepped back and looked around, the other constables running up, halting now on the far side of the corpse on the ground.

"They got Alex," he heard himself say. "I shot and missed."

"How many and which way?"

"Don't know, maybe two, maybe just the one. Went off towards those woods beyond."

"Did you get a look at them?"

"Aye, one of them. It was Sean O'Neill. Mind I lifted him yesterday at his home up the road. Alex said he was just a harmless poor bastard."

"He'll be over the border by now, anyway," said one of the others as they bent now over Alex, lifting him out of the puddle. Sinclair just stood to the side, staring off at the woods.

****

Our Ulster Covenant has been torn to shreds in Belfast, and we know that is mainly by the Belfast men and the surrounding districts that it has been torn to shreds. Belfast and the commercial districts thought they had made a bad bargain in admitting the men of Monaghan, Cavan and Donegal into their Covenant, and they were determined to get out of it. The Covenant did not mean what a plain man like myself thought it meant. It meant something quite different and it did not apply to the set of circumstances which have developed. I say, away with Belfast-made Covenants, I want to hear no more of them. The best thing you and I can do is to consign the whole matter to oblivion and try and forget that we ever entered into any Covenant.

Col. J. C. W. Madden at Drum Twelfth field, 1920.

****

Albert readjusted the light, hanging the Tilly storm-lamp from a nail in one of the crossbeams of the lean-to shed. The rain beat down incessantly, raising a din on the corrugated-iron roof and cascading off the grooves at the front onto the street of the farmyard. Albert cursed the dimness again, the swirling wind that threatened to topple the bucket as he raised it and poured the still-steaming milk into the large galvanised churn. The churn stood on a raised platform, an old landing-stone that used to sit near the front door of the farmhouse for dismounting horse-riders. Albert now wheeled over the small handcart and rolled the churn on its rim onto it, securing it in place with a piece of rope. Already, however, he knew he wouldn't roll the handcart down the lane to the roadway for the collection in the morning. He would wait until the rain let up and then he would have to face back out into the chilly night to complete the job.

It was all getting too much, he decided. Only five cows to milk now, but he had a springing heifer ready to drop her calf any day and a couple of stirks, young female cattle ready to be taken to the bull for the first time. The dairy herd could be back up to a dozen or more, he knew, as soon as Sinclair came home. Like everything else on the farm now, this was held in abeyance, just ready to be done as soon as Sinclair gave the word. But Albert found it a particular bother, the early milking and then the evening milking. He had asked Wee Willie Houston to stay around earlier to roll the cart down the lane on his way home, but his so-called helper had dodged off as soon as he knew it was going to rain. He would read him the riot act in the morning, but damned the bit of use that would be. Wee Willie, he had long ago found, was handy at avoiding work. Each day he only reinforced Albert's view of railway workers, but he dare not say that to Sadie for it would only remind her of poor Bob.

Albert removed his cap now and sighed as he wiped his forehead with the sleeve of his coat. Down the laneway, he could see lights turning off the main road and heading up towards the house, hesitating at the fork which led to the front or the back and then swinging around this way into the farmyard. A large black car pulled slowly into the yard and came to a halt across the way. Albert shielded his eyes with his hand as he put back his cap and tried to make out who it was as the door opened and a shadowy figure approached him. He was beginning to be frightened now, until a voice called out and the lights of the car were switched off. It was Robert James, calling, "Hey Albert, got a wee minute?"

Albert recognised the car, the big black Daimler owned by Col. Madden. He had often seen it trundling past him on the road in and out of Clones to Hilton Park. The driver sat in the front and Albert could tell from his shadow that he was wearing the peaked cap of his chauffeur's uniform.

"Aye surely, Robert James, what can I do for you?"

"The Colonel wants the committee members to come into Clones with him. There's something going on."

"Like what?"

"Cosgrave's arrived up from Dublin."

"Cosgrave? President Cosgrave of the government?"

"Aye, one and the same. He's to speak to a crowd on The Diamond."

"The night?"

"Aye, but he'll not stay long about, they say. There was a special constable killed out the road earlier on the day."

Albert was already retreating to the house, calling back, "Right, just houl on a wee minute till I clean myself up and I'll be with you. Come on in and say hello to Sadie."

"Och, I'll not. Quick as you can. The whole committee's to be there."

"Aye, two shakes and I'll be right with you. "

The sergeant's voice was quiet, but insistent: "This O'Neill was one of them? You're sure of that?"

He looked up from the form which was fastened into a clipboard on his desk, staring Sinclair straight in the face. Sinclair avoided his stare, looking past him to the table beyond where the corpse of Alex Johnson lay under a blanket, waiting for the van that would take him off to the morgue in Enniskillen.

"Aye, he was there all right," said Sinclair, wondering if Alex was still smiling cruelly under the blanket beyond. He had refused to look or even offer help as the others made a crude stretcher from a buttoned greatcoat and two sally branches they cut from a willow tree in the hedge. They had taken turns then, carrying the corpse back up the road to Kilturk where the lorry driver was still inside the post office drinking tea when they arrived. They brought the body back to Newtownbutler barracks, Sinclair sitting up front with the driver rather than sharing the back with the others. Since then, the place had been a hive of activity. Outside, the noise of lorry engines still revving and men's voices could be heard shouting inside and out as they ran about. Sinclair sat in the office, relaxed, as the sergeant debriefed him. Most of the others had already been in here and, as they emerged, Sinclair could see that some of the new men were visibly upset. He found himself wondering why they would feel that way. All he felt was immense relief that Alex was not among them, alive and kicking him or somebody else.

"You got a good look then?"

"Aye, right up close," Sinclair hesitated as he caught the sergeant's look, quizzical now. "I fired but I missed him."

Silence again. Sinclair turned his glance to the side, then down to his lap, his fingers playing with each other. The sergeant said softly, "Can't say I blame you, Armstrong .... Funny what can go through a man's mind at time like that, in the situation you were in."

"Aye," said Sinclair, resignedly, wondering again at his reaction out there on the road. He was close enough to see clearly, all right. O'Neill was standing still for that moment. He had him clearly in his sights, the familiar face, defiance in the eyes as he must have realised that he was caught there dead to rights. It was like a rabbit, caught in the glare of a lamp, waiting to be shot. But Sinclair remembered now that he could feel his body willing his aim off target, to the side and up as he let off that first shot. He let off the second and third and, as he ran for the body, his mind calculating already that he could not have saved Alex in any case. It was too late for that. But shooting O'Neill would have been like shooting himself. He remembered willing O'Neill to run, to get away. He also remembered the sneer in Alex's smile when he had turned over his face, a sneer saying, "You're way off target again, Sinclair."

"There will be an inquest, of course," the sergeant was saying.

"I know. When?"

"Shortly, I'd say. With Christmas coming up. Soon as they get a coroner. You'll have to give evidence."

Sinclair didn't even bother to think of what he might say then. "I don't mind," he told the sergeant. "Doesn't seem to matter any more really."

The sergeant nodded, and handed over the clipboard and pencil for Sinclair to sign the form.

The others were already there when Albert and Robert James arrived at Knight's house in Clones. They were crowded into the large bay window in the front drawing room. The room was in darkness, their forms obscured from outside view by the lace curtains which allowed in just enough light from the street lamps to let them to see each other in the gloom. The view of the market square outside was almost panoramic. A large flatbed trailer had been pulled up beside the ancient Celtic cross opposite, facing off down The Diamond towards the market house. A huge crowd was already milling around the area when Col. Madden's car had come slowly up from Whitehall Street. Recognising the car, most of the crowd had simply stepped aside to allow it to proceed. But one group of men had stood defiantly in front of it, their backs to the driver and the two passengers, until they were persuaded by a few stewards to allow it to pass through. As the car had inched forward towards the back of the platform, somebody had banged forcefully on its rear end, a thump that startled Albert. The driver had deposited them outside and they were let in by the housekeeper who directed them into the gloomy drawing room. As he and Robert James edged into the two vacant chairs to the side, to mumbled greetings from the others, Albert could see now that the driver was standing guard over the vehicle.

The others were looking intently over at the platform where men were arriving and taking seats at the rear, ranged opposite a podium at the front. Somebody was speaking to the gathering crowd, but Albert couldn't make out what was being said above the hubbub of the crowd and the murmur of conversation in the room. He looked around the semi-circle, making out Col. Madden at the far side, beside Knight. Two others sat between and Albert recognised them as Mr Beatty and Sam Carson, the other two members of the local party executive. Knight looked over at them as they settled, "Welcome, gentlemen, they're still at the preliminaries out there."

Albert peered closer, now seeing more clearly the group of figures at the rear of the platform. He tried to make out which one was Cosgrave, deciding in the end that he was the man in the middle, surrounded by a group of dark-clothed men.

"See they have a whole gaggle of Roman clergy up there," he whispered to Robert James, aware too late that his voice had carried in the room as the conversation died down.

"Aye, they like to make use of the captive audience," said Knight as he moved now to discreetly open one of the side panels on the window. The noise from outside rose sharply and then died down even more suddenly. Albert saw the figure in the middle of the platform rise and move to the front on invitation from the last speaker. A burst of applause rose tentatively from one section of the crowd , then died quickly. A few voices called out, but Albert could not make out what they were saying.

He knew now that the figure at the podium was the President of the Executive Council of the Dublin government.

"Would you look at the cut of him," he whispered to Robert James, now making sure that his voice was lower than before.

"Aye, hardly credit thon wee man with executing near eighty of his own within the space of a year, would you?"

Cosgrave was taking out a sheaf of notes and studying them on the podium as the crowd moved closer to the platform. Somebody shouted something about a "sell-out." There was a cheer from the side, much louder than the applause which had greeted Cosgrave. Albert whispered, "Doubt he'll need his firing squads to wriggle out of this one the night."

"Well most of thon crowd out there would be little or no use to him for that," said Robert James.

"Aye indeed, but it's a quare bad sign of him that he comes rushing up here from Dublin to make the excuses."

A "sshhh" from somebody in the group as they all strained forward to hear. Cosgrave had started to speak and the crowd noises had died down outside. The words carried through the open window, almost crystal clear now.

"....I come among you to demonstrate how seriously the Executive Council is taking this entire affair of the Boundary Commission. This lamentable result can only be explained by the persistent and unscrupulous use of threats of violence and political pressure ...."

Albert heard Robert James whisper, "Same boy would be an expert on thon, eh?"

Albert smiled, "Too true."

"....That the Boundary Commission was in course of formation, threats have been circulated, emphasised and encouraged by an influential section of the British press. This section of the press, while giving the most unstinted hospitality to the unconstitutional threats of the North, practically closed its columns to any reasonable arguments for the honest carrying out of the international agreement, supported by the law of both Great Britain and the Irish Free State ...."

"Up the Republic. Up DeValera," a heckler interrupted to cheers from a lot of the crowd.

"Och, thon's one escaped the firing squad," said Albert.

Cosgrave resumed: "Professor MacNeill as an honourable man has left the commission and has proved that so far as he was concerned, our confidence in him was not misplaced ...."

Col. Madden cleared his throat with a loud "Harrumph" of disapproval and Albert joined the others in a nudge and smile of assent for the expression.

"It has come to this," roared Cosgrave. "Our representative has lost faith in the other members of the commission and has felt himself in honour bound to disassociate himself from them...."

Another heckler, maybe the same one, cried out, "Not before his time. He's well used to backing down."

Albert smiled, remembering the stories of how MacNeill had issued the countermanding order in 1916, calling on the rebels to call off their Easter rising. He would never live down that retreat among the extremists on his own side. Now he was in danger of alienating the moderates as well.

"I must say that I also have lost faith in the other members of the Commission," Cosgrave said. "And I am forced to the conclusion that they allowed themselves to be swayed ..."

Knight was indignant now as he turned from the window to face the others. "Did you ever hear anything so childish. He produces the ball and insists that everybody else play with it. He even chose the teams. Now that he's losing the match, he wants to take it off home."

"He's scored an own goal on this anyway," said Albert, to murmurs of assent from the others.

"I've said it before," declared Madden. "They know absolutely nothing about administering their own affairs. When anything goes wrong, somebody else is always to blame."

They focused again on the platform speaker, noticing that a large section of the crowd was becoming more restless. A number of the Roman Catholic clergymen on the platform were glaring down in disapproval and several exchanged whispered words as Cosgrave continued: "We in the Free State government now feel that it is better to leave things as they now stand, rather than be a party to the grave injustice which could be perpetuated." He paused as shouts of "No" and "Traitors" erupted from the crowd. "We will of course, pursue the British government for some accommodation to ease the blow of this turn of events ...."

"Knew he'd have his reserve price," Albert remarked to the assembled gathering in the drawing-room, as Cosgrave outside called for "restraint and dignity by all the people in Ireland, and particularly those who are most closely and most directly affected ...."

A heckler roared, "Tell that to the Specials."

The final moments of the rally outside presented a scene of general disarray as others joined in. Several walked off, their faces showing obvious signs of disgust. But Cosgrave, with the assistance of members of the newly formed Civic Guards managed to conclude the meeting and depart the platform with some decorum. As he hurriedly prepared to return to Dublin, around him lay the tatters of a strategy his government had pursued relentlessly since the inception of the state. The Boundary Commission had been portrayed as the key foothold in the 1921 Treaty - the one Michael Collins and others since had referred to as the "stepping stone to national unity." The measure, in large part, had secured the support of many nationalists, most crucially those in the areas along the frontier. The border had been dismissed as a temporary measure, one that could not sustain the scrutiny of an international commission using the same criteria as had been employed in boundary disputes throughout Europe after the Great War. Now the Free State was accepting that its writ would never run beyond Clones.

As the crowds dispersed outside, Albert turned to Robert James and remarked, "I wonder where their stepping stone has gone."

"Aye," said the other man, "seems we're all in danger of falling off it."

****

We, the people of Drum, are pleased to see Col. Madden here and we wish to let him know how glad we are that he is on the County Council - a place where we will keep him. We are glad to have him on the Council where he can tell those rebels and Sinn Feiners that we are going to hold out for our rights. We in Drum are not a bad sample of Unionists when compared with Belfast where they are Home Rulers now

Rev. Robert Burns at Drum Twelfth field, 1920.

****

Champ, the staple dinner of Ulster households, uses a lot of potatoes. Peeled, washed, boiled, mashed to a creamy pulp with some milk and a dollop of butter and sprinkled with scallions. Albert enjoyed it scooped into a crater on top and a raw egg added that he could mix through with his fork to give it a bright golden hue. Washed down with mugs of buttermilk, it was ballast against the dank days of December, an almost abstemious Advent precursor to the excesses of Christmas fare. Sadie was wondering how many times she could convince Albert to eat champ - maybe three or four times a week, with the odd fry thrown in for breakfast or maybe his tea. The fry would have to include lots of potato bread too, another Ulster staple often made of leftover champ, mixed with a little flower, baked on the stove top and later fried. Albert loved the potato bread, heated up and slathered with fresh butter for his supper, the molten butter sliding off his chin in tiny rivulets as he tried to negotiate it into his mouth without dripping any. Then there was pratie oaten, fried in bacon fat on top of the stove for breakfast, potato soup .... Sadie was stuck now as she looked at the overflowing basket of tubers on the table.

Maybe, she thought, we should get in a few young pigs and fatten them up with potatoes. That would take care of a lot of them. The old pigsty was still there at the side of the barn, she thought, so there would be no big bother in fitting them up. But the thought of the smell, the frenzied squeals of the animals as they rushed headlong towards her when she filled their trough, did not exactly inspire her with enthusiasm for the task. Maybe somebody already in pigs, like Roy for instance, could take a load off Albert's hands. She didn't like to suggest it, of course. Roy had probably provisions enough for his animals and it would maybe be putting him in a position where he would feel obliged to take them. If she could think of some way that maybe they could do an exchange deal, that would be better. But they were already in Roy's debt for so much. He was already at Drumkirk for the ploughing, the hay-making and the threshing. Indeed, it sometimes seemed as if he was more often about the place than that useless helper Wee Willie Houston.

She looked over at Dorothy now, peeling potatoes as she was herself. The younger woman held the potato in one hand and carefully sliced off the outer layer, attempting all the time to undress the potato in a single length of skin. The process involved some concentration, a feat of will Sadie could not manage as she thought of how many more times she would have to undertake this chore in the days and weeks ahead. She, on the other hand, bore deeply into the potato itself, hacking off small slivers of peel that now formed a mound on her side of the table. She would use the skins to mix with buckets of wet coal slack to bank up the fire in the range. So it would not go to waste entirely, she thought.

"Will we ever see an end of these potatoes?" she asked. "We've enough out there to feed an army for the next two years."

"Aye, there's no shortage the year," Dorothy agreed, smiling. Her hands, like Sadie's were covered now in the dark grey, cloying soil which caked the potatoes. "I suppose you could say they're as cheap as dirt too."

Sadie was enjoying the visit. She was always relaxed in Dorothy's company and, not having to interrupt her own work, found that the younger woman was always anxious to help out.

"Pity Sinclair couldn't come over with you."

"Aye, he wanted to all right. But they're still on full alert until all this border business is sorted out."

"Will it last, do you think?"

"They say not. Sinclair may be looking for a new line of work soon."

"Well, he knows there's a place for him here. His father's getting so he can't manage by himself."

Dorothy laughed, her face brightening up a dull December day, as she flicked the knife at the basket between them. "I think he does very well. Sure, look at all the spuds he's grown for a start."

Sadie smiled back. "Aye indeed, daughter. If we could pay the bills with Kerr's Pinks we'd be right as rain." She resumed peeling the potato in her hand, not looking at Dorothy now as she almost mused, "But if Sinclair was about, I doubt he would make a better fist of turning them into money."

"It would make a nice change for him, surely," said Dorothy, as she too resumed the peeling. She laughed again, "See you have a big flock of turkeys out there as well."

Sadie thought of all the times she had cautioned Albert about thinking he could make a lot of money on the birds. Time and again she had tried to dampen his enthusiasm as he set about multiplying her own small stroke of fortune last year when prices had been good. Of course, he wouldn't listen. She knew her expression revealed her exasperation on that front too. "Aye, Albert reckons there will be a big market for birds again the year. Doubt we could be left with them, too, for he has little enough sense left."

Dorothy's giggle alerted Sadie to Albert's entrance. She hadn't heard the latch behind her and he was now closing the door. Then, as he removed his cap and walked around the table to sit down beside Dorothy, he said, "Is it my birds you're talking about? I'll be proved right about them in the end with the markets coming up."

"Aye," said Sadie, her voice dripping with indulgent sarcasm, "it'll make a fortune for you and tens of thousands more like you maybe."

"Do you maybe want one to take back with you Dorothy?" Albert asked, "I could have one ready for you in a few minutes, plucked and all."

"Och, doubt we wouldn't manage to eat one of them big turkeys you have out there," she replied. "Unless maybe we asked the whole of Newtown in for the Christmas."

"Expect you'll be moving off from there soon anyway. I hear the Specials is being disbanded," he said.

"That's the word anyway. The Bs and Cs are stepped down, but there's talk of the Bs being kept organised," said Dorothy. "But the As, like Sinclair.... That's the big question now."

Dorothy resumed peeling, aware now that Sadie had been working away at the spuds. Albert went over to the window and retrieved a newspaper. As he sat down again and opened it up, he remarked, "See from the paper where you're worth over £150 million now."

Sadie looked over and saw that he had buried his head in the newspaper. He was always doing that now. Making some obscure observation and seeing how she would react. He gave her little credit when it came to the business of news or politics now. As his interest in the farm waned, his interest in politics soared and he hated to think that Sadie might get a jump on him in that too. It had been the subject of much of their good-natured banter of late. She found that as he slowed down physically, he wanted reassurance that he had a lively mind still. Too often, though, his attempts at perspicacity in that field were as obvious as his floundering in the fields of Drumkirk. She hesitated momentarily, then decided to challenge him. If she did not respond, he would only be in a huff when Dorothy went home. "What are you talking about now?"

"About the agreement was signed in London yesterday," he said, delighted to show Dorothy that his knowledge was far-reaching. "It's all here in the paper, or didn't Mrs Anderson tell you about it, Sadie? The Free State's got out of paying its part of the Imperial War Debt."

"How did they manage that?" asked Dorothy.

"Backed down on the border. It was worth £150 million to them they found. Fermanagh and Tyrone mostly, I suppose."

"Doubt we wouldn't have seen too much of that money anyway," said Dorothy.

"Better off without it," Albert observed.

Sadie couldn't resist the jibe, "Aye surely, daughter, sure you'd only go spending it on high priced spuds and turkey meat, eh?"

****

Now I have no country.

Maj. Somerset E. Saunderson, December 1921.

****

It had been a long day, and for what seemed so little in the end. At the coroner's court in Enniskillen, Sinclair and a few others had sat about for hours before the cursory hearing into the death of Alex Johnson. It was the last inquest on a lengthy list and not the only police officer. Others in the large waiting room, which also served as a secondary morgue, moved around constantly, impatient with the delay, fearing that they might have to come back on another day, maybe even closer to Christmas. But Sinclair was being paid to be here and it was a lot better than waiting it out in a damp outpost near Newtownbutler.

At lunch time he had even gone off alone and visited the teashop that he had been in with Dorothy, Roy and Eileen way back when they were courting. Memories crowded in on each other. They had assumed a cohesive form. All that had happened since that day came back as a bad nightmare he seemed to have awoken from with the demise of the man on whose violent death he would shortly give evidence. In the end, a brief recital of what had happened seemed to suffice and the coroner recorded his verdict on the circumstances of the death. So that was it, thought Sinclair, as the book was closed symbolically on Alex.

He returned to Newtownbutler, signed off at the station and, after checking out the latest rumours on what was happening, went home. It was late. Life moves on, he thought as he closed the front door and slid home the bolt. Dorothy had already retired, and she called to him from the bedroom. He was anxious to join her, to hold her and be held.

Now, minutes later, he was undressing and telling her what they had said up in the barracks. They had not discussed the inquest. They probably would not do so, he believed, but she could see the change it had wrought in him already. For days past, since the shooting, he had been dreading any references to his personal acquaintance with the deceased. Nobody had asked.

"And this committee has been set up in Belfast to lead the strike," he was telling Dorothy now about the demobilisation of the special constables. "Hear tell they've taken over the barracks all through Antrim and in Belfast as well. They're holding the senior officers under guard and just going on about their duty."

"For what though, Sinclair? They've been offered the three months pay like yourself, haven't they."

"Aye, but they want a lump sum of £200 and they say they'll forgo the 'brew' for a year after they're disbanded."

"Och, they should have a titter of wit. Hope you're not going to get involved."

Sinclair laughed, thinking it was a lot different in Belfast than down here on the Fermanagh border. Already, the Special Constables living locally had been told they could transfer to the B Specials and still collect their allowances and keep their guns. Whatever about the city, the government had no plans to demobilise its garrison on the border. County command was also said to be finding jobs for special constables who needed them, to retain trained constabulary numbers and Protestant votes in the area. Things are a lot different in the country and there was not even a hint of confrontation at the barracks.

"Not much chance of that about here, I doubt. Anyway, I'm only straining at the bit now to get out and away from all this."

"Aye, I'll be glad to see the back of it all myself. I doubt the barracks life never suited me."

As he buttoned on his pyjamas, Sinclair felt a stab of concern. "Are you not happy then?"

"Och, no. It's not that. I'd sooner be here with you."

Sinclair climbed into the bed and, as he did so, Dorothy reached behind and pulled out one of the pillows she had been leaning against. He fluffed it with one hand and nestled in beside her, running his hand over her stomach and down her side, drawing her closer to him. She sidled down the bed and put her head on his chest. For a few moments, he basked in the warmth and comfort of her closeness. He felt the first stirrings of desire, but a thought niggled. Maybe now would be the time, he thought.

"Dorothy love?" he said softly, "We've hardly spoken about that since. You know, the ...."

"Oh that," she said, anxiously and he could feel her body tense in his embrace. "Well, I didn't want to bring it up ...."

"Just wanted to say I bear no grudge agin you, for .... you know ....

Course, I'd sooner it never happened."

"God, so do I. If only you knew ...."

"I do know. At the inquest the day, I suddenly seemed to understand. It seemed like it all happened to somebody else and I could look at it coldly. I know what you were going through, how much I hurt you, let you down and worse. I drank because I felt sorry for myself. I drank because I couldn't live with myself sober. I didn't think of you and it made everything just get worse for both of us. You were not to blame. I put you there. I am so sorry ...."

"It's behind us now and I'm sorry too," she said. "I never stopped loving you, not for a moment."

"Nor me you. Behind it all, that was what saved me in the end."

"Things are back like they were at the beginning."

"Well," he laughed, "Don't want to argue. But things have changed a lot over the last few years. Seems so long ago since that day at Clones fair, do you mind?"

"Aye," she laughed now. "Do indeed. Day we planned going to Enniskillen. You were afraid to ask your father."

"Don't suppose he knew how long I'd be away."

"Aye, four years. It's changed," she said, her voice serious, thoughtful. "But we'll be back there soon. It's our home, our real home."

Sinclair thought of home, Drumkirk, the land his family had farmed for generations, often only eking out a living on its stoney hillside soil. He could feel the contours of the land in his very being, the sense of blood, the sense of belonging. It was a feeling he had not found since he had left it. "Aye, matter a damn about the changes, it's still that."

Her voice now tentative, worried almost, "Sinclair?" He hugged her tighter, kissing the top of her head, relishing the scent of her hair. "I wasn't going to say anything for a few days. Until I was more certain like. But now seems like the time ...."

He felt tense, a hint of foreboding, "What love? Something wrong?"

"No, least I hope not."

She rolled her head off her chest and propped herself up on her elbow, looking down on him. Her expression soft, almost shy. "I think I'm .... well, I think I'm going to have a baby, our baby ...."

Sinclair felt a surge of joy and love consuming his entire being. He scrambled up into a sitting position as she did the same. He could see his smile reflected in her eyes, a wave of warmth passing between them. "Och, Dorothy love," he said, fumbling for words, words that would express his feelings. He felt overwhelmed by the miracle of it all. "That's just, well, it's just wonderful, powerful...."

He gathered her into an embrace, hugged her tight, drew back to kiss her passionately and felt her yield. They sank back into a supine position and he gathered her in his arms again. His overwhelming love had now become an overwhelming passion. He felt incredibly aroused by the woman he held in his arms. He wondered, momentarily if he could make love to her now, to them, Dorothy and his child.

As always after service now, Albert sought out the company of Roy McConkey. He enjoyed talking to the young man, his fresh wit, his banter. Most of all, he enjoyed the company of his son's best friend. Each time he talked to him, he could almost feel Sinclair's presence. Through Roy, he had come to appreciate the strength, the commitment, the resourcefulness of his own child. In the years of his son's absence, he had come to know, through Roy, his younger son's qualities, the very qualities he had ignored for too long as he had mourned Eric's death. The land at Drumkirk was always going to be Eric's of course, up until that day of the telegram from the War Office. After it, he despaired of the future, a despair fuelled by the events of those times - the rejection, the betrayal they all felt. But now he could see that Sinclair was the future, the rightful inheritor of Drumkirk, the next Armstrong who would plant the seed for generations to come. In Roy, he could feel confidence in that future, confidence in this tiny community that would uphold its way of life, its beliefs, its customs and faith, here in the drumlins that had been its home for centuries past and perhaps for centuries to come. From somewhere in the recesses of his mind, he recalled the words of scripture: "Therefore he said unto Judah, Let us build these cities, and make about them walls and towers, gates and bars, while the land is yet before us; because we have sought the Lord our God, we have sought him, and he hath given us rest on every side. Chronicles II, 14; 7."

He hurried along now, Sadie in his wake, towards Roy who stood smoking at the side of the path. Nearing him, he said, "How're you Roy, was just thinking inside there. You'd miss the Rev. Burns about these days. With the border deal, he would be giving then a quare roasting about God and mammon, eh?"

Sadie's voice, reprimanding, as Roy smiled at his discomfort, "Albert Armstrong, you mind what you say. That man's not a great preacher, but he's a God-fearing Christian and a man of the cloth. That's all matters at the latter end."

"Och, Mrs Armstrong," said Roy, placating her. "I know what Albert means. Mr Burns was a great man to give out and not give way. This man's a wee bit soft for about these parts."

"Suppose if he hadn't gone then, he'd be away now anyway," said Albert.

"What about Sinclair and Dorothy?" asked Roy. "Home this week?"

Albert's face lit up in a smile, "Aye, Tuesday they're coming."

"With the roads closed, they'll take the train to Clones," Sadie added.

"That's just powerful," said Roy. Then, laughing at Albert. "Sure, you'll be fit to put your feet up then. With Sinclair about to run the place."

Albert scowled. It was part of the game with Roy now. "Huh," he said derisively, "doubt I'll have to teach him all he's forgot. I'm not done yet. Not by a long shot."

Sadie joined in, "Would you listen to thon, Roy? He'll not lie at peace till they carry him off that land in a wooden box."

"Well, it's my land and generations before me," said Albert. "Maybe it's Sinclair's turn now, but she needs more than one pair of hands to keep her in shape. Else she'd be covered in whin bushes before you'd know it."

****

Therefore shall you keep all the commandments which I command you this day, that ye may be strong, and go in and possess the land, whither ye go to possess it; And that ye may prolong your days in the land, which the Lord swore unto your fathers to give unto them and to their seed, a land that flowest with milk and honey. For the land, whither thou goest in to possess it, is not as the land of Egypt, from whence ye came out, where thou sowedst thy seed, and wateredst it with thy foot, as a garden of herbs: But the land, whither ye go to possess it, is a land of hills and valleys, and drinketh water of the rain of heaven: A land which the Lord thy God careth for: the eyes of the Lord thy God are always upon it, from the beginning of the year even unto the end of the year. **Deuteronomy 11; 8-13**

****

For years afterwards, they would call it the great homecoming, with family and neighbours lined up on the railway platform as the train pulled in. They gathered from a distance of only four miles. But they had come across a great divide, through a deep chasm of betrayal and reconciliation. From Babylonian captivity, from bondage to pharaoh, the wandering in the desert was over at last. The prodigal would have his fatted calf.

When he talked about it to Reilly later that day, Hughie Maguire said that it was as if the whole of Drum was there at the station, a great gathering of Orangemen to rival last year's Twelfth. "You would think it was ould Eddie Carson himself was coming in," Maguire said.

"I'd say they're sorry it wasn't," Reilly replied.

But there were no regrets, no recriminations, no false hopes of salvation at the hands of man. The past had mingled with the future, the present with the conditional. They had come here as settlers to do God's work and they would continue to put their trust in His almighty reason. Their horizons were curtailed, cut short by a boundary they had never asked for, a barrier that would exclude them from those who had pledged to succour them even in their darkest hours. For now they would be content to forge their destiny here in these hills they had made their own. While others would shun them, suspect them, betray them for their own ends, He who changest not would abide with them here in the land He had chosen for them.

Dorothy felt she belonged among these people she had come to know and love. As she stepped from the carriage and saw them, she felt as if the child leapt in her womb. These were the people of her child's father, her child's people, her people. Sprung from the same stock, the Armstrongs and Halls were nourished on the same branch. They had come here hundreds of years ago with the hope of freedom to practice their religion, their laws, their way of life. From the border marches, they tamed this unruly land. They held strong against adversity and prospered in their chosen land. Together they would forge a new destiny for themselves in a new borderland .

The words of Simeon sprang to Albert's mind as he saw his son stepping onto that platform. "Now thou canst dismiss thy servant O Lord," his brain intoned while his heart was bursting with joy and relief that the Armstrongs would continue in Drumkirk. There among the hills they would continue to build, in their own way, a new Jerusalem. As Eric begat Albert who begat Eric who begat Albert and so on down the generations, Sinclair would provide a new generation of the family, a fresh offshoot, a strong limb forged in fire and tempered in trials and tribulations.

Sadie cried tears of joy. Reunited with her child, a man now with his own wife by his side, she thanked the Lord for his safe deliverance. Through the long dark days of his absence from their home in Drumkirk, she had pined for him and feared for him. Through sleepless nights and long days, she had refrained from expressing too much hope for his return, conscious always that his father would be heartbroken if he should stay away. She had provided wifely strength even as she had felt maternal loss and concern. Now Drumkirk would live again in their youth.

As he fell back into the embrace of his people, Sinclair felt another great burden lifted from his shoulders. The sense of security they provided was the sensation he had longed for through all those dark and dreadful years. Lured on by the promise of the kingdom they had all aspired to, he now knew that he had found his heart's desire in the home he had left. For all its shortcomings, for all the broken promises, for all the uncertainties of his people's place in the new and alien order, this was where he truly belonged.

So they gathered on the station platform, Sinclair and Dorothy telling how they had bought first-class tickets for the short journey. Sinclair pointing out that the expense was justified - wasn't he taking home his bride for the very first time? They laughed, hugged and talked, joined now by Col. Madden who had also stepped down from the first-class carriage of the train from Enniskillen, content to stay a while and enjoy this great reunion. Together, they emerged, passing by Reilly the news vendor coming to collect his copies of *The Impartial Reporter*. Doffing his cap, Reilly smirked: "Good day Colonel, or should I be extending Christmas greetings, seeing as how President Cosgrave sent them to Sir James?"

Barely out of hearing, Madden turned to Albert and remarked, "Damned upstart that news vendor."

"Aye indeed, Colonel," Albert replied. "The national rulers, such as they are, are formed from the same mould."

Madden harummphed, "Bad enough we had to put up with their damned guns. Now we have to endure their witticisms as well."

Sinclair, in ebullient mood, joined in, "Aye, you'd be hard put betimes to say which was worse."

So when Madden offered to give them a lift home in his large car, saying he had room for four at least, they had hesitated only momentarily. Albert wondered about his pony and trap. It would certainly be fitting to the occasion to travel in style. After all, as Sinclair had said, it was a bride's homecoming and more. Roy, ever at their side, ever faithful, ever resourceful, said he would drive the trap to Drumkirk and Robert James could take theirs.

The trunk was loaded in the black Daimler, the driver instructed to go first to Drumkirk and they prepared to board. Sinclair turned to Dorothy, whispering, "Hey Dorothy love. There's only room for four. Should we tell them?"

She smiled, patting her stomach unconsciously, "Aye, well it'll not take up much space for ...."

Their whispered exchange had been overheard. Albert cried out, "You mean there's ...." while Sadie simply gathered Dorothy into a warm embrace, a bond of mothers and mothers to be. "Och daughter, that's just powerful altogether."

Albert grabbed Sinclair's shoulder and smiled broadly at his son.

"You see," said Sinclair. "We're not done about here yet."

"Now you're talking like a man after my own heart," his father replied.

A shrill train whistle, a puffing engine, the train for Belfast was departing the platform. They climbed into the black Daimler and headed home, home to Drumkirk, the home of the Armstrongs.

In that day shall the branch of the Lord be beautiful and glorious, and the fruit of the earth shall be excellent and comely for them that are escaped of Israel.

And it shall come to pass that he that is left in Zion, and he that remaineth in Jerusalem, shall be called holy, even every one that is written among the living in Jerusalem. ***Isaiah 4, 2-3***